PRAISE FOR *A WICKED YARN*

"Knit together an interesting older protagonist, an astute knitting group, a friend accused of murder, [and] a daughter with secrets, and you have a purl of a mystery."
—Sherry Harris, Agatha Award–nominated author of the Sarah Winston Garage Sale mysteries and the Chloe Jackson, Sea Glass Saloon mysteries

"Such a cozy combination—knitting and murder. A delightful, well-crafted mystery!"
—Essie Lang, author of the Castle Bookshop Mysteries

"This heartwarming mystery knits together family and friends in pursuit of a cunning killer."
—Maya Corrigan, author of the Five-Ingredient Mystery series

"Charming, crafty, and so very cozy! Emmie Caldwell has stitched together an entertaining, well-plotted mystery that's as cozy as a favorite sweater. The clues are artfully woven into the story, and Lia and her daughter, Hayley, are a dynamic sleuthing duo. *A Wicked Yarn* is bound to delight fans of crafting cozies!"
—Sarah Fox, author of *Much Ado About Nutmeg*

Knits, Knots, and Knives

A Craft Fair Knitters Mystery

Emmie Caldwell

BERKLEY PRIME CRIME
New York

BERKLEY PRIME CRIME
Published by Berkley
An imprint of Penguin Random House LLC
penguinrandomhouse.com

Copyright © 2022 by Mary Ellen Hughes
Penguin Random House supports copyright. Copyright fuels creativity, encourages
diverse voices, promotes free speech, and creates a vibrant culture. Thank you for buying
an authorized edition of this book and for complying with copyright laws by not
reproducing, scanning, or distributing any part of it in any form without permission.
You are supporting writers and allowing Penguin Random House to continue to
publish books for every reader.

BERKLEY and the BERKLEY & B colophon are registered trademarks and
BERKLEY PRIME CRIME is a trademark of Penguin Random House LLC.

ISBN: 9780593101728

First Edition: December 2022

Printed in the United States of America
1   3   5   7   9   10   8   6   4   2

Book design by George Towne

This is a work of fiction. Names, characters, places, and incidents either are the product
of the author's imagination or are used fictitiously, and any resemblance to actual persons,
living or dead, business establishments, events, or locales is entirely coincidental.

For Terry

Chapter 1

L et's hope for the best."

Lia turned to her petite next-door neighbor, Sharon, and shot her a look of sympathy, aware of all Sharon's husband had been dealing with lately. As they began their stroll of the Schumacher grounds together, however, Lia couldn't help feeling excited. The long-awaited day of the annual Battle of Crandalsburg reenactment had arrived.

As a relative newcomer to the town, this would be Lia's first experience with the event, and as a vendor with the Crandalsburg Craft Fair she would be a participant of sorts, not just an onlooker.

The Schumacher barn, owned by the family for generations and the regular home for the craft fair, was historical, having been used as a hospital during the actual Civil War battle. Each year that scenario was re-created inside, and vendors' booths, including Lia's Ninth Street Knits, had been moved outdoors, a short distance away.

In addition, all the vendors had added Civil War–era items to their usual fare. For Lia and her fellow Ninth Street Knitters, that had meant weeks of knitting woolen socks and scarves from patterns followed by women of that period. Most would be worn that day by many of the reenactors, while some socks would be available to buy at Lia's booth.

"I feel like I should be wearing a hoopskirt while I'm making these," Maureen had said at their last meeting, with the others agreeing. Lia herself had often felt transported back in time as she knitted at her home, the cozy pre–Civil War house she'd moved to after her husband Tom's untimely death.

That feeling returned as she and Sharon entered the living history section of the grounds. A woman stirred porridge in a large pot that hung over an open fire. She looked up and smiled at them. No hoopskirt for her. She wore a plain, long cotton dress with an apron. A kerchief held back her hair.

A young man dressed in suspendered Union blue pants and gray shirt sat outside a tent playing a whistle-like instrument that reminded Lia of the recorder her daughter, Hayley, had learned to play in fourth grade. A second man whittled at a piece of wood nearby. Lia and Sharon paused to listen to the high-pitched notes, Lia recognizing "Tenting on the Old Camp Ground."

"I'm glad the weather is cool enough for those woolen shirts and jackets the men have to wear," she said.

"Yes, lucky for them that the battle occurred in October," Sharon said. "They'll have to do a lot of running in those heavy uniforms."

"And the women have to work in those long dresses over campfires. And in the sun."

"Makes you wonder how they all managed back then, doesn't it?" Sharon asked. "But it's been kept as historically accurate as possible, that is, until Sprouse took over."

Lia nodded. She knew about the shift in leadership of the reenactors that had caused disruption lately. Sharon's husband, Jack, had been involved with the group for years after discovering that an ancestor, Captain Josiah Kuhn, had played an important part in the battle. As group leader, Jack had been a stickler for absolute accuracy, down to the underwear worn by the soldiers and the food they ate during the two-day event. No burgers or Cokes would be seen in the campgrounds, or even wristwatches worn while in uniform.

Arden Sprouse, on the other hand, had dismissed such details as unimportant. With the significant financial contribution he brought to the reenactment himself and from donors he'd rounded up, his opinions ruled, much to Jack's dismay. Jack stayed in the group but had been demoted from captain to an unnamed sergeant, while Sprouse took the role of Captain Anderson, a person whose connection to the battle appeared iffy but whom Sprouse claimed as a newly discovered forebear.

Continuing their stroll, Lia and Sharon came upon Olivia Byrd, the young mother who sold her homemade soaps and essential oils each weekend next to Lia's craft fair booth. For living history, she had volunteered to demonstrate soapmaking as done in the mid-1800s. Dressed in period costume, the sleeves of her calico dress rolled up, Olivia definitely looked the part, especially standing next to a huge black pot hanging over the makings of a campfire. Her normally anxious expression was glowing for a change. It brightened even more when she saw Lia.

Lia marveled at the difference in historic Olivia. The

woman Lia saw each weekend was reserved—sweet, but often fretful. Today's Olivia was energized and clearly enjoying herself to the hilt. For the first time, Lia fully understood why Olivia did what she did. Her friend absolutely loved making soap, and that included even the crudest form of it.

"Looks like you're ready to go," Lia said. The event would start admitting spectators within half an hour.

"I can't wait," Olivia said. "Soap wouldn't normally have been made near a battlefield. But I'll be able to demonstrate how it was done back then, from simple wood ashes that every house collected and animal fats. Lye from the ashes and fat, the two basic ingredients. Isn't it amazing? A formula that was stumbled upon who knows how long ago, and we still use it today—with certain refinements, of course."

"Of course." Lia thought of the lovely scents that floated over from Olivia's booth from her own soaps, as well as the various oils she used in place of animal fat.

"You'll be a good teacher," Sharon said, which brought a pleased flush to Olivia's cheeks.

Lia seconded the thought, then noticed a crowd gathering in a field off to the left. "What's going on there?"

"Oh! That must be the bayonet fencing demo," Sharon said. "Come, you have to see this."

They bid good-bye to Olivia and hustled over to the area as Sharon explained what Lia was about to watch. "Our soldiers can't have bayonets on their rifles during the reenactment. It's much too dangerous, even with dull ones. So every year, two volunteers demonstrate how they might have been used during a battle. But they do it very carefully."

Lia and Sharon made it to the roped-off area and joined

the crowd gathered around the large circle. In the center were two uniformed reenactors, one in blue, the other in gray. Each held a long rifle with a menacing-looking bayonet at the end. A third man off to the left explained what they were about to do and how it would be done in slow motion for safety's sake.

Lia watched, fascinated but at the same time disturbed to think that this was once done in real life, person to person, in deadly fashion. Seeing the glint of the steel edges, she also worried about a current, accidental injury.

"They practice this for hours," Sharon said softly, perhaps sensing Lia's fears. "It's all carefully choreographed."

Lia nodded. The demonstration was impressive, and when it ended the crowd showed its appreciation with enthusiastic applause. The two uniformed soldiers acknowledged them, then turned to each other and shook hands.

"That's Jack's rifle," Sharon said, indicating the one held by the gray-uniformed fellow. "It's a reproduction, but still cost him a pretty penny."

"Good of him to lend it." Lia glanced around but didn't see him. "I hope it'll be carefully looked after."

"Oh, yes," Sharon assured her. "They'll do one more fencing demo, but in between they'll hand both rifles over to Jack. The other one belongs to Lucas Hall."

She said it with a sniff, prompting Lia to ask who that was.

"Arden Sprouse's son-in-law. His is an actual antique. He probably bought it just to show off, pretty much like his father-in-law."

Lia thought it best not to stay on the subject and instead said, "I'll need to be at my booth in a few minutes. I'd love to take a peek at the hospital setup first."

Sharon also wanted to see it, and they headed toward the barn. As they passed by the living history area again, Lia noticed a woman sitting at a spinning wheel some distance away and asked about her.

"That's Ronna Dickens," Sharon said. "She's spinning flax, not wool, in case you wondered. A friend of hers weaves it into linen, which is then made into clothes for some of the reenactors."

As they reached the barn and walked in, Lia barely recognized it. Craft booths had been replaced with lines of cots occupied by life-sized bandaged mannequins. There was also a surgery of sorts, which consisted of a wooden table covered with several instruments.

Most were tools for amputations, the most common treatment of the time, doctors having little knowledge of how to treat bullet wounds. Lacking antibiotics, more patients died from infection and disease than on the battlefield. As a former surgical nurse, Lia shuddered at the thought of what the soldiers must have gone through.

"I'm glad we were born when we were," Sharon said, looking over the grim display.

"Amen to that," Lia said. "But thank goodness at least for Florence Nightingale."

"Why? She wasn't here, was she?"

"She was a British nurse who worked during the Crimean War, once they actually allowed her to, that is. It wasn't considered seemly at the time. The first thing she and her nurses did was scrub down the field hospitals, which apparently were filthy. She saw the survival difference in patients who were bathed from those who weren't and argued for better hygiene. This carried over to our Civil War practices and probably saved lots of lives. Soldiers were ordered to bathe regularly, something many weren't in the habit of doing, and it helped keep down the spread of disease, at least to some extent."

"Wow." Sharon shook her head. "You could be running this part of the living history, Lia."

Lia shook her head, smiling. "I've had my fill of surgery," she said, having worked several years in the field. "I'm happy to stick to knitting. Which reminds me, I'd better get over to my booth."

"I'm going to look for Jack," Sharon said. "See how he's doing. I'll catch you later."

They split up, and Lia headed over to the vendors' booths—separated from the living history and battle reenactment areas but close enough for spectators to wander over to. The booths were gathered under a large canopy, essential protection from possible rain, but remained open on all sides to the currently lovely fresh air. Jen Beasley, who hosted the weekly Ninth Street Knitters meetings at her home in York, had driven over with her husband, Bob, to help move the groups' sweaters, afghans, and shawls to the new setting as well as deliver the mounds of soldiers' socks and scarves. Pretty much everything, therefore, was in order, and all Lia had to do was handle the sales, as she'd done each weekend for the group for the last several months.

Lia greeted her fellow vendors as she walked by but didn't stop to chat, as all were busily readying their booths. Having much less to do, thanks to Jen and Bob, Lia had time to relax and look over her new surroundings once she made it to her own spot.

"We lucked out with the weather," a voice said, and Lia turned to her left to see her friend and craft fair manager, Belinda, approaching.

"Wow, didn't we?" Lia said. "The storms they predicted for last night didn't materialize, thank goodness."

"Would have been a soggy mess in these fields," Belinda said, her gaze taking in the mowed acres surrounding them.

"I know one person who might not have minded," Lia said. "My neighbor Jack Kuhn. From what I understand, the actual battle was fought in mud. Jack is big on historical accuracy."

"That's fine for him and his soldiers," Belinda said. "Our craft vendors prefer dry, tidy land. I heard about the ker-fuffle in the reenactment group. So that was your neighbor?"

Lia nodded. "It was a bit of a power struggle between him and the new guy, Arden Sprouse. Sprouse won out. I don't know anything about Sprouse, but Jack's a great guy and I understand he's put a lot of time and effort into the reenactments."

"He has." Maggie Wood said from her quilt booth, which had been set next to Lia's. "And it's a darned shame how Sprouse treated him. I fault the others, too, who should have stood up for Jack. But Sprouse's money apparently spoke louder than loyalty."

"So who is Arden Sprouse?" Lia asked. "Has he lived in Crandalsburg a while? If so, why has he just now become so involved?"

"He and his family showed up after he bought the Hub-bard Hotel a few months ago," Maggie said. "He has some other businesses, but what those are, exactly, I have no idea." Her lips curled derisively. "I don't mind newcomers joining in. But I don't much care for people who show up in our town and decide to start running things their own way." Maggie's already florid complexion had reddened close to the shade of her long, curly hair. The quilter was never one for soft-pedaling her opinions.

"Guys," Nicole warned from her booth to Lia's left. "That's Mrs. Sprouse heading over right now."

Heads turned toward the figure Nicole indicated with a

head jerk, Lia's included. She watched as the stout fifty-something woman made her way gradually toward them, dressed in period costume that indicated participation in the day's event. She paused for a few moments at Gilbert Bowen's candle booth, where she chatted briefly before moving on.

Lia's group turned their gazes away from the woman as she approached, except for Lia, who continued to watch. When their eyes met, Mrs. Sprouse smiled an open, dimpled smile. Lia returned it.

"You must be Lia Geiger!" Arden Sprouse's wife said. "I've heard so many good things about your wonderful knits. I'm Heidi Sprouse."

"I'm glad to meet you," Lia said. "Have you met our craft fair manager?" Lia introduced Belinda, who had turned back, and the two took in Heidi's compliments on the fair's offerings.

"I haven't managed to visit before, but I intend to make up for that," she said. Heidi talked enthusiastically about the craft booth items she'd already seen. "Arden would love the metal sculptures, I know."

At Heidi's mention of her husband, Lia felt a twinge of guilt on Jack's behalf, though she wasn't chatting with his nemesis. She supposed Jack would forgive her for being amiable with Arden's wife, who couldn't be blamed for her husband's actions. At least so far.

"I see you're dressed in costume," Lia said. "Are you playing a role in the activities?"

"Oh!" Heidi said, flapping a hand dismissively. "A very minor one." She tucked a stray gray-brown lock back into her cotton bonnet. "I like to look after our young men—you know, just making sure everyone has what they need. My son-in-law is one of them, you know. I guess you could say I play a Civil War mother. Or maybe the mother those poor soldiers would have liked to have close by."

She shook her head. "Of course, someone like that wouldn't have been near the battlefield. More likely helping at the hospital. But I'll be backstage, so to speak. No one to be noticed."

Heidi pulled a cell phone out of her skirt pocket and checked it. "I'd best get back. I just wanted to take a quick peek at your craft fair. But I'll be here again, you can count on that! So nice to meet you!"

Heidi bustled off, swerving toward two more booths on her way out as though unable to resist another look.

Lia leaned toward Maggie, who'd kept back among her quilts but who must have heard most of the conversation.

"What do you think? She seemed nice."

"I suppose," Maggie conceded, though reluctantly. "At least she's not taking over center stage like her husband. But . . . oh, I don't know. I'll wait until I see more."

Lia thought she'd do the same, if only out of loyalty to Jack.

Chapter 2

Crowds began filling the grounds, spreading out among the living history areas and the craft fair tents. Lia had plenty of interested browsers and a few sales of her smaller items, like mittens and caps, that could be carried easily. One woman surprised her by writing down the descriptions and prices of some of Lia's items in a little notebook, explaining, "I have to budget myself. I keep a list of everything that interests me in each booth. At the end of the day, I'll decide on what I want that's within my limit. I drive a long way to get here," she added. "I can only make it once a year for the reenactment and the craft fair. So I plan."

"Very wise," Lia said, hoping one of her knitted pieces would make it in.

Another shopper oohed and aahed over a colorful knitted throw but groaned over the weight and bulk. "I can't lug it around, but I also don't want to go all the way over to my car. I'm parked pretty far away."

"I can hold it for you with a small deposit," Lia offered. Diana, one of the Ninth Street Knitters, had worked long and hard on the throw, and Lia wanted to see her efforts rewarded.

The shopper jumped at the solution, and Lia tucked the multicolored throw out of sight, the buyer's name pinned carefully to it.

Lia thought about how pleased Diana would be to hear about that at the next Ninth Street Knitters meeting. The group of five had been gathering for years at Jen's house and only recently added knitting for modest profits to their knitting for pleasure. That began after Lia moved to Crandalsburg, when staying at the house she and Tom had shared for over twenty-five years became too painful after Tom's death.

Belinda, who knew her so well, had recognized the need for a change before Lia did and encouraged the move, throwing in the offer of running a weekend vendor's booth at the craft fair. It all had worked out extremely well, for which Lia was very grateful.

One particularly happy result was her daughter's recent relocation to Crandalsburg, staying temporarily with Lia before finding her own apartment. Hayley's move had come about because of disenchantment with her first postcollege job at a large marketing firm in Philadelphia. She'd found her niche working at the nearby alpaca farm, where she was in charge of handling occasional events on the grounds and promoting the farm's wonderful selection of alpaca yarns, those luxuriously soft and warm fibers that were Lia's favorite knitting choice.

Lia looked forward to Hayley joining her to watch the battle reenactment later in the day, along with Hayley's boyfriend, Brady McCormick, an officer in the Crandalsburg police force. It would be a new experience for all three, since Brady had lived in Crandalsburg only slightly longer than Lia.

Lia wouldn't be surprised if Pete Sullivan, Brady's boss and Crandalsburg's police chief, also came by. She seemed to be running into him more and more at large events, which, of course, as police chief, shouldn't be totally unexpected, though it was almost always off duty. She just wasn't sure if he'd always been that active in the community and she'd only noticed it after finally meeting him, or if it was fairly new. It also wasn't something she could comfortably ask.

But Pete was a nice guy, and if they ended up in conversation at these events, it was always enjoyable, so Lia intended to avoid overthinking it, at least for now.

As she glanced around the open-air craft fair, Lia spotted Sharon heading toward her. Her friend didn't look happy, though when she noticed Lia watching, she managed a smile. A not-too-convincing one.

"Something wrong?" Lia asked as Sharon drew near.

Sharon huffed. "That Sprouse family."

Uh-oh. "What happened?"

Sharon came up to Lia's booth and stood, shifting her weight from side to side. "I went over to the camp area to see Jack. This has always been such a wonderful event for him. I was hoping he'd be able to put aside the problems and changes that he hated and find enough to enjoy."

Lia waited, hoping it wouldn't be too awful.

Sharon drew a deep breath. "Jack was checking uniforms. You know what a stickler he's been about them?"

Lia nodded. She also knew some of the terms. "Farbs" was one, given to those who thought that blue jeans or tennis shoes worn with a uniform jacket was enough. It never was for Jack. He, on the other hand, might be called a "stitch counter" but only behind his back, and from what Lia understood not by any of his regular group. They felt the same as Jack, that sloppiness in a reenactment was unacceptable.

"Arden Sprouse and his son-in-law, Lucas, came sauntering by." Sharon curled her lips distastefully. "One's as bad as the other, though I guess you can't blame it on genetics. Maybe more like *birds of a feather*. Anyway, Arden started laughing at Jack, saying things like, 'Still polishing those buttons, Kuhn? Careful. The sun's out today. We don't want the reflections to blind the spectators.' Jack said he wasn't concerned with how shiny the buttons were, but that they'd better be the right buttons, not those plastic ones that were showing up.

"Lucas scoffed at that," Sharon said. "He claimed Jack was the only one who cared about nitpicky things like that. That the crowd just wanted a good show with lots of yelling and smoke. I could see Jack's temper rising, but he held it in and just turned back to what he was doing."

"Good for him," Lia said, appalled at the men's rudeness. "Those two don't sound like the kind who'll stick with the reenactment long. With luck, they'll both move on to something else. Maybe demolition derbies."

"I don't know," Sharon said. "Sprouse has sunk plenty of money into this. He must see it as long-term."

Lia thought about that. "He did buy a hotel in the area," she said. "It could be that he sees the reenactment as good business for the tourists it draws."

Sharon groaned. "That and liking an opportunity to puff himself up. That 'Captain Anderson' that he claims is a maternal ancestor. Jack doesn't believe the original Anderson had much to do with our battle or that Sprouse is his descendant. He thinks Sprouse just wanted any reason to dress up and wave a sword."

"Does he have an authentic uniform?" Lia asked, thinking if he didn't, it would be another thorn in Jack's side.

"As far as I know." Sharon smiled wryly. "I probably would have heard if it wasn't."

"Probably," Lia agreed with a grin. "Want to join us to watch the battle? Hayley will have blankets to sit on."

"Sure!"

Lia thought about jokingly adding that if they were lucky Sprouse and his son-in-law would be the battle's designated victims. But from what she'd heard, that wouldn't necessarily be bad. Volunteers often begged to be one of the pretend casualties. Sprouse might love the chance to perform an overblown, theatrical "death," which would only annoy Sharon, Jack, and many others even more. Best not to tempt fate.

Chapter 3

Hayley walked into the vendors' area, calling, "Almost ready, Mom? Brady's saving us a spot on the slope. We should have a good view of the battle."

"Great! Yes, I'm done here." Lia pulled out her cashbox to transfer the contents to her tote. Bill Landry, the craft fair's security person, would be standing guard while the vendors left their booths, but it didn't hurt to be extra cautious.

"You have a couple of blankets, right?" Lia asked. "Sharon will be joining us."

"Yup, and Brady thought to bring plastic cloths for underneath in case the ground was damp."

"Clever guy."

"And we'll be facing east—no sun in our eyes."

"He thinks of everything. Or was that your idea?" Lia asked. She slung the tote over her shoulder as she came out from behind her counter.

"His, I have to admit, but not begrudgingly." Hayley grinned. "Not when it makes my day that much better. Want me to carry that tote? It looks heavy."

"No, it's fine, thanks. Just bulky." Lia waved to Bill at the other end of the open-air tent, grateful for his presence. She was the last of the vendors to leave, having had a last-minute customer—not anything she would begrudge, either, especially with a viewing spot saved and waiting for her.

They joined the flow of spectators heading to the battlefield, passing the living history area. Lia was glad to see several people pause for Olivia's soapmaking presentation, knowing how much effort her craft fair friend had put into it.

Hayley glanced over as well. "I've learned a lot today that I never knew about the Civil War time period," she said. "My history classes went into things like what led to the war and all the generals' names. But I never got a sense of what everyday people went through."

"Schools have only so much time," Lia said as they walked past a candle-making demonstration. "Education can't stop after graduation. There's so much more to learn."

"I know I'm glad I didn't live back then," Hayley said. "It must have been a tough time." She paused, thinking. "Then again, the twentieth century and this one haven't exactly been problem-free." She followed that with a laugh. "I wonder what people a hundred years from now will think? Things feel pretty good to me right now, but will they look back on us with pity?"

Lia looked at her daughter. "Interesting thought. What might they pity?"

"Oh, maybe things like how we had to spend hours in a car or plane to get from one place to another?" Hayley suggested. "You know, like instead of being beamed through a device in a few seconds?"

"Right now," Lia said, as they came to a halt for some kind of holdup, "I wouldn't mind being beamed over this crowd so I could sink down on one of your blankets. I've been on my feet for hours."

Hayley glanced around before taking Lia's arm. "C'mon," she said, pointing to a line of trees. "Let's slip through here. Before Brady came, I wandered around and got the lay of the land."

The dense tree line they wound through opened into the reenactors' camp, which was a beehive of activity. Hayley kept to the edge and out of their way, taking what she assured Lia was a shortcut to the spectator area. Lia caught sight of Heidi bustling about, looking, as she'd described herself, motherly, as she helped young soldiers with things like their uniform buttons and buckles. Rifles were being handed around—long ones, but with no bayonets attached.

Lia spotted Jack carrying two rifles with bayonets and realized they must be his and Lucas Hall's, which had been used in the fencing demonstration. She described the demonstration to Hayley as she watched him hand the rifles to an older man outside a tent, probably to be looked after by him during the battle reenactment, when Jack would wield a safer weapon. Her lip curled over the term *safer weapon*, which struck her as an oxymoron, but then she shrugged. At least in the current situation it was appropriate.

A group of men farther away began pushing a cannon, a sight one didn't see every day. The camp Lia and Hayley were edging past held Union soldiers. Lia assumed a second camp, somewhere in the area, had Confederates. The thought of each side lining up to attack was both unnerving and sad, and Lia had to remind herself again that it was all pretend.

They left the camp behind as Hayley led the way to the sloped viewing area, crowds gradually filling in spaces there.

"There's Brady," Hayley said, pointing to an oak tree where Brady stood waving. Hayley waved back and began winding her way upward between other spectators' blankets.

After the sober thoughts Lia had while passing through the camp, she was glad to see that most people settling in seemed fairly serious, not laughing or excited as though what they were about to see was on the level of a football or soccer game. They seemed to understand, as Lia did, that the reenactment was a learning experience as well as a tribute to all those who risked or lost their lives on this spot so many years ago.

"We made it!" Hayley said as they reached Brady. "Had to go out of our way a bit to get past a traffic jam."

"Hello, Brady," Lia said. "Thank you for setting all this up."

"No trouble, Mrs. Geiger." Brady's red hair glowed in the sun, which Lia was glad to see came from behind them. Despite several summer months spent outdoors, Brady was barely tanned. With his complexion, careful sun blocking was called for, which Hayley had assured her Brady was diligent about.

Brady invited Lia to sit on one of the blankets he'd spread out, but she declined for the moment. "I should keep an eye out for Sharon, my next-door neighbor." Just then her cell phone dinged.

Where r u? Sharon texted.

Lia quickly texted their whereabouts as best she could describe. Within minutes Hayley cried, "There she is!" All three waved and shouted until Sharon finally spotted them, then made her way up.

"Thanks!" she said. "The crowd got so big all of a sudden. I didn't think I'd ever find you."

"Another reason I'm glad to be in this century," Hayley said, wiggling her cell phone.

"She's become aware of nineteenth-century shortcomings," Lia explained. "Let's sit down," she said. "My feet need a rest."

"Mine, too." Sharon took a spot next to Lia, and Brady and Hayley settled down on the second blanket.

Hayley leaned forward and asked, "How's Mr. Kuhn doing?"

"Jack's fine," Sharon said. "Busy day for him!" she added, obviously trying to stay positive.

"Water, anyone?" Brady asked. He pulled bottles out of the cooler next to him. Food wasn't allowed in the viewing area, but water was.

Lia and Sharon each took one. As Lia twisted the cap off hers, she spotted a figure walking in their direction and smiled in recognition. Pete Sullivan.

She watched for a while, curious to see his destination. As police chief, he knew and was known by many people, and she saw him pause occasionally to chat. But he continued on. As he drew closer his gaze swept the area. He saw Lia watching, grinned, and took a few more steps.

"Hi there," he said. "I think I've climbed as far as I can. Got space for one more?"

Brady jumped up immediately. "Yes, sir! Plenty of room."

"Please join us," Hayley said. She began to pull out a beach towel to add to Brady's and her blanket, but Pete walked over toward Lia. He spread his jacket on the ground and sank down. He let out an *oof!* though Lia doubted it was from fatigue. He was an energetic fifty-something, and though his hair was silvery, it set off an only slightly lined tanned face.

Lia introduced Sharon to Pete after handing him a water bottle that Brady passed over.

"You're just in time," Sharon said. "The battle should start soon."

Pete nodded. "Your first time seeing it?" he asked Lia.

"Yes, and I've been so impressed with the whole event. The volunteers are all doing such a professional job."

"Lia knitted authentic socks for the reenactors," Sharon said.

"Just a few pairs," Lia said. "My knitting group pitched in to make many more."

"Socks?" Pete asked. "What's special about the socks?"

"The original ones were all homemade, for one thing," Lia said. "If the reenactors want to be completely authentic, they do so down to underwear and socks. Women back then supported their troops, and that included knitting for them. Some even knitted colors or patterns at the top that indicated their county. It was a very patriotic effort."

"That makes sense," Pete said. "I just never thought of that before."

"Sharon's husband is a longtime reenactor," Lia said. "I learned most of what I know from him."

"He'll be in the battle?" Pete asked Sharon, who nodded.

"I can usually pick him out," she said. "When I do, I'll let everyone know," she said, adding with a smile, "you can count on it."

"Ooh, here they come!" Hayley said.

All eyes turned toward the field as a line of navy blue–uniformed men marched forward to the steady beat of drums, their rifles held against their shoulders, the Stars and Stripes held high. One man strutted several feet ahead, turning back every few steps to wave his sword as though urging them on.

"That's Arden Sprouse," Sharon said dryly.

A second group, approaching from the far right, caught Lia's eye. These clearly represented the Confederate troops, with their gray uniforms and the Stars and Bars flying.

"Are all these reenactors from Crandalsburg?" she asked.

"Oh no," Sharon said. "Groups come from all over. I believe the Confederate ones this year are from North Carolina. Not too long of a trek, but we've had some travel from as far away as California to represent either side."

Lia nodded. The number of men below kept growing, something she hadn't fully expected. Crandalsburg would definitely have needed additional volunteers.

"There's the cannons," Pete said.

Lia winced as she saw the deadly weapons roll forward. As she watched, a memory came to her. It was a documentary she'd once seen that showed photos of open carriages filled with gentlemen and parasoled ladies lined up at a safe point to view one of the early battles. The attitude of the day seemed to be that of watching a simple competition, though how that could be boggled Lia's mind. Just anticipating what she knew on this day was safe and harmless still made Lia highly uneasy. She didn't understand those spectators of long ago wanting to witness what would truly be a bloody scene.

The lines of opposing sides stopped with plenty of distance between them. At a given signal one cannon boomed, sending up a huge cloud of smoke. A second cannon answered. Then soldiers shouted as they fired their rifles, multiple cracks and booms sounding as gunpowder filled the air.

Some men dropped to the ground, but others rushed forward as more cannon shots fired. The distance between the two sides quickly closed as hand-to-hand combat commenced. Fortunately, at least for Lia, the increasing smoke blurred the scene, though she could still hear the screams of those pretending to be wounded.

It was all too realistic. Lia tensed and sometimes closed her eyes, only to snap them open at startling noises. She looked over at Hayley. Splayed fingers partially covered her eyes. Brady, however, leaned forward to watch intently.

"I can't find Jack," Sharon said. "There's too much smoke."

"Are you okay?" Pete asked Lia. He was looking at her with concern.

She nodded and tried to smile but then grimaced as the wail of a "wounded" reenactor pierced the air.

"It upset me, too, my first time," Sharon assured her. "Now I just focus on the details." She turned back to the battle to continue her search for Jack.

Sharon's words helped to calm Lia, and she tried viewing the scene as a performance. As a onetime surgical nurse, she hadn't expected to become so stressed. But her work had been in a much more quiet, sterile environment. She doubted she would have done well in a MASH situation.

Finally a bugle sounded. The shooting ended, and each side withdrew, though as the smoke cleared it revealed dozens of men lying on the ground, some raising an arm but many more motionless. Horse-drawn wagons rolled onto the field, and white-coated men jumped down from them to begin tending to the wounded, though any aid in the actual war would have been minimal, leading to the extremely high number of casualties.

The crowd began to stir, and Lia's small group stood and stretched.

"Gosh, that was more realistic than I expected," Hayley said. Brady put an arm around her for a sympathetic squeeze.

"It makes for a good history lesson," Pete said, with Sharon nodding in agreement.

They discussed the battle details for some minutes, Sharon having advised waiting for the crowd to thin. Her gaze occasionally swept the field, still searching for Jack. Pete had his back to the battlefield, but Lia faced it and was the first to notice a commotion at the far end of the field near a clump of trees. Sharon noticed it, too, and caught Lia's eye worriedly.

Just then Pete's cell phone buzzed. He glanced at the screen and swiped at it, barking, "Sullivan." The others waited as his expression quickly tensed.

"I'll be right there." Pete looked at Brady. "McCormick, come with me. There's a problem."

Sharon's fingers clenched Lia's arm, and Lia turned to her. Her friend's face had gone white.

Chapter 4

Lia stuck close to Sharon's side. Clearly something very bad had happened. Pete and Brady had rushed down the slope to the center of the activity, next to the small clump of trees. It wasn't long before sirens sounded in the distance.

"I have to go there," Sharon said, her voice tense. Lia nodded, though she wondered how near they could get.

"Go ahead, Mom," Hayley said. "I'll pick up our things."

"You've tried Jack's phone?" Lia asked Sharon.

"He's not answering." Sharon began to push through the crowd, which stood frozen in place, eyes fixed on what was happening down below.

"Ma'am, you have to stay back," a uniformed officer said as they reached the battlefield, stopping Sharon from getting any closer to the tree area. Several of the uniformed reenactors were helping block off the area, presumably until more police arrived.

Sharon spotted one she knew and worked her way over

to him, Lia close behind. "Matt, is it Jack? Please, I can't find him. Is he hurt?"

The burly man with a chest-length beard, who might have looked fearsome in a hand-to-hand battle except for his gentle eyes, leaned forward to reassure her. "It's not Jack."

Sharon sagged with relief, then instantly asked, "What happened? Somebody's hurt. Who is it?"

The man hesitated. He glanced around before saying, "It's Arden Sprouse."

Sharon's mouth worked, but when no sound came out Lia asked, "How bad?"

There was a long intake of breath before the man answered. "He's dead," he told them, adding, "That's all I know."

That evening, Hayley stopped at Lia's house before heading to her own place. She looked as tired as Lia felt. The Battle of Crandalsburg reenactment had been closed down soon after the discovery of Arden Sprouse's body, which for Lia and other craft fair vendors meant closing up their booths. Hayley had pitched in, helping Lia pack her socks, sweaters, and other items into protective boxes or bags to be left under guard until they could be moved back into the Schumacher barn, whenever that might be. She'd then gone on to help the living history people, as much unexplained activity continued in the battle area.

Lia hadn't seen Heidi Sprouse, but Arden's wife had been in Lia's thoughts a lot. She hoped the poor woman was getting the support she needed. Lia still didn't know exactly what had happened to Arden. Heart attack automatically came to mind because of his age and added weight, and Lia found herself hoping that would be the explanation. That, or some other natural cause. But that immediate call to Pete Sullivan, along with the looks on the faces of the reenactors near the scene, had been telling her otherwise. She forced herself to stop speculating. An exact cause would come out before long. There was no need to overthink until then.

"How're you doing?" Hayley asked.

"I'm fine," Lia said from her seat in her knitting chair. "And thank you so much for your help. Any word from Brady?"

"Nothing yet. He'll get in touch when he can." Hayley had learned by then what to expect, or not expect, from her police officer boyfriend when he was on duty. "Did Sharon finally locate her husband?" she asked, as she headed to the kitchen in search of something to drink. Though her stay with Lia hadn't been particularly long before she found her own apartment, Hayley continued to make herself at home at Lia's house. Which was fine with Lia. "Want anything?" Hayley called as she opened the refrigerator.

"No, thanks, and yes, Sharon did find Jack. Or rather, he found her. He'd come down with one of his migraines just before the battle and had to sit it out. Or rather rest it out. He'd gone to an empty tent to lie down."

"Bummer. I hear those things can really knock you out. Bad timing." Hayley carried her bottle of peach green tea into the living room and flopped down, twisting off the cap. Lia's tan-and-white ragdoll cat, Daphne, immediately ran over and jumped onto her lap.

"There's meds you can take when you feel one coming on that help," Lia said. "I don't know if Jack had anything like that with him or not. But he still might not have felt up to participating in the battle."

Lia wondered if the extra stress Jack had been under helped bring on the migraine. The reenactor organization would be changed now, with Sprouse gone. How exactly was yet to be seen.

She asked about Hayley's work. As the relatively new marketing director for the Weber Alpaca Farm, Hayley was in the process of launching a new program, designed to spread the word widely on the wonderful alpaca yarns processed at the farm. Hayley hoped to educate and bring in more knitters, both to the Webers' yarn and gift shop and to their website for online orders.

Hayley was explaining her plan when Lia's phone rang. It was Belinda. Her friend rarely called just to chat, so Lia excused herself and swiped to answer. "Hi, Belinda. What's up?"

"Bad news," the craft fair manager said without preamble. "Arden Sprouse was murdered."

"Oh no." Lia had dearly hoped that wouldn't be the case. "What do you know?"

"Only that it probably happened sometime during the battle reenactment. I happened to pick that up as I was leaving the barn tonight. Lia," Belinda said. Her voice then rose an octave. "Another murder! On the grounds of the craft fair!"

Lia knew what her friend was thinking. The craft fair had barely recovered from the murder of Darren Peebles, Belinda's ex-husband, only five months earlier.

"Belinda," she began, hoping to soothe her, "that was so different. Darren's murder happened right in the middle of the craft fair barn, the building he'd threatened to buy and tear down. Sprouse has no connection to the craft fair at all. He was there for the reenactment."

"I know, but just you wait! Media reports will link his murder location to us and bring up Darren, just as people were starting to forget."

Lia knew that was a good possibility, but there was nothing she or Belinda could do about it.

"We already took a big hit," Belinda wailed, "having to close down the entire operation for the rest of the weekend. A whole day lost for all my vendors."

"One day," Lia said. "We'll survive it. And don't forget, Belinda, a man lost his life. His family is dealing with so much worse."

There was brief silence. Then Belinda said, "You're right. I wasn't thinking of the family. I'm sorry for them, of course." Another pause. "But—"

"I know. You're worried about the craft fair. You're used to looking after us. But don't worry just yet. It might not be bad."

Belinda sighed heavily but agreed that there was nothing she could do for the moment. They ended the call, and Lia looked up to see Hayley watching intently.

"Arden Sprouse was murdered," Lia told her.

Hayley blew a low whistle and hugged Daphne closely. "Wow," she said softly.

Chapter 5

The next morning Lia had barely finished her coffee when her phone rang. She sucked in her breath when she read Sharon's name on the screen.

"Lia, can I come over?" her neighbor asked.

"Of course." Lia didn't ask what was up. She set her mug in the sink and went to the door to let her in.

Sharon declined Lia's offer of coffee and got straight to her concerns. "The police have called Jack to come to the station." She sank onto the sofa.

Lia took the chair across from her. "Did they say why?"

"Only that they have a few questions." Sharon twisted the ends of her blue cardigan together. Daphne approached, but Sharon's nervously bouncing knees turned her instead to the kitchen.

The morning news had reported on Arden Sprouse's death and that it was considered a homicide but offered no further details.

"Did Jack have any more information about what happened to Sprouse?" Lia asked.

"Sprouse was stabbed." She huffed. "Remember how he led the group of soldiers out, marching in front and waving his make-believe sword? All for show, of course, since nobody needed to be led. Well, once the shooting started, he apparently turned off and left the field. I didn't catch it, and with all the shouting and smoke only a few of the men around him did, though there was too much going on by then for anyone to notice where he went. But it must have been to those trees off to the side. That's where he was found, anyway."

"Stabbed," Lia repeated. "Did they find the weapon?"

"No." Sharon looked at Lia plaintively. "I just don't know why they want to question Jack again! He said he told them all he knew yesterday. The police were talking with everybody, and it took forever. When he came home he was wiped out."

"I can imagine. So he told them about his migraine and having to find someplace to lie down?"

"He did, but there isn't anyone who can back that up. Everyone in the area was pretty busy getting ready for the battle. Jack said when the migraine hit, he knew he couldn't do anything except lie down, and he just wanted to get out of the way. With his head pounding, he needed a dark place where he could hunker down until it passed."

"Surely someone must have noticed," Lia offered. "It just might take some time to find out who."

"Lordy, I hope so." Sharon said as she rubbed at her arms. "It's common knowledge how Jack felt about Sprouse and all his changes to the group."

"Sharon, anyone who knows Jack also knows he wouldn't be capable of murder."

"It's certainly the truth," Sharon said. "But," she said, her voice rising, "couldn't someone argue that the murder wasn't planned, that it happened in the heat of the moment? Heaven knows Sprouse had a way of stirring people up. He seemed to take pleasure in it and went out of his way to do it."

"Surely Jack isn't the only person who was agitated by the man. Please don't worry too much, Sharon. The police are probably calling a lot of people back. They couldn't cover everything they needed to with the huge number of people at that crime scene. It'll take many more questions to get the facts straight."

Sharon smiled at that, weakly, but it was still an improvement. When Daphne wandered back, she actually reached down to pet the cat. "Thank you, Lia. I knew I could count on you."

"Want that coffee now?" Lia asked.

Sharon's smile grew wider. "No, I'll go and let you get back to whatever you were doing."

Lia assured Sharon she was welcome anytime and walked with her to the door.

As Sharon stepped onto the porch, she paused. "I just thought of something." She turned back to Lia, a hopeful look on her face. "Jack never carries a knife. It's just not his thing. And he wouldn't dream of carrying one during a reenactment. That should settle things right there."

Lia managed an agreeable nod, though she wasn't as confident as her neighbor on that point. Sharon had overlooked another possibility. But Lia wasn't about to point it out, not until a lot more information was released.

Lia got an unexpectedly pleasant call that afternoon in the midst of her ongoing uneasiness. It came from the woman who had taken meticulous notes on the items that interested her the day before, as she browsed through the craft fair stalls.

"I got your number from the fair manager," the woman said after introducing herself as Penny Gardner. "She said it'd be okay to call you. I wanted to buy the layette yesterday. The white one with the little butterflies?" she reminded Lia. "But everything shut down before I could. Remember I said I had come a long way?"

"I do remember," Lia said.

"Well, I can't drive back to get it. I just don't have the time. But I really want that set. A niece is expecting her first, and I'd like to have it for her baby shower. Do you still have it?"

When Lia told her she did, Penny said, "Wonderful! Here's my idea. If I send you a check, would you pack it up and mail it to me? I'll pay the extra cost, of course."

"Absolutely. I'd be very happy to." Lia heard the sigh of satisfaction on the other end. She recited her address and estimated the shipping costs, not concerned if it was on the low side. Anyone who went to the trouble this woman did to buy one of her Ninth Street Knits deserved a little perk if it came to that.

"Are you contacting any other vendors?" Lia asked. "I remember you were checking them all out."

"I'm going to call the jewelry lady," Penny said, a smile in her voice. "A little present to myself. There's a couple of other things I'm still thinking about." She sighed. "Such a hassle that they closed the event down so suddenly. I'm not sure what happened. Some kind of accident?"

"Yes, a rather serious one," Lia hedged. "But I don't have too many details yet."

"Well, that's unfortunate. I hope that person, whoever it was, will be okay."

Arden Sprouse wouldn't be, but Lia was more concerned about Jack. Despite the reassurances she'd given Sharon, not knowing all the facts yet, Lia wasn't at all sure that Jack would be fine. But she thanked Penny and promised to send off the layette set soon, happy at least for that bright spot for Penny, herself, and Tracy, the Ninth Street Knitter who'd made the pretty set. Who knew what might come next?

W hat came next turned out to be bad news, and it came in the most public way possible: through the local television station.

"We have breaking news on the recent murder of local businessman Arden Sprouse," the young female reporter said as she looked sternly into the camera. "Police have confirmed that the murder weapon that killed Sprouse at the Crandalsburg Battle reenactment on Saturday was a bayonet attached to a Civil War rifle belonging to one of the battle reenactors. At this point no charges have been filed. Police Chief Peter Sullivan has stated that the investigation is ongoing. Join us for more news tonight at eleven."

Belonging to one of the reenactors. As far as Lia knew, there were only two rifles with deadly bayonets on the grounds: Jack's and Lucas Hall's, both of which had been used for the bayonet demonstration. That narrowed the field considerably. But the reporter also stated that no charges had been filed. That told Lia that the police didn't have enough evidence to do so. Yet. But Lia had watched Jack hand two rifles with bayonets, presumably his and Lucas Hall's, to an older man. With both rifles likely valuable, they must have been left with him to be guarded. If they were, then how could either of them have been used to murder Sprouse?

Lia could think of several answers. The one she liked least was that either Jack or Lucas had been seen to retrieve it. But if that were the case, wouldn't one have been immediately charged? Then again, what about the man who'd taken charge of the rifles? Wouldn't he be a suspect?

Lia looked out her front window. Jack's pickup was there, parked behind Sharon's blue Impala. They both were home.

Lia picked up her phone and hit Sharon's number. When her friend picked up she asked, "Mind if I come over?"

Chapter 6

When Sharon opened the door, she asked Lia, "You heard?"

"The breaking news? Yes." Lia looked past Sharon to see Jack pacing, his hands jammed into his pockets.

Jack paused for a second to say, "C'mon in, Lia," before resuming his walk.

"Jack," Lia said as she stepped in, "I know you're completely innocent of this crime."

That stopped the man's pacing, and some of the tension left his face. "Thank you for that, Lia. I hope you're not the only one."

"Of course she won't be," Sharon said. She went up to her husband and hugged his shoulder. "The whole idea is ridiculous. Anyone could have used it."

Lia looked from one to the other. "So it was your bayonet, Jack?"

Jack nodded grimly. "Sprouse's blood was on it."

Lia's stomach clenched, but she did her best to seem unfazed. "Can we talk about that?" she asked. "About how that could have happened?"

Jack waved Lia to one of the chairs in the living room. He and Sharon sat together on the cheery flower-printed sofa, an incongruous background to the stiff postures and tight expressions of the two people on it.

"Sharon told you about my migraine?" Jack asked.

Lia nodded. "And that you had gone to an empty tent to lie down. Before that, I saw you turn over the two rifles—yours and Lucas Hall's—to someone. I assumed it was for safekeeping. Who was that man?"

"Herb Weaver. He's been in our reenactment group for years, long before I joined. A great guy, probably over eighty. He gave up doing the battlefield action when his hip gave out, but he still loves to help out as much as he can."

"Bad hip and in his eighties," Lia said. "So, unlikely to have used your rifle bayonet against Sprouse?"

"Definitely not Herb," Jack agreed firmly. "I know he disliked Sprouse and felt as appalled about what he was doing to the group as I did. But besides not being physically up to it, Herb would never act with any kind of violence. The old joke was if Herb accidently bumped somebody too hard during a reenactment, he'd stop and apologize. Unfortunately . . ." Jack rubbed his chin.

"Yes?" Lia prompted.

"Well, Herb's mind isn't as sharp as it used to be. I didn't think that'd be a problem when I put the rifles in his care. I wasn't really worried about theft—Lucas either, as far as I could tell. We just wanted Herb to keep them out of the way of careless damage or being accidentally mixed in with the other rifles. At the time I still intended to take part in the battle reenactment, as did Lucas, but definitely not with those two weapons. We had to leave them with someone. Herb assured me he'd keep a close eye on the rifles."

"But he didn't?" Lia asked.

"Not the entire time." Jack heaved a sigh. "He got hungry. He heard there were johnnycakes being handed out at living history, and he went over to get some. There were several people who verified that," he added.

"So anyone could have slipped into that tent while he was gone and grabbed your rifle," Lia said. "That's good."

"Yes, except there I was, alone in my tent during the battle reenactment when Sprouse got stabbed. Everyone knows about the problems between us, which were only escalating. Anyone who chooses to can decide that I faked a migraine to stay behind and murder Sprouse." Jack rubbed his thinning gray-sprinkled hair and sank his head in his hands.

"But not the police," Sharon stated firmly.

"So far," Jack said.

"I don't believe they will," Lia said. "Not at all. The police would need more evidence to charge you, Jack, which they obviously haven't found because there is none."

"Exactly what I've been telling him," Sharon said. "Pretty soon they'll find what they need on the actual murderer, and it'll all be over."

Jack put his arm around his wife for a grateful squeeze. But he didn't appear convinced by her statement.

Lia tried to look positive, for Sharon's sake, but her thoughts were aligned more with Jack's. Arden Sprouse's murder appeared to have been planned for an extremely crowded area, which could make relevant evidence hard to find and the murderer difficult to uncover. She worried that if the murder was never solved, Jack could be stuck in a very gray area of lingering suspicion. That wouldn't be as terrible as being charged, of course, but it wasn't a good place to be in, either. Not at all.

After returning home, Lia got a call from Hayley.

"Mom, do you still have that slow cooker you used to use?"

Lia pictured her older slow cooker, the one she often cooked with until she won a shiny new one in a charity raffle. She'd kept the other one, as she had kept far too many things—*just in case*—though the expected *case* had never appeared.

"I do," she said, the memory of having packed the thing during her move from York but storing it in her new basement coming to her.

"Does it still work?" Hayley asked.

"It should. Did you want it?"

"I could really use it. I got spoiled coming home from work every night to your ready-made meals."

"You often fixed dinners on the weekends when I spent all day at the craft fair," Lia reminded her.

"Yes, but I don't have that kind of time during the week. I don't know how I managed when I lived in Philly. Ate out far too much, I suppose. But that gets expensive."

Hayley had taken a pay cut when she left her job in Philadelphia for the position at the Weber Alpaca Farm. She'd accepted the cut for a job that made her much happier. Her living expenses were lower in Crandalsburg, but some things remained the same: car costs and insurance, to name only two. Lia was glad to see her daughter looking for ways to manage her budget.

"Let me check out the pot. If it's in good shape, I'll run it over. Is there anything else I can bring?" Hayley had moved most of her belongings out of Lia's house, but a few boxes remained until Hayley decided to either keep or chuck their contents.

"Not today," Hayley said. "I promise I'll get to those other things soon."

"No hurry," Lia assured her. After having Hayley's personal and work-related things fill every spare nook and cranny of Lia's little house, it currently felt almost cavernous. Besides, she was aware of boxes of unused items in her basement that she'd intended to go through for months, a task that seemed to slip farther down on her to-do list with every passing day. She ended the call and headed downstairs to make at least one small dent in that hoard, thanks to Hayley.

Lia dug out the slow cooker and after a quick check found it to be in good working condition. She washed it up, then grabbed her purse and keys to drive it over, dropping in a generous bagful of the chocolate chip cookies she'd baked a couple of days ago—one of Hayley's favorites.

When Lia pulled up to the house Hayley had moved to, she thought how lucky her daughter was to have snagged the apartment there. The owner had converted the entire upper floor into a separate living space, adding a small kitchen before dividing the rest into a bedroom, bathroom, and sitting area. Hayley had a private stairway that led from the backyard, which she had permission to use—with specific rules, of course, none of which were unreasonable.

The owner, a woman in her mid-sixties, lived in the lower apartment. Hayley had told Lia that Marlaine Griffith had grown up in the house and never married. She'd turned the house into separate apartments after inheriting it from her parents, telling Hayley she didn't need the space and that, besides the extra income, she liked having someone else on the premises.

"But only females," she'd declared, because apparently men were too noisy, and they didn't know how to look after a place properly. Ms. Griffith had no intentions of being anyone's housekeeper.

A woman who knew her own mind, Lia thought as she climbed out of her car, soon spotting the landlady energetically raking leaves.

"Good afternoon, Marlaine," Lia called. She'd chatted with the woman often enough to be on a first-name basis, though the chats had been short and mostly about the weather.

Marlaine, dressed in loose jeans and a sweatshirt, looked up and returned the greeting briskly while continuing to rake. Lia had picked up early on that Marlaine was someone who focused closely on the job at hand and was not to be distracted from it, so Lia continued on down the flagstone walk at the side of the house that led to Hayley's staircase. Hayley had apparently seen her from her window because the door at the top of those stairs swung open with Hayley calling, "Come on up, Mom."

When she made it to the top, Lia handed her daughter the slow cooker. "Thank you for taking this off my hands," she said. "If there's anything else you can use from my basement, I'll be delighted to turn it over. Just let me know."

"Thanks. So far I'm good. Oooh, cookies!" Hayley said as she spotted them. "Thanks again! Want to help me chop up a few veggies for this handy thing?" she asked, leading the way inside. "I plan to have everything ready to toss in tomorrow morning. Then my dinner will be waiting when I come home. And the next day, and maybe the next one, too."

"Sure." Lia rolled up her sleeves and washed her hands at Hayley's sink. As they chopped, she described her talk with Jack and Sharon.

"Gosh, poor Jack," Hayley said, trimming the leaves off a second leek.

"I don't suppose Brady has mentioned anything about the murder, such as there being a strong suspect?" Lia asked.

"No, not a thing. I get the feeling they're pretty stuck, what with the wide-open possibilities. You know, because of all the people in the area but no witnesses or clues."

"Other than knowing it was Jack's bayonet that was used." Lia gathered up her parsnip peelings to dispose of.

"Right. Other than the bayonet. Odd that they found that so soon, though, isn't it?"

"It is," Lia said, "now that you mention it. I'll ask Jack if he knows how that came about."

"And I'll ask Brady." Hayley paused, then turned to Lia with a lopsided grin. "I have a feeling we're getting involved in this investigation, Mom. Are we?"

"Only to the extent of trying to get a few points straight. Did you want some of those cut up?" Lia asked, pointing to a bag of red-skinned potatoes.

"Yes, five, please, peeled and diced. But isn't that how we got pulled in pretty darn far the last couple of times? One thing kept leading to another."

Lia rinsed off her first potato. "I'm sure our excellent Crandalsburg police will soon have this situation, this murder, well in hand."

"Except . . . ?" Hayley prompted.

"Except," Lia said, "if Jack Kuhn isn't completely cleared of any wrongdoing, something will have to be done."

"By you?"

Lia picked up her peeler and smiled at her daughter. "We'll see."

Chapter 7

The next morning, Lia carried her coffee into the living room to catch the news on TV, a routine that was usually a relaxing time for her. But that day she felt some tension as she took her seat, wondering what might come out next about Arden Sprouse's murder.

The program began with the report of a garbage truck accident causing a traffic backup on the turnpike, followed by one of a local house fire, then a video of the governor visiting a Harrisburg senior center. Lia took a sip of her coffee and ran one hand over Daphne's back as the cat snuggled next to her. When they went to a commercial, Lia took a second sip.

The news anchor returned, and a couple of upcoming political bills were discussed. After that, a photo of Arden Sprouse flashed on the screen as his murder at the reenactment was recounted. The dark-haired woman behind the anchor desk reported, "Lucas Hall, son-in-law of Arden

Sprouse, has spoken out for the first time on this horrific tragedy, which has affected his family so terribly." Lia set her mug down on the table, a fortunate move.

She soon saw the man identified as Hall—thirtyish, tall, and fit, with hair combed slickly back from his face in a style Lia happened to find off-putting, especially when combined with an aggressively scowling expression, which Hall displayed. But she reminded herself that his wife's father had just been murdered—obviously nothing to smile about it. She also tried to clear her mind of Sharon's tale of Lucas's taunting of Jack so she could listen with an open mind.

The young male reporter spoke into a handheld microphone as he introduced Lucas, who stood outside a large home, presumably his own. The reporter began by asking how he and his father-in-law happened to be at the reenactment. Lucas's answer implied that their role was much larger than Lia knew to be accurate. If Sharon was watching, Lia could imagine her color rising. But that was nothing compared to what came out next.

"The police," Lucas cried, "need to stop diddling around and arrest Jack Kuhn now for the murder of my father-in-law!" He jabbed his finger at the camera. "Kuhn is a complete maniac. The vicious verbal attacks he made against my father-in-law are common knowledge, all because Arden stepped up to fix the problems in the reenactors group. Verbal attacks apparently weren't enough for Kuhn, and now my father-in-law is dead. Kuhn needs to be arrested and locked up for it!"

The reporter proceeded to recount the known details of Arden Sprouse's murder, and to Lia's mind seemed to be confirming Lucas's horrible words, as if no other explanation other than Jack being the perpetrator was plausible.

Lia clicked off the television and sat staring at the blank set, appalled at what she'd just seen and heard. Daphne, as though sensing her mood, began licking at Lia's hand, which distracted Lia enough to relax a bit, and she ruffled Daphne's fur. "I wish you could cool everyone down with that."

Lia glanced at her coffee mug, wondering if she might have thrown it at the television screen had it still been in hand. Probably not, but she couldn't speak for Sharon or Jack if they'd happened to see what she just had.

Spouting such drivel on TV wouldn't help find Sprouse's murderer, who was probably chuckling somewhere right now after hearing it. But who could that be? Lia had been so focused on who it couldn't be—Jack—that she hadn't considered who actually could have stabbed Sprouse. Most of what she knew about the man, she'd learned through Sharon and Jack, and some from Maggie, who'd mentioned Sprouse as having various business holdings.

It was time to find out more. Surely a man of his kind, who had his finger in a lot of pies and loved the control, had made enemies beyond the reenactors. If Lia could come up with names, it might at least help take that unfair focus off Jack.

Her next question was, Where to start?

She received help with that before long from Jen Beasley.

"How are you doing?" Jen asked when Lia picked up her call. "Bob and I only recently learned about the murder and the entire reenactment event being closed down. How distressing! Did you know the man?"

"I didn't," Lia said, "but I met his wife—now his widow—just that day, before it all happened."

"The poor woman." Jen clucked sympathetically.

"Yes, I'm sorry for her and for the rest of his family, too, of course. But I'm not happy with what her son-in-law stated on TV a short time ago." Lia described Lucas Hall's televised interview and how much it could hurt her friend and neighbor Jack.

"It was your neighbor's bayonet?" Jen said, dismayed. Lia hastened to explain how it could have been used by almost anyone while Jack was dealing with his migraine.

"Oh, I see," Jen then said. "Well then, Lucas should have kept his mouth shut instead of pointing a finger like that so publicly. Your friend could sue him for slander for pulling a stunt like that."

"I suppose so, but right now it's probably the least of Jack's problems. Lucas Hall might be only one of many who believe Jack is a murderer. It's something he absolutely doesn't deserve. But the only way to end this is to find out who hated Arden Sprouse enough to murder him. I don't know enough about the man to know where to look."

"Well, there's one person who could give you some insight." Jen said. "Ronna Dickens."

"Who's that?"

"A woman I ran into after Bob and I helped move all the knitted things to your outdoor booth on Saturday. We didn't stay around long, you know. We've seen the reenactment several times before. But I spotted Ronna setting up her spinning demonstration in the living history area and went over to say hello. She taught a class I took a couple of years ago when I thought I'd have the time to spin my own yarn." Jen chuckled lightly. "Silly me."

Jen's mention of the spinning demonstration reminded Lia that Sharon had pointed the woman out. But how would a yarn spinner connect to Arden Sprouse? Jen explained. "Ronna and Sprouse have butted heads a few times."

"Over what?"

"The environment. Ronna is passionate about it. Sprouse apparently less so. But she could explain that better than I can."

"I'd love to hear it. Where can I find her?" Lia asked.

"Eco Alley."

"What?" Lia asked

"It's her shop. It's right there in Crandalsburg. You haven't seen it?" Jen asked.

"I guess I haven't. What sort of shop is it?"

"It carries a big variety of things that are all eco-friendly," Jen explained. "Meaning, well, you know, I'm sure. Nothing that harms the environment. It's an interesting shop to scour through. You sometimes find things you never knew you needed."

"So how does spinning yarn connect with that?" Lia asked.

"Oh, Ronna just got into spinning for the joy of it. She became expert enough that she was asked to teach, and so she did. I think you'll find her an interesting person." Jen gave Lia the address of Eco Alley, after which their conversation switched to a side problem created by the reenactment closedown.

"All those Civil War socks we knitted," Jen said. "I know many were preordered by the men. But we made extras for you to sell at the booth. Then it was closed down."

"I know," Lia said, letting out a small sigh. "We lost that sale time right when I expected the highest interest to come, after the battle scene. But they're still beautiful socks. I'll keep a few handy at the booth with a special label on them and will just have to store the rest. There'll be future reenactments, won't there?"

"I certainly hope so," Jen said, a trifle ominously. "But murder can have repercussions that nobody can foresee."

That was certainly true, Lia had to agree. On that somber note they ended their call, with Lia hoping to redirect at least one of those dire effects away from the decent man who lived next door to her.

Chapter 8

Lia found Eco Alley in a little shopping center tucked between a vegan juice bar and an acupuncturist. A fitting spot, she supposed, to draw like-minded shoppers. A peek through the front window showed a shop jammed full of merchandise as Jen had described. Lia was curious to explore it. But most importantly she hoped to talk with Ronna Dickens.

Lia stepped inside and immediately turned sideways to let another customer exit the close quarters. She glanced around for the shop's proprietor. The small checkout counter near the front was unmanned, but Lia heard voices coming from the back and headed there—not an easy task, as racks of clothing stood close to one another, followed by several merchandise-packed shelves and tables.

When she reached the area of the voices, she found that one of them belonged to a tall woman dressed in a sage green linen blouse belted loosely over a long printed skirt.

She tossed her long, gray-tinged hair out of her way as she held up a pair of brightly colored flip-flops.

"Now, these are produced from recycled rubber," she told her inches-shorter customer, a young woman in jeans and a tee, who stood listening with rapt attention. "Their manufacturing process is without chemicals, thus no harmful carbon emissions. And those"—she pointed to a group of slip-on flats—"are literally made from plastic bottles."

The younger woman turned to eagerly examine them.

"Let me know if you need help finding a size," the tall woman said. She looked over to Lia. "Hi! Can I help you?"

"Ronna Dickens?" Lia asked.

"One and the same. Salesperson or customer?" Ronna asked with a cautious smile.

"Neither," Lia said. "That is, I think I'm a potential customer, as soon as I have a chance to browse through this interesting place. But I'm a friend of Jen Beasley, who took one of your spinning classes."

"Oh yes! You're interested in a class? I have the schedule." She waved Lia toward the front counter as she charged forward.

"No," Lia said, hastily clarifying. "I'm interested in Arden Sprouse. Jen thought you might be able to tell me more about him. And before you ask, I'm not a reporter."

Ronna's eyes narrowed. She pushed past Lia to step up to and behind the counter. The raised height, combined with her own, produced a commanding air as she took charge of the tight space. "Then why are you interested in Sprouse?" she asked, peering down at Lia.

Lia glanced back toward the shoe shopper, who remained hidden among the shoes. "You know, of course, about his murder?" she asked.

"Of course."

"There have been wild accusations thrown out about a particular person being responsible for it, as if he's the only possible suspect. I don't agree. I expect someone in Sprouse's position wouldn't have been limited to a single enemy, but I need to know a lot more about him to be sure of that."

"Oh, you can be sure." Ronna spotted her customer heading toward them with a shoebox, and she held up her hand. "Hold on."

Lia made way for the shopper and eased over to a shelf stocked with women's purses, tote bags, and cosmetic cases. A sign identified them as billboard bags. Intrigued, Lia read the explanation that came with it. Apparently, the attractive pieces before her had been made from discarded vinyl materials of billboards that would otherwise have been sent to landfills. *Wow!* She sidled over to another shelf that held compostable dinnerware made from bamboo. *Interesting idea.* She next glanced over an entire table filled with toys made from recycled milk jugs. *Shoes and toys. Who would have thought?*

She had just begun browsing through the organic and fair-trade-certified clothing section when the shoe customer completed her transaction and left.

Ronna beckoned Lia back as the shop door closed. "You wanted to know about Sprouse's enemies? You're looking at one right now." Her stern expression broke into a grin. "At least I was for a while, and who knows? If things hadn't gone my way, I might have wanted to shoot the man myself. Oh, wait. He was stabbed, right?"

Ronna stepped down from behind the counter and idly lifted the sleeve of a plaid shirt hanging nearby. "Love these things. Cost a bit more, but they last forever."

"There was some kind of dispute between you?" Lia asked. "What about?"

"Hmm? Oh! Destroying the environment." Ronna dropped the sleeve to face Lia. "The man had no conscience as far as the environment goes. He bought this hotel, Hubbard House. Know it?"

"I've heard the name," Lia said, thinking back to Maggie's mention.

"Family-run. Nice little place," Ronna continued. "But apparently too little for Sprouse's taste. He wanted to expand, add on a restaurant, a swimming pool, family cottages, things like that. The problem was the land he wanted to do it all on has a lovely creek running through it with some rare and endangered plants that would have been obliterated by the bulldozers he'd bring in."

Lia saw Ronna's problem. "You sued?"

"First I tried talking with him. I can be reasonable, within limits. But that got me nowhere. So I turned to our esteemed mayor, told him no way could he support that plan, and explained exactly why." Her lip curled. "Talk about stonewalling! Sprouse's so-called improvements would bring more money to Crandalsburg. Visitors, who would spend more money, yada, yada. That same old song and dance. It's all about money. But bringing in a lawyer who threatened to sue changed his tune."

"That must have been satisfying," Lia said.

"Definitely." Ronna nodded, then paused, thinking. "You know, I can think of one enemy Sprouse made with that hotel deal other than myself. Gil Hubbard."

"Hubbard? Of Hubbard House?"

"That's the one," Ronna said. "I'm not saying Gil killed Sprouse, but he had good reason to." At Lia's questioning look, Ronna explained. "He got a raw deal, at least from what I've heard."

"In what way?"

"Well . . ." Ronna walked over to the toy table and started straightening the boxed stacking cups and toy boats. "Gil was in the worst place for a seller—one who's desperate to sell. His wife had been sick for a long time—cancer—and Gil let the hotel run down while he looked after her. A string of bad luck didn't help, things like a small fire and some kind of injury lawsuit from a guest. Then the medical bills piled up.

"Gil and Sprouse knew each other from way back, as I understand it, maybe school friends, I don't know, which might have led Gil to expect some extra consideration. I'm sure he needed to get enough from the sale to at least cover his debts. He also wanted to be kept on as manager, which Sprouse initially agreed to.

"But Gil underestimated Sprouse. Besides grinding the purchase price down to rock bottom, he also kicked Gil to the curb as far as the manager position. So Gil's unemployed, and at his age probably unemployable, still in debt, and I would assume very, very angry."

Lia shook her head in sympathy. "Is Gil the kind of person who would turn that anger into violence?" she asked.

Ronna shrugged. "Who can say what anyone's capable of when they've reached the end of their rope? Kick a dog, even a good one, often enough, and they'll eventually turn on you, right?"

"Some would, I suppose."

Ronna's store phone rang, and she headed over to get it. As she recited directions to her store to the caller, Lia mulled over Gil Hubbard's sad situation. Arden Sprouse, of course, was a businessman, successful enough to be in the habit of driving hard bargains. If Gil couldn't get a better offer for his hotel, he couldn't expect Sprouse to be overly generous simply because Gil needed the money. Reneging on the employment promise, however, was a different thing. That sounded coldhearted, though Lia reminded herself she didn't know all the factors that went into the decision.

Ronna finished her call and started shuffling a few papers. A new customer walked in and after a brief discussion headed farther back. Lia picked up a set of reusable storage bags that had caught her eye and brought them over to the counter to pay.

After getting her bag and receipt, Lia thanked Ronna for talking with her and turned to leave, but she stopped before reaching the door to ask, "How is Gil Hubbard's wife doing?"

Ronna looked up from her paper shuffling. "Huh? Oh, the wife?" She shrugged, then said, "She died." With that, she resumed her task, dismissing Lia, who winced at the terse delivery. Perhaps Arden Sprouse hadn't been the only coldhearted person in the environmental dispute. Lia lifted a hand in silent farewell then, and left.

Chapter 9

When Lia arrived home, movement at the side of her neighbors' house caught her eye. Jack was digging in one of Sharon's flower gardens. Apparently he'd been at it a while, since he propped his shovel to take a rest, whipped off his hat, and wiped a sleeve over his brow. He nodded and smiled when he noticed Lia heading up her walk.

"Planting spring bulbs?" Lia asked as she veered closer.

"Sharon bought them last week. Thought I might as well put them in, now that I have the time." At Lia's questioning look, he explained. "A job I scheduled to start work on this afternoon was canceled."

"Oh." Lia knew Jack's home improvement business was usually booked weeks in advance. Cancellations were rare.

"Yeah," he said, noting Lia's expression. "They didn't say so, but I could read between the lines, or rather hear it in their voices. They didn't like the idea of a possible murderer working in their house."

"Oh, Jack. That's so unfair. All because of what Lucas Hall spouted on TV this morning, I suppose?"

"Probably. But their loss," he said, forcing a laugh. "They'll have a hard time finding anyone else for a while."

"And no one who'd do it as well," Lia said. She'd been impressed with Jack's work in his own home—beautiful hardwood floors and an expertly redone kitchen.

"Well . . ." Jack shrugged and reached for his shovel.

"May I ask a quick question before you get back to work?"

"Sure." Jack leaned an arm on the shovel's handle. "What about?"

"Your rifle. I wondered where the police found it. I'm guessing it wasn't left near the body since that wasn't reported right away. Did they have to search hard for it?"

"No, actually it was Herb Weaver who came up with it."

"The eighty-year-old who took charge of the two rifles?" Lia asked.

"Right. Sorry, I thought I'd mentioned that. Both rifles were in his tent. Herb might not have noticed the blood on the bayonet on mine if it hadn't been for all the commotion when Sprouse was found. It had been wiped but not thoroughly. Herb spotted what was left on the blade after taking a close look."

"So someone took your rifle while Herb was out of the tent, used it against Sprouse, then put it back?"

"Yup."

Lia frowned, thinking about that. "But that someone went to the trouble of wiping the bayonet, as though they didn't want the weapon identified. Why?"

"I can think of one reason." Jack shifted his weight. "They used my rifle, then deliberately left just enough blood on the bayonet to implicate me. The police could assume I was in too much of a hurry to put the rifle back to do a thorough job of wiping it."

"But maybe the actual murderer was the one in the rush," Lia argued. "Was the rest of the rifle wiped clean?"

"Of fingerprints? No," Jack said. "Apparently mine were still on it."

"And probably the fellow who used it for the bayonet demonstration," Lia said. "Plus Herb's."

"Probably," Jack agreed. "But they both have verified alibis for the time, whereas I . . ."

"Jack," Lia said, "I've begun looking for enemies of Arden Sprouse. It looks like you have at least one, too, something I can't imagine."

"Nor can I," Sharon said, coming toward them, a carton of bulbs in her hands. She set them on the ground. "Jack, would you bring the hose over for me? It's in the shed."

Once Jack left, Sharon said, "I caught some of what you were saying. I don't know who's got it in for Jack—leaving evidence of the murder on his rifle. Whoever it is won't succeed in getting him charged with murder. I'm convinced of that. But they're hurting him in other ways."

"Jack told me about the job cancellation," Lia said.

"Yes, and that's hard. But something else hurts even more."

"What's that?"

Sharon glanced in the direction Jack had gone. "His re-enactor group," she said. "They've asked him to step out."

"Oh no!"

"Temporarily," Sharon said with a look of disgust. "That's how they put it. Until things are sorted out." She shook her head, blinking away tears. "After all he's done for them."

Jack reappeared from the back of the house, dragging the partially rolled-up hose.

"Thanks, honey," Sharon said brightly.

Lia understood that Sharon didn't want to discuss Jack's latest blow any further in front of him, but it turned her stomach to hear about it.

"I'll leave you to your planting," she said, matching Sharon's cheeriness as best she could. But her face darkened as soon as she turned away. What would happen next to her poor neighbor? Eggs thrown at his house? Reporters camped in front? This shouldn't happen to someone who hadn't done a thing to deserve it.

When she went into her house, she was greeted immediately by Daphne, whose purrs helped soothe Lia as she snuggled the cat in her arms. But pleasant as that was, it wasn't any help with Jack's problem. Lia set Daphne down gently and pulled out her phone to call Belinda.

"How are things going around the craft barn?" Lia asked when her friend picked up. "Are they still working on the crime scene?"

"No, it looks like they've finished there. The tents and some of the living history things are still in place, but I think we'll have the grounds back by the weekend for the craft fair."

"That's good." The vendors needed to catch up on their lost day. "Are you there now?"

"No, I'm at home. Why? Want to come over?"

"I could pick up lunch. Or is it too soon for you?" A glance at the clock told Lia it was eleven thirty.

Belinda laughed. "You just reminded me that I didn't have breakfast yet. Lunch would be great."

"Good. The usual?"

"Chinese?" Belinda asked. "We always get that. How about something different? Chad and I tried a new place, Xenia's. They just opened up. Nothing fancy, but they have great Greek food."

"Okay with me. Why don't you order for both of us? You know my tastes by now. Just tell me how to find the place."

Lia made notes on Belinda's directions. As she hung up, she thought about how Chad, Belinda's boyfriend—a label her friend refused to use—had broadened her interests. Come to think of it, *boyfriend* was a silly way to refer to a man in his fifties, close to Belinda's and her ages. *Gentleman friend* seemed a bit much, too. Lia smiled, knowing the exact term for a relationship was unimportant. How they felt about each other was, and she saw warm feelings between the two, which in turn made Lia happy. Her friend hadn't had a lot of success in the romance department. It was time for an upward turn in her life.

When Lia knocked at Belinda's front door, an aromatic bag of carry-out food in hand, she didn't have to wait long for the door to swing open.

"Thank goodness!" Belinda said, reaching for the bag and pulling Lia in with it. "I've been starving ever since I called in the order, thinking about that food!" She hustled down the hall to the kitchen, leaving Lia to close the door behind her and follow with a grin.

"You know, you really shouldn't skip meals," Lia said as she helped Belinda unpack the carry-out. Belinda wasn't big on cooking, but she usually managed to have things on hand—sandwich fixings or heat-and-eat freezer meals.

"I know. I just got tied up with all the adjustments needed at the Schumacher barn this week," she said, referring to the many midweek classes and special events she scheduled besides the weekend craft fair.

"But I thought you said the investigation had wrapped

up." Lia got two plates from Belinda's cupboards and grabbed silverware.

"It has. Water?" Belinda asked. "Or coffee? It's all I have."

"Water for now," Lia said. "Maybe coffee later. So what still needed adjusting at the barn?"

Belinda dropped ice cubes into two glasses. "The yoga class would have been this morning. As of yesterday, I couldn't guarantee the space would be freed up, so I had to squeeze them into another time slot later this week. That required some juggling and plenty of phone calls." She added water to the glasses and set them on the table.

"Will you be going to the barn soon? An out-of-town customer asked me to mail something she had intended to buy on Saturday but didn't get the chance before we had to shut down. I wondered if you could pick it up for me."

"Sure, I'll be there tomorrow. What should I look for?"

Lia described the layette and where Belinda could find it among the other knits. "That'll be great. Then I can send it off to her before the weekend." Lia began working at the take-out boxes. "Let's see what we're having for lunch."

"That's the moussaka," Belinda said as Lia lifted the first lid. "It's ground beef, potatoes, and eggplant." She opened the second box herself. "This one's shrimp *yiou-vetsi*. I thought you might like it, but if you'd rather take the moussaka . . . ?"

"No, I love shrimp." Lia exchanged her box for Belinda's. "You did great, and I'm impressed that you can rattle off those Greek names."

Belinda grinned. "Chad and I had a little game going as we read the menu, which helped." She transferred the moussaka to her own plate.

They dug in, with Lia soon declaring her dish was delicious. After a few bites she brought up Jack's increasing problems stemming from the murder.

"That poor guy," Belinda said. She took a sip of her water. "I understand what he's going through."

Lia knew she would, her friend having struggled through similar repercussions after the murder of her ex-husband. "I don't want to see Jack being stuck in never-ending suspicion if the police can't solve this murder," she said.

"It's early days, Lia."

"Yes, but unless someone comes forward to confess, I don't see a big chance of this crime being solved." Lia scooped up a forkful of orzo, then said, "Think about it. Hundreds of people in the area, everyone's attention on the battle reenactment, noise, smoke, soldiers running about, trampling evidence until all that's left is the blood left on Jack's bayonet."

Belinda nodded. "So what do you want to do about it? I assume you're heading in that direction."

"Well, yes, a little." Lia hedged until she saw Belinda's lip begin to curl. "How can I not?" Lia defended herself. "If I poke around, I might find something that would help Jack!"

"I know. Far be it from me to say not to," Belinda said, grimacing, "since I know it would do no good. But will you at least report to your police friend and stop before you get yourself into anything dicey?"

"Pete?" Lia squirmed a bit. She knew she would need to keep the Crandalsburg chief of police informed. She also expected he would want her to leave all investigating up to them. She liked Pete and didn't want to cause friction between them. But she also felt she knew where the line was between doing some good and getting in the way. Or worse.

"Yes, Pete," Belinda prodded.

"I'll share anything I think is important with Pete," Lia said cautiously. "And," she added, "I'll always be careful."

That seemed to satisfy her friend, so Lia asked, "Now, what can you tell me about Gil Hubbard?"

"Gil Hubbard?" Belinda jerked her head in surprise. "Where did that come from?"

Lia explained how Ronna of Eco Alley had pointed to Hubbard as a probable enemy of Sprouse. "What do you know about that?"

Belinda scraped at her plate thoughtfully before eventually looking up. "I was sorry to see Gil sell his hotel. He'd run it for years, though I admit he let too many things go in the last few years. He could have kept the business going better with improvements here and there, as the town was growing and events like the reenactment were drawing more visitors."

"I understood his attention was focused on his wife and her illness for some time." Lia shared what Ronna had said about Hubbard being forced to sell to Sprouse in desperation due to mounting debts, only to have Sprouse renege on a promise to keep Gil on as manager.

"I didn't know that." Belinda frowned. "It's a shame, but unless the agreement was written into a contract . . ."

"It sounds like Gil relied on an old acquaintance keeping his word."

"Poor Gil." Belinda shook her head.

"Yes, poor Gil, unless of course he turned to murder," Lia said. "What would you say? Is he capable of that?"

"Physically, yes. He seems in pretty good shape. But would he?" Belinda shrugged. "I don't know him well enough to say. You'll have to talk to a closer acquaintance. Maybe Hayley's boss could tell you."

"Hayley's boss?" Lia asked in surprise. "Mr. Weber?"

"Yes. Gil has been working at the alpaca farm for a while. When I heard that, I assumed it was just something to do to keep himself busy after an early retirement. But from what you tell me, it sounds like he needs the money. And maybe Carl Weber took pity on him."

"What does he do there?"

"No idea." Belinda stabbed at her food. "Ask Hayley. She might know."

Lia nodded as her mind ran with that new information. If Gil Hubbard was employed at the Weber farm, it was obviously a convenient place for Lia to take his measure—fine if it led to ruling him out. But what if it didn't? The idea of Hayley working daily in close proximity with a possible murderer was not a pleasant one—to say the least.

Chapter 10

Back home and feeling a need to gather her thoughts, Lia turned to knitting, her favorite method of getting her brain cells working. She was currently working on bookmarks, a project suggested by Belinda after she'd joined the book club where she'd met Chad.

"One of the club members uses a really nice knit bookmark," Belinda had said. "I'll bet you could sell plenty of them at your booth."

After knitting all those socks for the reenactors, Lia had been ready for a change, and she tried a few patterns. She settled on one she liked and soon knew the steps by heart, making the bookmarks in several colors and often using leftover yarn, which made her feel very efficient.

She picked up her needles and cast on the stitches, this time using a medium blue yarn. Daphne came over to curl next to her feet as she settled into her work. While working the first row, Lia considered what to do about Gil Hubbard. The poor man had troubles enough, having lost his wife and his hotel. Lia certainly didn't want to add to that with unjustified hints of wrongdoing—that is, assuming the man was innocent. If he was guilty of murder, though, she needed to dig that out, clear Jack's name, and see Gil transferred from Hayley's workplace to prison.

How could she accomplish both goals? By the time she'd finished the blue bookmark as well as a multicolored one, Lia thought she'd come up at least with a place to start.

She waited until Hayley was likely to be home and done with her supper—the one that would have been ready and waiting for her in Lia's old slow cooker. Having dined lightly herself after the huge lunch she'd had at Belinda's, Lia fixed a hazelnut coffee, then set it down to cool as she called her daughter.

"How was your dinner?" she asked as Hayley picked up.

"It was great! I could smell it as I came up my stairs. What a luxury, leftovers for tomorrow, and all I need to wash up is one plate."

They chatted a bit about Hayley's day before Lia moved on to the reason for her call.

"Is there a man named Gil Hubbard working at the farm?" she asked.

"Gil Hubbard?" There was a long silence until Hayley finally said, "Oh! Gil! An older guy? Balding? Kind of a sad face?"

"I don't know what he looks like, but the sad face fits." Lia explained what she knew about the man and why she'd asked.

"Gosh, I had no idea. I'm not sure I ever heard his last name, and if I did I probably wouldn't have connected it to the Hubbard, not with the kind of work he's doing at the farm. He's been doing general cleanup and maintenance—you know, mucking out the stalls and such."

"Mucking out stalls?" Lia said, surprised.

"Among other things. But he's been working with the alpacas more, now that the college kids we had for the summer are back in class."

Honest work, Lia thought, but quite a change for a man who once ran his own hotel. She knew the job opportunities at the Weber farm were few and that the Webers handled the business end of the place themselves, which eliminated that possibility. But couldn't Gil have found something—anything—closer to his abilities?

Both Ronna and Belinda had said that he'd let his hotel run down during his wife's illness, whose ultimate death must have been a blow. Lia wondered if depression, along with the limited job opportunities in a small town like Crandalsburg, had led him to settle on such menial work. Or had it been the other way around, that he'd applied widely but had been consistently turned down, perhaps because of unspoken ageism? That, along with his other losses, could certainly lead to depression.

But if it hadn't been for Arden Sprouse, Gil wouldn't have been in that downward spiral in the first place. Did he see it that way and want revenge?

"Do you know if Gil was working at the farm on Saturday, the day of the murder?" Lia asked.

"No, but I could find out. You think he might be the murderer?"

"All I know is that he had a pretty strong motive. If he has the alibi of having been at the farm, that'll be the end of it, and honestly I hope he does. But if it turns out he was off on Saturday, do you think you can ask Mr. Weber about him? He might have hired Gil as a friend, and perhaps he could give you an idea of the kind of person he is and what he might be capable of."

"Or . . . I could talk to Gil myself," Hayley said.

"I'd really rather you didn't," Lia said. "Until we know more about him, it'd be safer to keep your distance."

"But, Mom—"

"Just as a favor to me?" Lia asked. "For now?"

Hayley let out an exaggerated huff, which Lia suspected was for show, then agreed. "I'll talk to Mr. Weber and get back to you."

"Thanks, dear." Lia wished her a good evening and ended the call.

She had barely set her phone down when it rang. Startled, Lia checked the caller's name. It was Pete Sullivan.

"Hello, Pete?" Lia answered tentatively. Had he somehow picked up that she was looking into the murder of Arden Sprouse? Then she shook herself, aware of how ridiculous that was. But why was he calling?

"Hi, Lia," Pete said. His upbeat tone relaxed Lia, and she reached out to pet Daphne, who'd sidled up to her. "I hope I'm not disturbing you?" he asked politely before getting to the reason for his call. "There's going to be a photography club excursion on Wednesday, the day after tomorrow. It's something I thought you might enjoy, a scenic photo shoot at Parkridge. I know this is last-minute, but I wasn't sure until today that I could make it myself. Jen and Bob are planning to go," he added, as though for added incentive.

"Oh!" Lia said, caught off-balance by the unexpected change of subject—at least within her own mind. She remembered her single visit to the photography club with the Beasleys. Bob was a member, as was Pete, whom she'd met for the first time that night. The group had discussed possible trips of this sort. Had she shown interest in them at the time? She couldn't remember, exactly. But Parkridge did sound like an intriguing spot to visit.

"It looks like perfect weather for it," Pete threw out as she hesitated. "You seemed to enjoy hiking," he added, "so I thought you might like to join us."

Pete was referring to the hike they'd taken together up Long Run Falls, though that had been for a very different purpose. Pete had taken Lia there to explain the reasons the police had ruled the way they did about a woman's fatal fall. It had been a more somber excursion, but what he suggested now did appeal to Lia.

"Are you sure nonmembers can go?" she asked. "I don't even have a real camera anymore. Any photos I'd take would have to be with my cell phone."

"No problem," Pete assured her. "Family and friends come along on these things all the time."

Lia learned it would involve a full afternoon and evening. Not a huge time to be kept from her investigating, not that she'd mention that to Pete. And the fresh air on a beautiful fall day sounded so good.

"Then I'd love to go," she said.

Pete sounded delighted as he gave her a few more details, including when he'd pick her up—pleased, she told herself, only because of the rare chance he had to participate because of his job. She had simply been added to the excursion as one of the friends he'd mentioned who were always welcomed.

Which was fine.

Chapter 11

Hayley called the next day during her lunch break. "Gil Hubbard wasn't working at the farm on Saturday," she informed Lia.

"Oh dear," Lia said.

"Yeah, I know. And on top of that, one of the women who works in the gift shop said she saw him in the crowd at the reenactment. She said she called out to him to join her and her family, but he just waved and shook his head."

"Did this woman say if she knew Gil well?"

"She doesn't," Hayley said. "She just recognized him from seeing him around the farm and was being nice. But I did ask Mr. Weber about him."

"And?"

"Well, it confirmed my opinion that I've got a great boss," Hayley said. "He hired Gil to help him out. He said he felt bad that he couldn't offer him anything better paying with his budget currently stretched pretty thin. But then he said something odd."

"Oh?" Lia perked up. "What was that?"

"He said even if he could have offered him an office position, he thought working outdoors was better for Gil, for now."

"In what way?" Lia asked.

"Mr. Weber didn't go into details. He just said he felt Gil needed his space to let off steam once in a while."

"Is that how he put it?" Lia asked. "Letting off steam? Because that sounds like an anger problem, more than grief."

"That's how he put it, and I agree that's what it sounded like. It made me worry about the alpacas, and I asked if it was safe for them. But Mr. Weber assured me they were good for Gil. Calming. You know how sweet they can be around people."

Lia did know, and that it was a big part of why Hayley wanted to work there.

"But he also warned me not to bring up anything about Gil's previous work to him. That it was a flammable subject for him."

"Flammable," Lia said.

"Yeah, strong word, right?" Hayley asked. "Hey, I gotta go. Just wanted to let you know what I found out."

Lia thanked her and stood thinking after the call ended. Gil Hubbard had been on the reenactment grounds, apparently wandering by himself. He had bitter feelings toward Arden Sprouse and according to Hayley's boss he was in an agitated state. All strong reasons to consider him a suspect.

But then she reconsidered. If Gil came to the reenactment to kill Sprouse, why would he use Jack's bayonet? Would he even have known where it was? Why take a chance on find-

ing it and not just bring his own weapon? Unless . . . Lia
stared out her front window. Unless he had acted on impulse?

Jack and Sharon were out in their yard, this time busily
raking leaves. Lia hesitated, then grabbed a light jacket and
stepped outside. A strong breeze tousled her hair, and she
flipped the jacket's hood forward as she headed toward the
border between the two properties, a line dotted with a row
of evenly spaced, low-growing azaleas.

Her neighbors glanced up and smiled, both immediately
pausing their work as Lia slipped between the shrubs to
join them.

"A breezy day for gathering leaves," she said as she held
on to her hood.

"Good for staying cool," Sharon said.

"I won't keep you," Lia said. "I just have a quick question."

Jack let his rake drop next to a pile of leaves. "To tell the
truth, I'm ready for a break. And a drink. Sharon's got a
pitcher of iced tea ready. Why don't we head over to the
screened-in porch?"

"Sounds good," Sharon said. "C'mon, Lia," she said as
she turned toward the back of their house.

"Just for a minute," Lia promised as she got in line to
follow.

Jack held the screen door for the women, then stepped
in as Sharon continued on to her kitchen, waving away Lia's
offer of help.

"Just take a seat," she said. "I'll be right out."

Lia did as she was told and settled on a cushioned porch
chair as Jack took the settee. He appeared in good spirits,
which might be attributed to the fresh air and exercise. She
hated to spoil that with her questions, though she doubted
thoughts of the murder were ever far from his or Sharon's
mind.

"Here we are." Sharon carried a tray with three filled glasses on it and set it on the white wicker table before handing them out. She sank into the second chair and took a long drink of tea, then sighed. "Oh, that tastes good." She took another sip, then turned to Lia. "So, what's on your mind?"

"Gil Hubbard," Lia answered simply. "Do you know him?"

"Gil Hubbard?" Jack looked puzzled, but Sharon nodded.

"The Hubbard Hotel?" she reminded her husband.

"Oh, *that* Hubbard," Jack said.

"I know who he is but not well," Sharon said to Lia.

"Enough to recognize him?" Lia asked.

"Bald? Fifty-something? I noticed him at the reenactment."

"Did you? Do you remember where?" Lia asked.

"Sure. It was when we were watching the bayonet demonstration." Lia's pulse quickened as Sharon went on. "He was standing across the way from us. Remember how the crowd kind of curved around the roped-off demo area? He kept a little apart from everyone. I knew his wife had died recently, and I felt sorry for him."

"What was his manner?" Lia asked. "Did he seem sad?"

Sharon thought back. "Not sad, exactly. More tense. He seemed very focused on what the guys were doing with the bayonets." Sharon gave Lia a searching look. "Why do you ask?"

"I've learned that Gil had pretty hard feelings toward Arden Sprouse." She explained what Ronna had told her about Sprouse's treatment of Gil.

"I'm not surprised," Jack said. "On the other hand, Sprouse was a businessman. Gil might not have got a better deal from anyone else."

"Maybe not," Lia said. "But it sounds like Sprouse made promises that Gil counted on. He was let down at a pretty bad time for him. Justifiable or not, he might have been looking for revenge."

"It's a new suspect, Jack," Sharon said. "I'm sorry that it's Gil, but if he was the one who murdered Sprouse . . ." She stopped herself from going further, but Lia knew she badly wanted someone, anyone other than Jack, to be identified as the murderer—and soon.

"It's only a start," Lia cautioned. "Gil has a motive, but I need to connect him to your rifle, Jack. We can place him at the demonstration. Could he have followed you when you carried both rifles to Herb Weaver?"

Jack shook his head. "If he did, I wouldn't know. I don't know the guy by sight, and there were plenty of others around for him to blend in with."

"But it was possible?" Lia asked.

"Sure, he probably could have."

"Then I believe we have a suspect," Sharon said. She looked excited but Jack less so.

"There's not a thing more on Hubbard than there is on me," he said.

"But we know it wasn't you," Sharon argued.

"And we don't know that it was him. Not yet," Jack added. "But maybe . . ."

"What?" Both Sharon and Lia asked.

"Maybe someone saw him hanging around Herb's tent. If we could find that out . . ."

"Ask Herb!" Sharon was on the edge of her seat by then. "Ask some of the guys who would have been around there."

Lia saw Jack's reluctance. He'd been asked to step away from the reenactors' group "until things were sorted out." That surely stung, and the thought of contacting any members after that must be painful, especially since there was no guarantee it would bring out anything useful.

"Let me ask," she said. "Give me names and numbers."

Jack still hesitated. "I don't know . . ."

"Let her, Jack," Sharon urged. "Lia would be good at getting more out of them." She turned a worried eye to Lia. "If you're sure?"

"I'm sure. I just need you to point me in the right direction."

At that Sharon scrambled out of her seat and into the kitchen. She returned with Jack's phone, which she handed to him.

"Pick out the names and send them to Lia. Then we'll go over where she should start."

Chapter 12

Jack had been less reluctant about Lia talking with Herb Weaver, the man who'd been in charge of Jack's and Lucas's rifles, and he called to set up her visit. He'd told Herb only that she was a friend, and he'd appreciate Herb talking with her. Lia found the place with little trouble, a modest but well-kept ranch-style house just outside the Crandalsburg town limits.

Herb answered her knock swiftly and invited her in even before she introduced herself. She did so as she followed him to a cozily stuffed living room, not surprised to see plenty of Civil War memorabilia about. Jack had mentioned that Herb was a widower, and Lia suspected the framed period photos, the folded flags, and the glass case of smaller items had gradually made their way up from a basement den where they might have originally been consigned.

Herb was pretty much as Jack had described, adding to her vague memory of having seen him in front of his tent:

eightyish, stout, and with sparse white hair. He had a noticeable limp from a bad right hip, but also soft brown eyes
and a kindly face. Lia declined his offer of coffee as she
took a seat on the blue-and-tan plaid sofa.

"Thank you for seeing me, Mr. Weaver—"

"Herb, please," he begged.

Lia smiled. "Herb, I want to talk to you about that afternoon at the reenactment."

Herb's brown eyes grew troubled. "What a terrible day."

"It was, though it started out so well."

"Our reenactments have always been perfect. Never any
kind of problem before," Herb said. "No accidents of any
kind. Everyone working together and getting along. Until . . ."

"Until?" Lia asked.

Herb shifted uncomfortably in his chair. "I hate to say
anything bad about the dead, but . . ." He shifted again. "It's
just . . . things were much better before he came in. Sprouse,
I mean."

"That's what I understand, too. He made changes that
not everyone liked."

"It wasn't just that," Herb said. "We used to all work together so easily as a group. No disagreements that couldn't
be worked out. We all got along. Then he took over, and all
of a sudden people were taking sides and, and . . ." Herb
leaned back in his chair, his hands pressing at his thighs. "It
just wasn't as good as it used to be."

Lia could see how deeply that had affected the older
man, watching an organization that had meant so much to
him for years start to fall apart.

"And now," Herb said. "Asking Jack to leave? Instead of
standing by him as comrades? I could hardly believe it! I
didn't like it, not at all, and I told them so." Herb shook his
head. "Not that any of them paid any attention."

"I'm glad to know you stood up for Jack," Lia said. "And I'm sure you weren't the only one. I know Jack well enough to believe his story about the migraine."

Herb winced as he shook his head. "I'll never forgive myself for leaving those rifles out of my sight."

"You couldn't know what would happen," Lia said, wanting to soothe the older man's distress. What was done was done. Now they needed to work on the effects. "I wondered if you noticed anyone hanging around the tent where the rifles were kept. Someone who wasn't part of the reenactment?"

"A stranger?" Herb asked. "No, I can't say I did."

"Perhaps not a total stranger," Lia said. "Do you know Gil Hubbard?"

"The hotel guy? Sure, I know who he is."

"Did you see him in the area around the time Jack gave you the rifles?"

Herb rubbed his white-bristled chin. "I don't think so. But, you know, I had other things on my mind then. If I'd been watching out for him, I might be able to say one way or the other."

"I understand," Lia said, though she'd hoped for more.

"It was that son-in-law who was around more than I liked," Herb said, a look of distaste on his face.

"Lucas? Why? What was he doing?"

"Laughing and joking with people like it was all some kind of party. We don't do reenactments for the fun of it. It's serious stuff. People died. Lots of them. But to him it was just one big costume party. His father-in-law, too. And to say what Lucas did about Jack on TV? Terrible!"

"I agree. He had no right to accuse Jack like that, no matter how upset he might have been. Were he and Arden close?" Lia asked, thinking about the emotion and vehemence in Lucas's on-screen accusation.

"I don't know about close," Herb said. "But they were two of a kind, that's for sure."

"In what way?"

"Money. That was what they cared about. Not people. Money and all the things that come with it."

"Luxuries?" Lia asked.

Herb nodded. "And influence. You got enough in the bank, people kowtow to you. That's what they liked. You could see it." Herb's eyes flashed. "I wondered, watching the two, if Lucas married his wife only to be brought into Arden's business. I often felt sorry for her, the way he treated her."

"How was that?" Lia asked.

Herb drew a long breath. "He just didn't treat her like he cared. You'd hear it in how he talked to her, ordering instead of asking nicely. And when he didn't need something from her, she was ignored. He was just plain cold. That's gotta hurt a person, don't you think?"

Lia did. She suspected Herb had been the opposite with his own wife, which made him notice Lucas's shortcomings.

"I have to say," Herb continued. "If my son-in-law treated my daughter like that, he'd get a good talking-to. But it didn't seem to bother Arden."

"Was Arden the same with his own wife?" Lia asked.

Herb's expression changed at the mention of Sprouse's wife. His eyes softened as the disapproving frown disappeared. "Now, Mrs. Sprouse, Heidi, she's a real gem. I didn't like Arden taking over the group like he did, but Heidi almost made up for it the way she fussed over all of us. Like a mother hen. I never saw him treat her badly, but on the other hand he wasn't exactly lovey-dovey. Like I said, people weren't important to him. But it was different with her. She cared."

Lia had gotten a similar impression of Heidi Sprouse during the brief time they'd met. She had known couples who seemed mismatched but somehow got along well enough. Perhaps the Sprouse marriage was like that?

"So, Lucas worked for his father-in-law?" she asked.

"Not just worked *for*," Herb said. "He was like second-in-command, from what I understand."

"I see. And now that Arden Sprouse is dead, does Lucas take over?"

Herb spread his hands in a who-knows? gesture. "Could be," he said. "Depends on how Arden set it all up, I suppose."

"Right," Lia agreed. But if it had been arranged in Lucas's favor, that gave him quite a motive for murder, she thought. She'd come to Herb for help on one suspect and had been pointed to another. Though she wasn't quite finished with Gil Hubbard. Lia still intended to talk with others on Jack's list. But now she had a few more questions to ask them.

Lia was grateful for Herb's time and also liked the man, so when he offered to show her his vegetable garden, she accepted, expecting a few fading plants left over from summer still producing a tomato or two. But apparently Civil War reenactment wasn't Herb's only interest. What he had was a large, tidy plot actively producing fall vegetables, and he walked her around it to point out turnips, beets, and more. The older man explained that one of his grandsons helped with the work that Herb's bad hip kept him from doing.

Lia thought Herb had both an amazing garden and an amazing grandson and said so, which made Herb beam. They parted on Herb's invitation for Lia to come back in a week or so when he'd have some mustard greens ready to give her. Lia thanked him, unsure if she really wanted mustard greens, never having eaten or cooked them herself, but thought it might be worth a try if only as a reason to visit this lovely man again.

H er next stop was the hardware store run by Frank Burns. Jack had informed Lia that he and Frank hadn't always seen eye to eye, but that he was a fair and sensible man: *I know he would have been in the area around Herb's tent. He might be able to tell you if Gil Hubbard was there, too.*

Stepping into the hardware store, with its array of home repair supplies, brought back thoughts of the many times Lia had accompanied Tom when he needed a certain tool or part for one of his projects. She noticed that these small memories had begun to make her smile instead of causing pain as her life without Tom went on. She didn't take it as a sign of forgetting or loving him less. Tom would always be part of her heart. But Lia knew he wouldn't have wanted her own life to end when his had. Tom, in his wise and wonderful ways, would have urged Lia to move forward, which she had, struggling mightily at first but helped so much by the caring people around her. Now it had become easier to look back on all those good years with gratitude, to enjoy each new good day, and to look forward to what was yet to come.

"Help you, ma'am?"

The voice shook Lia from her musings. She smiled at the man behind the counter and asked, "Frank Burns?" He was about Jack's age, though stouter and more serious-looking.

"I am," he said with an expression that asked why that was important.

"Jack Kuhn suggested I talk with you," Lia explained, stepping closer. "It's about what happened at the reenactment. Would that be okay with you?" Lia hadn't spotted any customers in the modestly sized store. She hoped that would give her a few minutes.

Burns looked uneasy and ran a hand through his thick, dark hair. "If it's about Jack being asked to leave—"

"No, it's not. Right now I'm interested in who you might have seen in the area around Herb Weaver's tent after he took possession of Jack's and Lucas Hall's rifles. You know, of course, that Jack's bayoneted rifle was used to kill Arden Sprouse."

Burns grimaced. "That was shocking news."

"To me, too," Lia said. "Someone would have had to sneak it out of the tent while Herb was gone. I don't believe it was Jack."

"I don't either," the hardware store owner said to Lia's relief. "Jack's a good man. I didn't think ousting him from the reenactors was called for. But I can't come up with any way to help him out of this."

"Perhaps if his friends work together, we can discover the truth of what happened. As a start, can you tell me if there was anyone hanging around who shouldn't have been there? Or perhaps just someone behaving out of the ordinary?"

"What would be out of the ordinary?" Frank asked. "We were all, or most of us, gearing up to run onto a battlefield and yell bloody murder."

"How about anyone who seemed to have other plans? Or strangers hanging around?"

"There were some people I didn't know. There always are. Friends or relatives of reenactors come by." Burns straightened a package of painters tape hanging lopsidedly from a nearby rack.

"Do you know Gil Hubbard?" Lia asked. When Burns shook his head, she shared the description Hayley had given her along with the details Sharon had added. "He would probably have been keeping to himself, not talking to anyone."

Burns thought back. "Bald guy in a Steelers sweatshirt? Yeah, I think I remember him! We get guys coming around who are interested in volunteering. I think I was going to ask if that's what he wanted but got distracted by someone needing to check with me on the lineup."

"You think the man you saw was Hubbard?" Lia asked, growing excited, though Burns quickly tamped that down.

"I don't know the guy so I can't swear it was him. He just fit your description. Even if you showed me a photo, I'm not sure I could say it was the same person. I saw him for a couple of seconds at most."

"I understand. But it's worth making a note of. If more comes out, it could be significant."

"Tell you what," Burns said. "I'll ask around, see if anyone else remembers seeing Hubbard, and if so what he was doing there."

"That would be very helpful," Lia said. "But please be discreet in your questioning. Nobody's accusing Gil Hubbard of anything at this point. We're just gathering information that might lead to clearing Jack." Burns had struck her as a person she could trust, as Jack had also implied.

"I'll be sure to make that clear," Burns said. "There've been enough wild accusations as it is."

"Yes," Lia agreed. "You saw Lucas Hall's interview?"

"Heard about it." Burns looked down, shaking his head in disgust. "Idiot."

"He seemed determined to call out Jack," Lia said. "Unnecessarily so. I'd be interested to know how well he can account for his own movements."

"Not something I can answer, but maybe I can find that out, too."

Lia gave Burns her contact information and left, hopeful that she would soon hear more from him.

Chapter 13

Jen had called Lia the night before about the photography club outing. "I'm so glad you'll be coming! Bob and Pete worked out that the four of us should ride together to Parkridge, so we'll meet at your place and take Pete's bigger car."

She'd said they'd be there around one, so Lia was ready and watching, expecting Pete to arrive first since the Beasleys had the longer drive. It felt like ages since Lia had gone on an excursion of this sort, and she was looking forward to it. But it concerned her a bit that her neighbors might wonder why the Crandalsburg chief of police was showing up at her place. Lia gave Sharon a heads-up explanation beforehand.

"It's just a group outing that I'm going on that Pete Sullivan happens to be a part of. Purely social."

"Okay," Sharon had said. "Good to know. And if the subject of Arden Sprouse's murder happens to come up . . . ?"

"Unlikely," Lia said. "We'll be surrounded by photo club

members most of the time, all wanting to talk about cameras." Not to mention Lia hadn't found anything solid to bring up yet.

As soon as she saw Pete's silver Equinox pull up, Lia opened her door, ready to hail him in. But then Bob pulled up right behind him. Bob and Jen immediately began transferring their gear to the Equinox, so Lia grabbed her backpack, checked to make sure Daphne wasn't at her heels, and stepped out to join them.

"What a perfect day!" Jen said as Lia approached, looking at the clear blue sky.

"A few clouds would actually be better for our photos," Bob said.

"There'll be shady areas by the time we get there," Pete said, coming over and greeting Lia with a bright smile. "Want to put your backpack in the trunk with the other gear?"

"Sure," Lia said, letting him take it. "I won't need what's in it until we're in the park. I'm really looking forward to this!"

"The group will be stopping at a great place on the way home for dinner," Jen said. She proceeded to describe the restaurant to Lia as Bob and Pete arranged their camera bags. A discussion of photo opportunities began between the two men. As it continued, Bob automatically slid into the front passenger seat, and Jen, still talking to Lia, drew her into the back with her.

Lia saw Pete pause, then give a small shrug before climbing into the driver's seat, making her wonder if, as his guest, she should have joined him up front, though she didn't see how she could have gracefully managed it. Calling out "shotgun" didn't seem particularly appropriate or even necessary in this friends group.

They drove off, and Lia thought no more about it as the conversation turned to the afternoon ahead, with Lia learning more about the state park she'd be visiting.

"There's remains of an old iron furnace," Bob told her. "Just the stone walls left standing. But with the archways and empty framed windows it looks almost like an old castle."

"Wedding parties often have their photos taken there," Jen said.

"It's at its best in spring and summer," Pete added. "With all the wildflowers blooming. But the fall leaves should have turned enough to give us plenty of color."

"It sounds beautiful," Lia said.

The drive itself was beautiful, and Lia enjoyed the changing views outside her window, which included fields of grazing cows and pretty farmhouses, rolling hills, and bridges curving over sparkling blue water, sometimes dotted with small boats. Eventually they arrived at Parkridge, marked with a large green welcoming sign circled by a low stone wall. Pete turned in and followed the arrows to the parking lot next to the visitor center.

"We're all meeting up here," Bob told Lia. "There'll be maps and snacks."

They climbed out and stretched before heading inside, where Lia counted about a dozen photo club members mingling. Several hailed their group.

"You made it!" one particularly jolly man called out. Red-cheeked and weighted down with bags, he wore a bulging multipocketed vest that only added to his already round shape.

"Got enough equipment there, Len?" Bob asked jokingly.

"Ready for anything," Len answered, grinning as he patted his vest proudly.

"Such as alien landings?" Pete asked.

"You never know. When it happens, I'll be the one getting the best photos."

"Okay, guys." A woman Lia recognized as the club president clapped her hands to get the group's attention. "Everyone here?" She got a rumbling affirmation as she also counted heads. "Great! Here's the plan. We'll drive to the iron furnace first. It's a central spot, and you can leave your cars there if you like. Take your best shots and bring them to the next meeting to show them off. We'll vote, and the winner gets a gift certificate for pizza at Angelo's!" She paused as several cheers rang out.

"After that, you're on your own to wander through the park for whatever interests you. Plan to leave by four thirty. We'll meet up at the Tyrolean Inn for dinner. We have the party room reserved, and a great buffet dinner of bratwursts, knockwursts, and weisswursts will be waiting for us. So don't be late! Questions?"

Len raised his hand. "I need to know which is the best-worst."

People groaned and chuckled as Len went on to insist straight-faced that it was important, and he also needed information about the beer selection. Lia grinned, and the club president rolled her eyes, then clapped the group back to order.

"Everyone, grab a map and let's get going. Good luck, and have a great time!"

The members headed for the parking lot, and Pete joined a queue of four other cars along a winding road, several others having carpooled as they had. He had been right about the leaves turning. The park was a blaze of golds, reds, and yellows, making Lia wish she had a good camera to capture it all. Lacking that, she drank it all in live.

The gray stones of the iron furnace remains were a dramatic contrast to the color.

"I can see why wedding parties come here," Lia said, gazing as they left Pete's car. "It makes a beautiful backdrop."

"I've seen photos on the website," Jen said. "That empty window makes a perfect frame for bride-and-groom shots."

Bob and Pete got busy taking their photos. Lia watched as the members carefully kept out of one another's way and took turns for certain shots. When several had had their fill and wandered away, Bob beckoned to Jen and Lia to pose near the structure. They did so, arm in arm, then Pete waved for Bob to join the two. After he took the shot, Lia stepped away and suggested Pete take one of just Bob and Jen. As a cloud changed the light, Bob led his wife over to the bride-and-groom window frame, where they posed nicely.

"Your turn," Bob called and waved Pete and Lia over as he picked up his camera.

Lia expected Jen to stay in place, but she followed Bob, leaving Lia to pose alone with Pete at the window, feeling just a bit awkward. *It's just a photo*, she told herself. *Never mind the romantic connection.* They both smiled, Pete's hand lightly around Lia's shoulders, and it was over in seconds.

"Okay!" Bob said, lowering his camera. "Where to next?"

Lia and Pete stepped apart, and the two men pulled out their maps to consult. Lia joined Jen to head back to the car, neither concerned with giving input.

"They'll choose by photo ops," Jen said. "But I'll enjoy the scenery wherever we go."

Lia drew in a deep breath of the crisp fall air. "I agree. They can't go wrong in a place like this."

The next spots called for more challenging hiking, which Lia welcomed. All she'd done lately were walks around her neighborhood, which she wouldn't categorize as intense—nothing like this brisk, pulse-ramping exercise—and it felt good! It also made her hungry.

She obviously wasn't alone in that. After the guys took several shots from a hill they'd all just climbed, which overlooked a picturesque pond, Jen said, "I'm starting to salivate thinking about all those wursts and potato salads ahead for us. You fellows about ready?"

"I am," Pete said as Bob nodded vigorously.

"Good! Let's go." Jen led the way down the hill and to the car. Before long they were packed up and heading out of the park.

Chapter 14

There was little conversation as they rode toward the Tyrolean Inn, less from fatigue, Lia suspected, than from thoughts focused on the food ahead. As Pete eventually slowed at the restaurant, Lia took in its dark, wood-trimmed exterior, brightened by window boxes brimming with orange and yellow mums.

"Oh, how charming," she said.

"It's just as pretty inside," Jen said, unbuckling her seat belt and grabbing her purse.

"Most importantly, the food's good," Pete said. He held Lia's door and walked with her behind the Beasleys.

They were greeted inside by a hostess in a traditional dirndl dress, her hair woven into two long braids. She led them to the wood-paneled room reserved for the photo club. Several members were already seated at two long, rectangular tables covered in checkered tablecloths and set a comfortable distance away from a glowing fireplace.

Lia's group slipped into four spots next to and across from Len, the man who'd been prepared for an alien landing. He'd apparently left most of his gear elsewhere, though several of his vest pockets still bulged.

Bob introduced Lia to him, but before they had a chance to exchange more than a greeting, two Tyrolean-dressed waitresses appeared with pitchers of beer, which they distributed among the tables. Pete filled Lia's glass and his own, as chatter at the table naturally focused on the excursion and photos until the hostess invited them to the buffet that awaited in the outer area.

Chairs scraped as sixteen hungry people quickly got in line to fill their plates. Judging by the initial reactions, no one was disappointed. Besides the promised sausages, the steam table was loaded down with German potato salad, sauerkraut, spaetzle, red cabbage, mixed-greens salads, and more. As the group inched along on each side, traditional *Volksmusik* serenaded them from overhead speakers.

"A live band plays on weekends," Jen told Lia. "With dancing. It's a lot of fun!"

Back at their party room, they all dug in with raves over the food and much passing of the beer pitchers. Conversation didn't fully resume until dessert time, when many in the group leaned back in their chairs over coffee. Lia had chosen a chocolatey torte to top off her meal, though some, Pete included, chose a sampling of the specialty cookies.

"So," Len said to Lia, looking highly contented after polishing off a fully loaded plate, "will we be seeing you at future meetings?"

Lia set down her coffee cup and shook her head. "I'm not actually a camera person. I just came along to enjoy the day." She smiled. "And the company." Pete glanced over and returned the smile.

"Lia's an expert knitter," Jen said, leaning past Bob. "She runs a booth for our knitting group at the Crandalsburg Craft Fair."

"Do you?" Len said politely. "Then I must have seen it—and you—last weekend. I was there for the reenactment and browsed around. That was before all the excitement, of course." He looked at Pete with mock indignation to add, "When your guys hustled us all off the grounds. I didn't even get a rain check on my ticket."

"Sorry about that, Len," Pete said. "Had to be done."

"I know, I know," Len said. "Just kidding. That must have been a hassle and a half dealing with a crime like that in the middle of a huge crowd. Any progress? I mean as far as who done it?"

The auburn-haired woman sitting on the other side of Pete spoke up. "Wasn't it that guy they were talking about on TV? Jack something-or-other? The son-in-law said so." She looked at Pete for an answer.

"We're still investigating," Pete said. He stuffed half a gingerbread cookie into his mouth as though signaling *enough said*.

"But I heard—" the woman persisted, causing Lia to address her.

"What that son-in-law, Lucas Sprouse, said on television was completely uncalled-for," Lia said. "I'm appalled that the station aired such an unfounded claim. I happen to know the man Lucas accused. He's a totally decent and honest person."

"Oh!" the woman said, leaning back.

Len broke in. "You know, I saw something that I didn't think much of at the time, but maybe it's something you'd want to look into, Pete." He glanced at Lia in a conciliatory way. "It had nothing to do with your friend, who I don't even know. This involved one of the women in the living history section."

"Oh?" Lia said, surprised. "What was it?"

"An argument with a man. And not your everyday kind. This was a sparks-flying, fists-balled sort. It took place out of the way, where they probably thought they were alone. But I had found a bit of shade and quiet for the moment, and they must not have spotted me. They were both clearly furious, but they also kept their voices down, so I don't know what it was all about.

"At the time," Len continued, "I shrugged it off. But when pictures of the murder victim started showing up on TV, I realized the guy I saw was him."

"And the woman was?" Pete asked.

"I don't know her name," Len said. "But I recognized her. She had been doing the living history spinning demonstration."

Ronna Dickens, Lia said to herself.

On the drive home, Lia sat up front with Pete. Bob dozed in the back while Jen seemed busy with her phone, so Lia brought up Len's story. She had seen Pete talking privately with the man before they left.

"I know who the woman was that Len saw," she said. "Ronna Dickens."

Pete nodded in a way that told Lia he already knew.

"I spoke to her on Monday," Lia said.

Pete looked over.

"She told me about their dispute—Sprouse's and hers. Not the argument Len witnessed. Their longtime one. It was about a creek with endangered plants that Sprouse would have destroyed. But Ronna stopped that from happening, she said, by threatening a lawsuit."

"Then why were they arguing at the reenactment?" Pete asked.

"I don't know. Maybe lingering animosities?" Pete didn't react to that.

"She pointed me to Gil Hubbard as a likely enemy of Sprouse," Lia said. "Do you know about his bitterness toward Sprouse after the loss of his hotel?"

After a brief pause, Pete asked mildly, "Lia, what have you been up to?"

"Jack and Sharon are good friends of mine," Lia said. "I meant what I said to the woman sitting next to you back there. She had already tried and convicted Jack in her mind, and she isn't the only one. Jack's had job cancellations. Friends have let him down. Everyone's looking at him with suspicion. He needs his name cleared."

Pete sighed. "Lia, it's an ongoing investigation. We can't completely exonerate people until we learn exactly what happened."

"But surely—" Lia began.

"I'm sorry. It's just the way it has to be. And I know you want to help your friend, but I'd really rather you left it up to us. I promise we know what we're doing." His tone softened. "And I don't want to see you put yourself in danger."

Lia was touched but at the same time felt the need to defend herself. "I don't intend to meet anonymous tipsters in dark alleys," she said. "I'm only asking questions."

When Pete was silent, she added, "And I may be able to find out things that the police don't, simply because someone thinks they're not important enough to report to you. For instance, did you know that Gil Hubbard, who I mentioned has a grudge against Arden Sprouse, may have been seen hanging around the tent where the two bayoneted ri-

fles were kept? He wasn't a reenactor and had no good reason to be there."

"May have been seen?" Pete asked.

"Well, the person who told me this doesn't know Hubbard personally and could only go by his description. But
he's going to check with others about it."

"So you've spoken to more people than Ronna Dickens
about the murder?"

"And I probably will, too," Jen piped up from the back.
She'd put her phone away and obviously had overheard.
"The Ninth Street Knitters support each other whenever we
can. We talk about a lot more than knitting when we get
together."

Pete groaned but asked, "Then will you please keep me
updated about what you're up to?"

"Of course we will," Jen said. "We don't go around
making citizen's arrests, do we, Lia?"

At Pete's pained look, Lia assured him that would never
cross her mind. "My only goal is to help speed things along
so that Jack Kuhn's life can get back to normal."

"And to see the actual murderer put behind bars," Jen
added.

Bob snuffled as he woke out of his doze and caught Jen's
last words. "Huh? We're stopping at a bar?" he asked, peering around bleary-eyed. "Why?"

"No, sweetie," Jen assured him. "I was talking about
prison bars."

That only puzzled Bob more, to Lia's amusement, but
he shrugged good-naturedly and asked if anyone knew the
score of the Bears game, the Hershey ice hockey team he
followed.

Jen pulled out her phone to check for him, and Pete turned

on the radio, not searching for sports news but settling on a soothing light-jazz station. Conversation came to an end, as the occupants eventually gazed out their respective windows, all four becoming lost in their thoughts as darkened fields whizzed by.

Chapter 15

The next morning, Lia was retrieving her mail when she noticed Sharon down the block, apparently heading back from a brisk walk. From the look on her face, it hadn't been particularly refreshing. Lia went to the sidewalk to meet her.

Staring down at the pavement rather fiercely, Sharon only became aware of Lia when she came within steps of her. She pulled up short and rearranged her expression into something resembling a smile, though not very convincingly.

"Good morning," Lia said. "Want to sit a bit?"

Sharon drew a deep breath before saying, "Sure." She followed Lia to her front porch with its two slatted rockers, a spot Lia always found soothing. She hoped it would work its magic on her friend now.

"How was your outing yesterday?" Sharon asked as she plopped into one chair.

Lia remained standing. "Very pleasant," she said. "Would you like a drink?"

Sharon shook her head, lifting the half-filled water bottle she held in one hand, so Lia took the second chair. They rocked in silence for a bit until Sharon said, "One of Jack's clients, someone he did significant work for, informed him she's withholding final payment."

Lia winced. "Why is that?"

"Jack said she's been a pain in the neck all through the reno job, changing her mind so many times at the last minute that he was forced to add labor and material costs. She then started finding faults that weren't there, he said. Now she's threatening to take him to court for what she's already paid, claiming shoddy work."

Sharon's rocking had sped up as she spoke. She planted her feet to stop, then looked over to Lia. "Jack thinks she's trying to take advantage of his situation. You, know, since the murder."

"How awful," Lia said. "Who is this woman?"

"Her name's Candace Carr. She's fairly new in town—bought a house with a lot of charm but also plenty of problems. Jack spelled them out clearly for her. She knew exactly what to expect."

"I'm sorry," Lia said. After another silence, she said, "I did talk to Pete Sullivan about the unfairness of what Jack's been going through. And I told him what I've started to dig up."

At Lia's words, Sharon straightened. "Anything good?"

"Nothing major so far, but a start." Lia told her what she'd learned about Gil Hubbard and of Ronna Dickens's spitting argument with Sprouse. "What do you know about Ronna?" she asked.

"She's very passionate about protecting the environment. I've been to her store. Have you?"

"I have. Interesting place, and yes, I picked up on that passion. But she told me she'd stopped Arden Sprouse from destroying a particular creek, so I'm wondering what their conflict at the reenactment was about."

"I can't help you there," Sharon said, leaning back and rolling her water bottle between her hands. "Do you think it might have led to Sprouse's murder?" she asked, hope slipping into her tone.

"One argument doesn't automatically lead to murder," Lia cautioned. "All it does, for me, is put her on my suspect list. But the police are aware of it, and of Gil Hubbard."

Sharon shook her head sadly. "It's awful to want people you know to turn out to be murderers. But someone has to be. And that person is letting Jack take the fall for what they did!"

"That won't last," Lia said. She reached over to give Sharon's arm an encouraging squeeze. "It can't. There is something out there that will prove Jack's innocence and convict the proper person. We just have to find it."

Strong words, Lia knew, meant to buck up her friend. But were they only words or could Lia back them up with results? She badly wanted to, and she would do all she could toward it. But would it be enough?

That evening, Lia drove to Jen Beasley's house in York to meet with her fellow Ninth Street Knitters. It felt like ages since she'd seen most of them, what with all that had happened, though it had been only a week. She had a lot to talk over.

As usual, as the one who traveled farthest, she was the last to arrive. The group had formed years ago, when Lia also lived in York. Their mutual love of knitting had drawn them together, but the strong friendships that developed continued to bind them. The four women had been a huge help to Lia with problems in the past, sometimes with new information and sometimes simply by listening. Tonight she'd take whichever she could get.

Lia walked right into the house—none of them having bothered to knock for years—and headed to the kitchen, where the others were spreading out their potluck snacks.

"Lia!" they cried in unison as she appeared.

"We heard about the murder," Maureen said, explaining the startling reception. "So terrible! For everybody concerned, of course, but another blow for the craft fair."

"I think the fair will be okay," Lia assured her as she added the cut veggies and dip she'd brought to Jen's countertop. "At least the media so far hasn't linked this murder to us. Perhaps because it didn't occur inside the craft barn. I can't say the same for my poor neighbor, but I'll get into that later, once we settle down."

The women filled their snack plates and chose their drinks before heading to Jen's living room, each automatically settling in her favorite spot. Lia's was the stuffed chair that originally had Daphne's cushion next to it. That was before she brought the ragdoll cat home as her new mom because of Bob's worsening allergies.

Maureen and Diana always had a million things to say to each other when they arrived and ended up side by side on the sofa to continue the conversation.

Tracy took the love seat for herself, spreading out multiple balls of yarn as she knitted her intricate layette patterns, and Jen's favorite knitting chair was her rocker, which the others knew and left for her.

As they pulled out their current projects, Lia said, "First, the good news. Tracy, I've sold your white layette with the butterflies. Belinda picked it up for me from the craft fair barn. I'll be mailing it to the buyer soon."

"Really? I'm so glad." Tracy beamed. The mother of twins, she grew skilled at knitting baby items before the boys were born. Now that her sons were in middle school, Tracy enjoyed knitting those items for others and was always delighted to hear they had found a good home.

"And, Diana," Lia said, turning to the forty-something brunette, "I have a deposit on your multicolored throw."

"Yay!" Diana cried. "I worked on that for ages."

"And it turned out beautifully," Jen said.

"The buyer will pick it up at the craft fair this weekend," Lia said. "She had intended to come back for it after the reenactment. But then everything was closed down so suddenly after the murder was discovered."

"What a nightmare that must have been," Tracy said, shaking her head.

"It was," Lia agreed, "and it continues for my next-door neighbor Jack." She described what he'd been going through since the murder was discovered—the lingering suspicion and its effects on his life and work. "I know Jack well enough to be convinced that he's simply the victim of bad circumstances, with his rifle and bayonet used as the murder weapon and having no corroborated alibi."

"Lia's already working on it," Jen said, loosening a length of yellow yarn from her wound ball. "And I know we'll all do what we can to help, right?"

"Of course we will," Diana said. "If we can," she added. "But I don't know a thing about Arden Sprouse."

Lia shared what she knew, that he was apparently a successful businessman who had bought the struggling Hubbard Hotel in Crandalsburg with big plans to expand it. "He also essentially took over the reenactment group and stepped on a lot of toes—some would say tromped—with his changes. Jack was a major opponent of those changes. Gil Hubbard is the hotel owner who probably felt conned, and Ronna Dickens fought Sprouse over the environmental damage he intended to cause."

Lia grabbed a quick sip of coffee before going on. "I'm eliminating Jack as a suspect, of course, but have Hubbard and Dickens on my list." She paused. "That's it so far." She waited as the group absorbed it all.

"Ronna Dickens," Maureen said slowly. "I know that name."

"She owns Eco Alley," Jen said. "A shop of environmentally friendly items. Maybe you've been there?"

"Never heard of it," Maureen said, shaking her head. "No, it's something else . . . Wait! I remember. She led a protest march in Harrisburg once, over something environmental, don't ask me what. But I remember the name because it's close to my brother-in-law's, Ron Dickenson. We teased him about it when she was arrested."

"She was arrested? What for?" Lia asked.

"For attacking one of the state senators. She really got in his face, from what I remember, and somehow he ended up on the ground. It might have been accidental, and I don't know if she ended up actually charged with anything. But I do remember videos of her loudly protesting as they led her away."

"Sounds like someone you don't want to cross," Tracy said, which prompted Lia to mention the quarrel Ronna had with Sprouse not long before his murder.

"Uh-oh," Diana said. "That looks like your murderer, Lia."

"But she needs proof," Tracy said.

"That's my problem," Lia said, nodding. "And the problem facing the police. Finding proof."

A silence fell over the room until Jen offered softly, "Sometimes that only comes with a second murder."

"What!" Diana sounded horrified.

"Not that I'm hoping for one," Jen quickly added. "But it might happen. Our murderer could feel threatened with exposure and kill again to prevent that. Or they might actually feel empowered by the first murder and decide to eliminate a second enemy. But overconfidence could make them careless, and—"

"And they leave behind evidence," Maureen finished for her. "Proof."

"Exactly."

The group pondered that for several minutes over the clacking of their needles. The thought that Jen might be right and another murder might occur was chilling. But for Lia, at least, it was all the more reason to discover who that evil person was.

And to watch her back carefully.

Chapter 16

Lia had barely made it through her front door after driving back from York, when her cell phone rang. It was Hayley.

"Hi, Mom. Did I time it right? You're back from your knitting thing, right?"

"Just walked in." Lia reached down to pat Daphne, who'd scampered over to greet her. "What's up?"

"Nothing special. Just checking in. If you need a minute, you can call me back."

"No, it's fine. I'll just grab some water before I sit. It's good to hear from you. How's work?" Lia asked as she headed to the kitchen.

As she filled a glass with water and added ice, Lia listened to Hayley's description of the marketing campaign she was working on for the alpaca farm. Some of the details went over her head, but what Lia cared about the most was the enthusiasm she heard in Hayley's voice.

"That all sounds great," Lia said as she returned to the living room and sank into her knitting chair. "I hope the Webers will be ready for the massive yarn sales that result."

Hayley chuckled. "We're thinking long-term, Mom, with maybe a modest initial uptick if we're lucky. I think they'll be able to handle that. By the way, I, uh, spoke to Gil Hubbard today."

"You did?" Lia asked, feeling a twinge of concern.

"Nothing much," Hayley assured her. "He was in the barn when I happened to pop in. I tell myself that Rosie feels neglected if I don't stop in at least once a day to see her," she said, referring to her favorite alpaca. "All Gil and I talked about was stuff like the weather. But he seems so sad. It makes me feel sorry for him, unless, of course, he happens to be feeling bad about stabbing Arden Sprouse. Did you come up with anything that could confirm that?"

"Nothing confirming, but his actions at the reenactment do look suspicious." Lia told Hayley what she'd learned about Gil's intense interest in the bayonet demonstration, then the possibility he'd been lingering near Herb Weaver's tent after the rifles were taken there.

"Darn. That doesn't sound too good."

"But I now have a second suspect," Lia said, sharing what she'd learned about Ronna, first from Len after the photo excursion, then from Maureen a short time ago at the knitters meeting.

"Good! Maybe Gil will be off the hook." Hayley paused. "So you went to this photo thing with Chief Sullivan? On a date?"

"Oh no, not a date," Lia said. "He simply invited me to come along with the group, which included our mutual friends, Jen and Bob." As she said it, Lia wondered if she was assuring herself rather than Hayley. Or both. She turned to a more comfortable subject: the discussion she'd had with Pete about both Ronna and Gil as murder suspects. "I promised I'd keep him updated on what I find."

"After he suggested you stay out of it altogether?" Hayley asked, her tone suggesting a grin.

"Yes, of course, which is what Brady has pushed sometimes, too. And I understand. They're the pros, though I still think I can contribute in my way. How is Brady, by the way?"

"Busy," Hayley said. "He's started taking on a lot of overtime lately, as well as moonlighting on security jobs. So instead of seeing each other, we've been texting a lot."

"I see." Lia knew Tom would approve the practicality of building up extra income and savings early on. But Lia felt a motherly twinge over what it might do to their relationship.

"It's all fine," Hayley said. "I'm pretty busy right now, too. We'll catch up. Oh, I almost forgot. I had an interesting conversation with my landlady."

"Ms. Griffith?" Lia asked. She held her water glass out of the way as Daphne looked ready to jump on Lia's lap.

"Yeah, except she wants me to call her Marlaine."

"Okay. So what was the conversation about?"

"Lucas Hall."

Lia let out a soft *oof* as Daphne landed. The ragdoll cat was cuddly but not exactly lightweight. "The Sprouse son-in-law?" she asked. "What about him?

"Marlaine doesn't have a high opinion of him, and she's had opportunity to get to know him. She's Heidi Sprouse's cousin."

"Is she? That's interesting."

"Yeah. They didn't grow up in the same town, but Marlaine said their families spent plenty of summer vacations together. When the Sprouses moved to Crandalsburg, Marlaine was invited over a lot."

"So what does she base this low opinion of Lucas on?"

"She didn't say, exactly, but she said she didn't like his looks from the moment she set eyes on him."

"Didn't like his looks?" Lia asked, a smile forming.

"I know," Hayley said. "But you've met her. She throws out an opinion in as few words as possible as if just the fact of her saying it makes it so."

"How did this come up?" Lia asked.

"Marlaine had just picked up her evening paper, which the delivery guy knows to set properly in the paper box instead of tossing it on her lawn, by the way. I had just come home, and she was reading the front page. It had a story about the murder with a photo of all the Sprouses, including the son-in-law. That's when she told me about her connection to them and her feelings about Lucas."

"But nothing beyond that?"

"Nope. Want me to see what I can get out of her?" Hayley asked.

"If you can," Lia said. "Though it sounds like that might be challenging."

Hayley laughed. "Like it was trying to get Dad to share his golf scores?"

Lia smiled at the memory. "Maybe not that hard."

"I'll see what I can do."

Lia noticed the time and wound things down. Hayley had a job to get ready for. When she hung up, Lia realized she had a voice message on her phone. It was from an unfamiliar number, but she pulled it up to hear.

"Uh, hi, Mrs. Geiger?" the voice began. "This is Frank Burns. Say, I, uh, asked some people if they knew Gil Hubbard and if they saw him hanging around our tents that day. One guy said he did, around the same time I thought I might have. Cliff Morris said he tried to talk with Gil, about, you know, all his troubles, lately—just wanted to offer his sympathy. Hubbard brushed him off, saying he had to be somewhere. But Cliff spotted him a little later, and Hubbard hadn't gone far. He looked like he had something really heavy on his mind."

The message ended with a hesitant good-bye, and Lia ran her hand over Daphne's back as she mulled that over. Had Gil been planning how to get the rifles from Herb's tent? Did watching the bayonet demo put the idea for murder in his head? Lia could see that happening, though whether he'd actually acted on it was something else again.

Should she pass this on to Pete? She'd promised to keep him updated with anything useful but wasn't sure this qualified. Gil hadn't actually been spotted slipping into the tent or sneaking off with Jack's rifle. No, she needed more.

Thinking of Pete turned her thoughts in another direction. During their conversation, Hayley had asked if their excursion had been a date. Lia had claimed it wasn't, but was that true? Did Pete see it as one, and if so, how did Lia feel about that? What would Hayley think? She had brought up her dad soon afterward, jokingly, but had there been another motive behind it?

But first and foremost, was Lia actually ready to start dating? When she was reminded of Tom in the hardware store, she thought about how he would have wanted her to move on. She'd congratulated herself on how she'd done so, to some extent, with her move to Crandalsburg and joining the craft fair.

But did moving on have to include dating? Did she want

that? If not, Pete needed to know. But he might be thinking only of friendship, in which case Lia needn't concern herself one way or the other. And yet—

Daphne made a protesting peep over the stroking, signaling *enough!*

"Sorry, Daph," Lia said. "Too many complicated things running through my head. Time to turn them off and just turn in."

At Lia's shift forward, Daphne jumped down agreeably. Lia took her glass to the kitchen, turned off the lights, and headed up the stairs. She'd get back to all those thorny thoughts another day.

Chapter 17

The next morning, Lia went online to see what she could find about Ronna's arrest in Harrisburg. There wasn't much to find. A small mention of the scuffle that ended with the environmentalist being led away, but nothing about charges. So the senator's ending up on the ground must not have been found to be her fault, or perhaps he declined to press the issue. Lia did discover a short video of Ronna's protests taken from someone's cell phone. The woman clearly didn't require bullhorns.

Lia then looked into Ronna's claim of having blocked Sprouse's environmentally hurtful plan for the hotel grounds. Lia searched through the Crandalsburg government website but found nothing concerning that, which probably shouldn't have surprised her. But perhaps Pete could help? Or Brady?

Lia closed down her laptop and concentrated on getting Tracy's white layette set ready for mailing. Belinda had dropped it off on her way to an appointment after one of her trips to the craft barn, along with a perfect-sized box she'd received from a delivery of her own. All Lia had to do was wrap the layette prettily in tissue paper, slip it into a plastic bag for good measure, then seal and label the box. She did so, taking pleasure in the task, first through handling Tracy's beautiful pieces, then from imagining the joy they would bring to both the gift giver and recipient. That was Lia's favorite part of knitting for the craft fair, seeing the eyes of a buyer light up over something she or one of her knitting friends had put so much heart into.

Lia leaned out the door to check the coolness of the day. She slipped on a lightweight jacket, then picked up her box to head to the post office. The car keys were in her hand, but the sun was shining so brightly that as she reached her Camry, she dropped the keys into her jacket pocket. It was too fine a day to spend behind a steering wheel when she had the time and the energy to walk a few blocks.

Her neighborhood was quiet, though a couple of people were raking leaves, and Lia responded to their friendly waves as she walked by. Her thoughts flew back to the night she'd gone door to door, frantically searching for Daphne. Not the best circumstance for meeting her neighbors, though it had been effective in eventually locating the cat. Happily, since then she'd come to know several neighbors even better.

Her thoughts went on to more memories as she walked, and before she knew it, Lia had reached her destination.

Belinda had once told her that the Crandalsburg post office had originally been a bank, which must have been cost saving when it came to the conversion. Tellers' windows became postal workers' spots, though Lia had no idea what became of the safe. Perhaps she'd ask sometime.

She got in line behind four other patrons, one of whom

held a tote filled with several small packages, so Lia prepared herself for a wait, studying a poster announcing an upcoming fundraising white elephant sale. It wasn't until she'd shuffled to the head of the line that she was addressed by a person who'd stepped up behind her.

"You're the knitting lady from the craft fair, aren't you?"

Lia turned, expecting to find one of her customers, and was surprised to see Heidi Sprouse. The widow of Arden Sprouse was in contemporary clothes rather than the Civil War–era dress she'd had on when they first met, but her friendly face and stout figure were recognizable.

"It's Lia, isn't it? "Heidi asked tentatively.

"Yes. Lia Geiger. May I say how sorry I am about your husband, Mrs. Sprouse?"

"Heidi, please. And thank you." She held up a thick pack of envelopes with a slight grimace. "Thank you notes for all the cards and flowers. People have been very kind."

Lia nodded sympathetically, then heard "Next!" She started to move, but Heidi stopped her with a touch on her arm.

"Wait for me, will you?" she asked.

"Of course." Lia took her package to the next available postal clerk and had it stamped and insured. She saw that Heidi had gone to the second window. When Lia was done, she waited for Heidi just inside.

"Thank you," Heidi said and led the way out. After a few steps, she asked, "Do you have time for a coffee? It's been such a hectic few days. I could really use a little downtime."

"Yes, certainly." Lia suggested Marie's. "It's right around the corner," she said.

"Perfect," Heidi said and took Lia's arm to start walking.

Within minutes, Lia was facing Heidi across a table at

Marie's cozy diner, a steaming mug of coffee in front of each and a sticky bun on the way for Heidi.

Heidi stirred cream into her coffee and took a long swallow before sitting back with a sigh. "Oh, you don't know how good it is to just sit down for something like this."

"I can imagine," Lia said. "Actually, I can more than imagine." She told Heidi about her own loss, though aware that, painful as it was, there at least hadn't been the horror of a murder on top of it.

"I didn't realize," Heidi said and gave Lia what was clearly a heartfelt condolence. "Seeing you apparently doing so well gives me hope."

"It does get easier over time," Lia assured her.

"That's good to know." Heidi's sticky bun arrived, and she took a bite from it. "So good," she murmured. "My cousin makes these, too."

"Marlaine?" Lia asked.

Heidi's eyes widened. "Yes. You know her?"

"She's my daughter's landlady. We met a couple of times."

Heidi grinned. "Not much of a chatterbox, is she?"

"She's . . . concise," Lia said, picking up her mug.

"Concise," Heidi said, chuckling. "You're being kind. But she's a great person. And a rock. I don't know what I would have done without her, these last few days."

"It can make a huge difference," Lia agreed. "And you have your daughter, too."

"I do." Heidi's eyes glowed warmly for several moments, then surprisingly turned chilly. "And then there's Lucas."

Lia nodded. "Marlaine isn't exactly fond of him."

Heidi shook her head. "I probably shouldn't say anything. He's my daughter's husband. But that's exactly why I'm bothered. You always want the best for your daughter, don't you?"

"Of course. But it's not always in our control."

"I know, I know," Heidi said, rocking her head. "I should just let it go. Julie seems fine, so that's all that matters." Heidi bit into her sticky bun again. After a sip of her coffee she said, "I just wish he'd learn when to keep his mouth shut. It was bad enough what happened to Arden, but to see Lucas spouting off about it on TV, when he doesn't know what the heck he's talking about . . ." Her voice trailed off.

"The man he was spouting off about is my neighbor Jack Kuhn," Lia said.

"Your neighbor? I've met Jack. He seems like a decent man."

"Jack's a good man," Lia said. "He and Arden had their differences over the reenactment group, but that's all it was—a disagreement."

"That's what I understood, too," Heidi assured her.

"Unfortunately, because of that and because it was his rifle's bayonet—" Lia stopped, biting her tongue for having brought that up. But Arden's widow showed she was made of sturdy stuff.

"I knew about the rifle—the police told me—and they asked me about Jack Kuhn, if he'd threatened Arden, things like that. I told them no. There had never been anything like that."

"I'm very glad to hear that. Unfortunately, Jack doesn't have an alibi that can be backed up." Lia explained about the migraine and his self-imposed isolation during the time his rifle was left unattended.

"You know, I remember seeing him looking awfully pale that afternoon." Heidi swiped a paper napkin at her mouth. "Marlaine gets migraines, and I recognized the look. I was going to speak to him, see if there was anything I could do. But then the crowd got between us, and I lost him. I'll be glad to tell the police that, if you think it would help."

"It wouldn't clear him, but it's something, and I know Jack would appreciate it, especially coming from you," Lia said. "He's been under a very heavy cloud of suspicion that's been hurtful and undeserved."

"Then I'll absolutely do it. And if there's any other way I can help, please let me know. I mean it. I want the truth about Arden's murder to come out and for none of us, Jack included, to be left hanging."

"That's very kind of you," Lia said, truly grateful. "I've been working toward that end myself. It has to be an overwhelmingly difficult crime for the police to solve, what with the pandemonium of the reenactment and the huge crowds. But if more people come forward with bits and pieces of what they saw, it might make the difference. It could fill in the picture of what actually happened."

Heidi smiled. "I knew when I first met you that you were someone I wanted to know better. You're clearly a good friend to Jack and probably to many others. I'm so glad we ran into each other today."

When the check came, Heidi snatched it up and headed to the cashier. Later, she surprised Lia with a small bakery box. "Sticky buns," she explained. "My little treat to thank you for the kind gift of your time today," she said, then winked. "They're almost as good as my cousin Marlaine's."

She bustled off then, with a good-bye wave.

Chapter 18

When Lia arrived at the craft fair parking area Saturday morning, she was amazed at how normal everything appeared. All signs of the reenactment and living history were gone, as was any indication of the crime scene. The effect was a bit bewildering, as though it all had been imagined. Except it hadn't. Arden Sprouse was dead, and his killer was still at large.

"Weird, isn't it?" Maggie's voice came from behind Lia as she stood in the parking area, musing.

"Definitely," Lia said, turning to her friend. "But better than if it were still roped off and the craft fair canceled."

"Agreed." Maggie shifted the weight of the quilt in her arms. "Life goes on," she said as she continued on to the barn.

It does, Lia thought, *but never as it was.* The violent crime that occurred had damaged more than one life. Healing wouldn't be as easy or quick as cleaning up the crime scene had been. But it would be aided significantly by catching the culprit. She was reminded of Jen's ominous words: *before another life is lost.*

Lia followed Maggie into the barn where the familiar, uplifting sights and sounds of crafters setting up their booths greeted her.

"Good morning, Olivia," Lia called to her craft neighbor. Lia was sorry to see an unhappy face.

"Hi, Lia," Olivia answered, barely enough energy in her voice to be heard.

Lia left her bag of knits on the counter and moved closer. "Feeling down?"

Olivia nodded. "It's just . . . I worked so hard getting ready for the living history. And then . . ." She shrugged.

"I know." Lia squeezed Olivia's hand. "It felt like having the rug pulled out from under you, right?"

"Yes!"

"But you were doing a wonderful job while you were there, Olivia. I could see how interested people were in your demonstration."

"You could?"

"Yes. And you reached a lot of them. Don't think of it as a loss or a waste of your efforts. It wasn't, and there'll be more opportunities for it in the future."

"I guess you're right." A smile tugged at the edges of Olivia's lips. "There's always next year." Olivia shook herself. "And I know I shouldn't even feel this way. I mean, my disappointment is nothing compared to what the Sprouse family must be going through."

"It's not nothing to you. You have every right to feel disappointed," Lia assured her. "It's totally separate from the Sprouse's grief and doesn't diminish it." Lia moved toward her own booth. "As a matter of fact, I saw Heidi

Sprouse yesterday, and she seems to be doing pretty well, well enough to care about other people at a time like this."

"She must be a very strong woman," Olivia said as she resumed lining up her essential oils and handmade soaps.

Lia nodded. "I get that impression." She got to work arranging her own booth, hanging colorful sweaters on a line at the side and spreading out caps and other small knits on her counter. As she did, she found herself thinking of the Civil War–era surgery that had occupied her spot just days ago, with its grim display of the only help wounded soldiers had available to them at the time. How much cheerier the barn looked now, though the lesson taught by the display was important. And the memory of the unsolved crime surely lingered in more minds than her own.

But as Bill Landry called out his usual heads-up to the vendors, Lia felt the familiar ripple of excitement flow through the craft barn. Shoppers waited outside the doors, and life, as Maggie pointed out, went on. Lia straightened the last of her items and watched as Bill prepared to swing the large doors open. Today, she decided, would be a good day.

Both Lia's and Olivia's booths were back in their original spots after some shifting a few weeks ago to fill a vacancy. Lia was comfortable snugged next to the side exit, where she'd first started. From her vantage point, Lia could see most of the booths lining the craft barn and during slow times enjoyed watching the interaction between shoppers and vendors as she sat and knitted.

She did so now, as the doors opened, knowing it would be a while before the first arrivals made their way over to her. Her current project was a headband–ear warmer, which she'd already made in several patterns and colors. They'd proven to be a popular item and were a quick and easy knit, so easy that she could pay plenty of attention to the activities around her while she worked.

As expected, many of the conversations that drifted her way concerned the reenactment and murder. At first she hoped that would have run its course by the time shoppers reached her, but on further thought, she realized there might be nuggets to be mined from the chatter. As she'd said to Heidi, bits and pieces could help fill in a picture. It wouldn't hurt to encourage as much talk as she could, while at the same time hopefully making sales.

Her first shopper, however, a woman in her thirties, was interested neither in chatting about the murder nor in buying. A knitter herself, she had stopped to chat about patterns and yarn shops and projects they'd completed. Lia made sure to mention the alpaca yarns available at the Weber farm and was pleased when her noncustomer asked for more information. It was a pleasant conversation, and Lia didn't mind in the least that it ended in no sale, at least not for her. It might work eventually for the Webers, which would be just fine.

She did make a couple of satisfying sales following that. Neither of those shoppers talked about the happenings of the previous week. But then someone arrived who brought up a more surprising subject. Lia was digging into her reserve box for replacement items when a woman of about her own age appeared and began fingering her way through the hanging sweaters.

"Good morning," Lia said, straightening. She laid the knit place mats she'd found on the counter. "Anything I can help you with?"

The woman tucked a strand of blond hair behind her ear and smiled. "Well, I don't see what I'm searching for. Unless you have more sweaters hiding somewhere?"

"I'm afraid not. What is it you have in mind?"

The woman laughed lightly. "Well, it's a sweater my next-door neighbor wears, and I love it. But all I know is that she picked it up some time ago when she was traveling." She described the general pattern, which sounded like an Aran cardigan. Lia pulled up one of her catalogues and flipped through it.

"Does it look something like this?" she asked, turning the book in the woman's direction.

Her shopper peered at the photo. "Yes . . . except hers has a collar." She turned the page. "Ah! That's closer to it. But it's missing pockets."

"Pockets can be easily added," Lia assured her. "And these can be made in just about any color or with colored trim. If you see something you like, I could take an order for it with a small deposit."

The woman turned another page. "Wow, lots of choices. Now I'm thinking I might like one of these better than something exactly like hers."

Lia smiled. "That's the beauty of made to order. Yours would be one of a kind. And you and your neighbor could wear your sweaters together without being twinsies."

The woman chuckled. "Something to think about, though right now she and I don't really see much of each other. She's pretty new to the neighborhood. I just happened to run into her when she had that gorgeous cardigan on. What would it cost to special order a sweater like this?"

Lia explained how it would depend on several things but gave her a likely range. It brought an astonished reaction.

"Yikes! I'd have to think about that a little," the woman said. "I guess I should have figured. Candace—that's my neighbor—seems to have plenty of money to spend. Including on her wardrobe."

Candace. The name rang a bell for Lia. Could that be the

same person Sharon had mentioned just two days ago? "Did Candace happen to have work done on her house recently?" she asked.

The woman looked up from the catalogue. "Yes, lots of it. Workmen coming and going all the time. It wasn't so bad when they were working inside, but then she had them add a deck in the back. Hammering from nine to four! No bother for her—she was away all day. But I work from home." She rolled her eyes in exasperation but then smiled. "I have to admit that it looked good once it was done."

"Then I think her last name is Carr. Am I right?" When Lia got a surprised agreement from her shopper, she said, "That work was done by my neighbor Jack Kuhn. Did Candace seem satisfied with it?"

"I'm sure she was. She had a bunch of people over, including several of us neighbors, to show it all off. Kind of an open house. She seemed quite proud of it." The woman paused. "You know, I just realized. One of the guests was that man who was killed here last week!"

"Arden Sprouse?"

"Yes. Candace worked for him. She said she'd moved to Crandalsburg when his company relocated here. I forget where she said they moved from, but it must have been beyond commuting distance."

"And it must have been an important job for her to be willing to move."

"No doubt." The woman turned one more page of the catalogue before checking the time on her phone. "Ugh! I'd better get going. Thank you for all this information on the sweater. I can see it will be a bit of an investment, and I'm going to have to mull over how badly I want it. Can I call you if I have more questions?"

"Of course." Lia pulled a business card from the stack she'd had printed. Her shopper gave her own name—Beth Daniels—and thanked her again before heading off, with her thoughts most likely on Aran cardigans, while Lia's remained on Candace Carr.

Chapter 19

Toward the end of the day, traffic in the barn slowed, and Lia wanted to stretch her legs a bit. Since she and Olivia were in the habit of watching over each other's booths when needed, Lia was able to take off and wander about. She chatted with several vendors along the way, bought a large chocolate cookie from Carolyn Hanson's baked goods, and continued on until she stopped at Mark Simmons's photography booth.

Mark was busy with a shopper, but Lia's eye was quickly caught by a display of the photos he had taken at the reenactment. Those of the battle were in black and white, giving them a Mathew Brady–like historical feel. Mark had even taken a few photos of reenactors in their uniforms, posed like the portraits of that era. The battle photos, interesting as they were, brought back the uncomfortable emotions Lia had felt at the time, and she moved on to shots of the crafters, chuckling as she found one of herself chatting with Maggie.

There were a few candids of the reenactors, taken in the tent area before the battle. Lia looked closely at those. She spotted Frank Burns in the crowd, but too many of the other faces were turned away from the camera. She recognized Heidi in one shot, mostly from the period costume she'd worn that day.

Then she saw a taller woman in a separate photo. Lia thought she recognized Ronna Dickens from the costume she'd worn for her living history spinning demonstration, but she wasn't sure. If it was Ronna, what was she doing in the tent area?

Len had said he witnessed Ronna arguing with Arden Sprouse in a much more isolated location. Had the argument begun near the tents? Lia studied the other figures but didn't find Sprouse, whose face she'd become familiar with from it being splashed all over the news media. However, she did spot Herb, standing outside the tent where Jack's and Lucas's rifles were stored. He and the tall woman were only feet apart. Had the rifles been in that tent at the time?

When Mark finished with his customer, Lia took that photo over to him.

"Mark, can you tell me what time this was taken?"

Mark looked at it and said, "Not offhand. All I can say right now is that it was sometime before the battle scene."

"What about the woman there?" Lia asked, pointing to the figure. "Do you know who it is?"

Mark was shaking his head when a voice behind Lia startled her. "That's Ronna, isn't it?" The voice belonged to Belinda's "gentleman friend," who was peering over her shoulder.

"Chad!" Lia said. "I didn't know you were here. You know Ronna?"

"Kind of. We've met a few times at Aymesburg," he

said, referring to the college where he taught. "She comes by once in a while to talk with Travis Parsons. He teaches courses for environmental science."

"That makes sense," Lia said and told Chad about Ronna's shop, Eco Alley. Lia's cell phone suddenly pinged, a text from Olivia signaling that Lia had a customer waiting.

"I have to get back to my booth," she said. "Will you be around? I'd like to discuss this some more."

"Sure. If you don't see me wandering about, I'll be in Belinda's office."

"Perfect." Lia hurried back to her booth to deal with her customer, eventually making a satisfying end-of-day sale of a child's pullover.

"For my niece," the young woman told her, as Lia bagged the pink cardigan with a large flower applique. "She *loves* anything pink."

"I'll bet her room is that color," Lia said, handing over the bag.

"It totally glows," her customer said with a grin. "She's five now. We'll see how long that lasts."

The woman took off, one of the final few shoppers to exit the craft barn, and Lia began closing up her booth. When she'd finished, and Bill had closed the doors, she glanced around for Chad. Not seeing him in the larger area, she headed down the side hall to Belinda's office. The door was open, and she could hear his voice as she approached.

"There she is," Chad said when Lia appeared in the doorway. "Settle this for us, Lia. Which has the best sushi? Asian Café or Fuji House?"

"I have no idea," Lia said, smiling. "I've only been to the Asian Café, and I didn't try their sushi."

"There you go," Chad said to Belinda. "It must be Fuji House."

"That doesn't settle it at all," Belinda protested good-naturedly. "But fine. We can go to Fuji House. He'll argue about it all night, otherwise," she said to Lia. "And I'm starving."

"Or we could try Mexican," Chad said, grinning.

"Enough! Want to join us?" Belinda asked Lia.

"No, thanks. I just came to ask Chad about Ronna Dickens," Lia said, explaining about the photo.

"Ah yes, Ronna," Chad said. "So, as I said, she would show up at the college every so often to talk with Travis. Our offices are next to each other, so I met her and sometimes chatted with them both. I say *chatted*, but you've met her," he said, "so you can guess that these weren't just passing-the-time chats."

"I'm sure," Lia said. "She has strong feelings about protecting the environment. And I think that's great and agree that we all should do what we can for the planet. But I've heard about a protest she led in Harrisburg that ended in some violence. Did she say anything about that?"

"Hmm." Chad rubbed his chin. "She mentioned protests, but I didn't hear anything about their getting rough. That's unfortunate if true. Though it does grab media attention. I'd rather see positive attention myself."

"Unfortunately," Belinda said, "peaceful protests and demonstrations seldom garner much attention."

"You're probably right," Chad said. "Sadly."

"This particular incident was fairly minor," Lia said. "A state senator ended up on the ground, and it's not clear that it was Ronna's fault. Whatever happened was apparently smoothed over. The cell phone videos only showed Ronna being loud and insistent."

"That I can believe," Chad said with a grin.

"Ronna told me about her fight against Arden Sprouse's

plan for the Hubbard Hotel grounds," Lia said. "Did you hear much about it from her?"

"About the creek and its endangered plants? Oh yes. That sure didn't go the way she wanted, did it?"

"It didn't?" Lia said. "I thought she prevented approval with threats to sue."

"Uh-uh," Chad said. "That didn't work. Her lawyer backed out for some reason. I didn't hear what that was, only the names Ronna called him and the places she thought he could go."

"Really?" Lia said. "Wow, that's the opposite of what she told me. But then I was a stranger asking questions at her shop, not someone taking a statement under oath."

"Maybe it hurt her pride to admit the failure," Belinda put in.

Maybe, Lia thought. But it also presented her in a better light to Lia at the time, after which Ronna was quick to point the finger at Gil Hubbard.

It sounded like Lia needed to look more deeply into Ronna Dickens.

Chapter 20

Lia's phone rang as she was driving home from the craft fair. It was Pete. She was on a quiet stretch of a two-lane road and might have answered, but she let it go and listened to the message instead. Pete was inviting her to a play.

"A friend of mine couldn't use these tickets for Tuesday night and offered them to me. I wondered if you might enjoy it?" He said he'd check with her the next day and ended the call.

Lia drove on in auto mode after that, luckily in sparse traffic, her thoughts spinning over Pete's invitation. This wasn't a join-the-group-with-our-mutual-friends sort of event but was a couple's evening out. In other words, a date. How did she want to respond? This, she was finding, was the hardest thing she'd had to decide in a long time, which seemed ridiculous but was true.

A horn blast from a passing car snapped Lia back to her

driving, which had apparently slowed unacceptably, and she set aside Pete's call to focus on the present. She had several hours before she had to answer him, after all, and Hayley was coming over that evening. First things first.

Hayley had offered to bring over dinner in her slow cooker. "I wanted to try roasting a chicken in the cooker with a lemon-pepper marinade. It makes a lot, so I thought I'd share."

"Sounds lovely," Lia said. "Brady, too?" she'd asked but learned that Brady was working another moonlighting gig. Hayley had said it lightly, but Lia wondered how she felt about seeing him less and less and having to spend another Saturday night with her mother. For Lia, it was great, but she wasn't a twenty-four-year-old.

Hayley was already at Lia's by the time she got home, having her own key to the house, and Lia was greeted with the delightful aroma of Hayley's chicken, warming in the slow cooker. On top of that, it was nice to walk into a lit living room with music playing and cooking noises coming from the kitchen. Lia had been pleased when Hayley found her own place, especially witnessing the pleasure her daughter took in making it her own. But Hayley's stay with her, short as it was, had gotten Lia used to the company. It sometimes came with too much activity. But living on your own often brought too much quiet.

Lia bent down to scoop up Daphne, who'd come scurrying over. "But having you helps a lot," she said as she nuzzled her face into the wiggling cat's thick fur.

"Hi, Mom!" Hayley came out of the kitchen to join the hug. "Good day at the craft fair?" she asked.

"Pretty good!" Lia said. She set Daphne down and brushed off a bit of fur as she listed some of the items she'd sold. She mentioned Olivia's low spirits, which gradually perked up, especially as customers arrived.

"Poor Olivia," Hayley said. "All the work she must have put into her living history demo."

"She's quite meticulous," Lia said, "which probably makes her worry twice as much as the rest of us over details."

"Lots of sleepless nights," Hayley said. "I had a few before the fundraiser event at the farm."

"But it turned out wonderfully," Lia said, remembering the first major event Hayley had organized at the Weber farm. It had raised money for the Crandalsburg Parks Booster Club with games, food, and carefully supervised visits with the alpacas, and had also been publicity for the farm itself. "Anything like that coming up in the future?" she asked, following Hayley to the kitchen.

"There've been inquiries about next spring," Hayley said, lifting the lid of her slow cooker. "We'll see." She poked a fork into her roasted chicken. "I think this is ready." She handed the fork to Lia. "What do you think?"

Lia pressed on the skin to see clear juices run out. "It's good."

They worked together to get the chicken and vegetables onto the dining table, which Hayley had already set, then settled down to enjoy it all, Lia raving sincerely over her first bites, as Hayley's cheeks pinked with pleasure.

Several minutes later, Hayley scraped the last bit of mashed potato from her plate with a satisfied sigh. "Well," she said. "That worked out pretty well."

"It was a winner," Lia agreed. She set her knife and fork down on her plate and leaned back. "So where was Brady getting dinner tonight?" she asked.

"At the Cranberry Hill Mall food court, I suppose. That's where he's working security. Again."

"Sounds like he's putting in a lot of extra work hours," Lia said. She reached down to pat Daphne, who'd come to lean against her shoe. "Is he saving up for something in particular?"

"I'm not sure," Hayley admitted. She took a swallow from her water glass. "He's been vague about his reasons. In case you're worried, I'm sure it's not to pay off debts. Brady's pretty smart about money, I think."

"I'm sure he is," Lia said. "He's smart in general," she added, but felt a small niggle, aware that Brady was also young and vulnerable to making the kinds of financial mistakes that came from inexperience. "How long since you've actually seen each other?"

"Well . . ." Hayley thought back. "We grabbed a pizza together at the mall last week during his break time. It's not as bad as it sounds. I mean, we text and talk a lot, so it's not as if we're drifting apart or anything." She stacked her utensils on her plate and pushed it aside. "But I do miss actual going-out times."

Lia nodded. "Any idea how long he'll keep doing this?"

"Not really. He's said things like 'not much longer' but not given an actual end date." Hayley straightened up with a bright smile. "In the meantime, I've found a running partner. A girl who lives across the street. Her name's Molly."

"Great! That makes it more fun, I'm sure."

"It does. And pulls me out of the house when I'm feeling lazy."

Lia didn't remember Hayley ever being lazy about jogging. The opposite, in fact, often having a need to run to burn off excess energy. But Lia was glad to hear she had company. Hayley and Brady had often enjoyed runs together—in the past.

Hayley began picking up dishes, and Lia got up to help. At Hayley's insistence, Lia kept some of the leftover chicken for herself but put all the vegetables into take-home containers for Hayley, happy to think of the ready-made meals she'd have waiting for her in the coming week. They made coffee and carried their mugs into the living room.

"I hear you've become friends with Heidi Sprouse," Hayley said as Daphne quickly jumped up to join her. When Lia looked up in surprise, she added with a grin, "My landlady mentioned it."

"Marlaine is more talkative than I realized," Lia said, setting her mug on the small table next to her. "I don't know about being actual friends yet, but we got to know each other a bit." She explained about going for coffee after running into each other at the post office. "Heidi seemed to need a break."

"That's nice. I mean going for coffee together. Did she bring up her son-in-law?"

"She did, as a matter of fact. She's not too fond of him, nor are any of the people I've spoken to lately."

"Marlaine added a little more to her comment about not liking the looks of him," Hayley said.

"Oh?"

"She thinks he has the strongest motive for doing away with his father-in-law. Apparently Arden set it up for Lucas to take his place as head of the corporation if anything happened to him."

"A strong motive indeed," Lia agreed. "A gentleman I spoke with, Herb Weaver, thought Lucas might have married Arden's daughter to get a foothold into the business."

Hayley's nose wrinkled. "What a creep," she said.

"It's only an opinion," Lia cautioned. "But Herb struck me as fairly astute." She smiled, thinking back to her visit with him and his offer of mustard greens from his garden, which she might take him up on. "Did Marlaine have anything more on Lucas to back up his motive? Anything she heard him say or is aware that he did?"

"Not that she shared with me," Hayley said. "At least not yet. She's been getting a little chattier by the day, so maybe I can pull out a clue or two."

"That would be useful." Lia told Hayley about how Ronna Dickens's claim of having prevented Arden from destroying rare and endangered plants had turned out to be false. "I don't know why she lied to me about that, but it was immediately after that she told me about Gil's problem with Sprouse."

"So she used Gil to deflect attention from herself," Hayley said, a note of hope for the unfortunate man in her voice.

"Apparently. But it doesn't make him totally innocent, yet. He still has his own motives. And hanging around the rifle tent makes him look pretty suspicious."

"Yeah, that's right." Hayley shifted her weight as Daphne decided to circle to a more comfortable position. "Well, I vote for Lucas. He sounds like a creep, and I'd rather have him be the murderer."

"It can only be what it is," Lia reminded her and picked up her mug for a sip.

They sat quietly for a few moments. Then Lia cleared her throat. "On another note," she began and waited until Hayley looked up from scratching Daphne's ears. "I've had an invitation from Pete Sullivan."

"Oh?"

"He left a voice mail, and I haven't decided how to respond. I wanted to run it by you, if you don't mind?"

"Sure. What's the invitation?"

"To a play. Pete said a friend gave him two tickets—"

"Hah!" Hayley laughed. "The old 'happen to have two tickets' ploy? But it's kind of cute, too." She stopped herself. "Sorry. You were saying?"

Lia rolled her eyes. "Yes, as I was saying, he invited me to join him to see a play. No details yet, but I'm not sure about accepting." She paused. "For one thing, I wondered how you'd feel about it. I mean, about me going out. With Pete. On what would, this time, be an actual date."

Hayley was quiet for a while. "Do you mean because he's Brady's boss? Or just going out on a date, period."

"The date part," Lia said. "Would you find it upsetting?"

"Mom, what I'd feel should have nothing to do with it."

"It would affect you," Lia argued, "and I wouldn't want—"

Hayley stopped her. "No, Mom. I don't want you to worry about that. Really. I'm a grown-up." She drew a breath. "Yes, I'm sad about losing Dad, and I will always miss him. I know you loved him. But I would never expect you to live the rest of your life in the past, and certainly not for my sake. Letting ourselves be happy wouldn't mean either of us loved Dad any less, would it?"

"No, of course not."

"So the last thing I'd ever want to do is hold you back from that. And if seeing Chief Sullivan, Pete, makes you happy, please go for it."

Lia smiled, impressed and a little surprised with how mature her daughter had become. "The thing is, I'm not sure I'm quite ready for a big step like this."

"Okay, so that's another thing altogether."

"It is," Lia agreed. *And something I need to figure out.*

Hayley's phone pinged. As she picked it up to check, Daphne jumped off her lap and padded over to Lia, gazing up at her with dewy eyes that seemed to say, *You'll always have me*. Lia laughed and gave her a squeeze as she lifted the cat.

"That was Brady," Hayley said. "He'll be working late tomorrow. No get-together for us—again." She sighed grumpily but then grinned at Lia. "For now. It'll end. Soon." Another deeper sigh. "I hope."

Chapter 21

Early Sunday morning, Lia carried her mug out onto her front porch for a breath of that day's mild October air. Leaves in the nearby trees had started to turn red and gold, and she savored the view as she took her first sip of fresh-brewed coffee. The morning paper lay on the walk, rolled up inside its plastic sleeve, and she stepped down to pick it up. As she did, she heard the Kuhns' front door open and looked over. Sharon, wrapped in a long gray cardigan over a tee and jeans, stepped out for their own copy.

"Good morning!" Lia called.

Sharon started, then grinned weakly. "Didn't see you there," she said. "Good morning." She bent down for the thick paper, then pulled her sweater tightly around her, though the air wasn't particularly chilly. Her hair had fallen over her face, and she pushed it back haphazardly. For a moment, Lia thought Sharon would scurry back into the house, but instead she stepped over to the tidy row of low-growing azaleas that divided their yards.

"How were things at the craft fair?" she asked.

"Back to normal," Lia said, coming closer. "From the look of it, you'd never know what had happened just one week ago. Our shoppers came back. Business was brisk."

"Good." Sharon nodded, clearly straining to be upbeat.

"I learned something from one of my shoppers," Lia said. "A neighbor of Candace Carr."

Sharon's look sharpened. "What?"

"Candace was apparently quite pleased with the work Jack did on her house, contrary to her complaints to him. She even had neighbors and friends over to show off the improvements."

Sharon smiled bitterly. "I knew she had no cause for complaint."

"This might help if she tries to take Jack to court to get any money back."

"Yes!" Sharon brightened. "Thank you." Then her enthusiasm flagged. "Though I suppose she could always claim the problems in the work showed up later. But I'll tell Jack. It should perk him up to hear that."

"How has he been?" Lia asked.

Sharon sighed. "Not good. He's never been at such loose ends. I try to find things around the house to keep him busy, but there's only so much. And I can see that nothing, really, keeps his mind off all the worries." Her eyes flashed angrily. "I wish the Sprouses had never set foot in Crandalsburg!"

"I do, too," Lia assured her. She saw Jack at their front window. "There he is," she told Sharon.

Sharon turned. "Probably wondering what's taking me

so long," she said with a small laugh. "Or wants me to eat my pancakes before they get cold. Jack's taken to cooking breakfasts, lately."

"Go ahead," Lia said, "and tell him about Candace. It's getting time for me to head to church before the craft fair." *Where she'd say a special prayer for her neighbor. As well as think hard about what she could do next to help him.*

J ack was still on Lia's mind when she arrived at her booth before the Sunday eleven o'clock opening, and he remained there for the next couple of hours, interrupted only by Lia's customers.

She arranged to take her lunch break with Maggie and looked forward to the liveliness she could count on the quilter to bring to it. This day Maggie brought a tale of two of her shoppers. "Sisters, I think. Dee-dee was interested in my big pinwheel quilt. Well, *interested* is not the right word," Maggie said. "I mean, this woman was practically drooling. But all the other one, Sylvia, could see was the price tag attached to it, and she was determined to talk sense into her sister. I just stood back and waited to see who would win out. My thought, of course, was it was Dee-dee's money to spend as she liked, but the super-practical—and bossy—Sylvia kept pointing out how much trouble it was going to be to care for and how she'd seen one just as nice in polyester at Walmart for a much lower price.

"Dee-dee heaved a big sigh, and I assumed that had done it. She suggested that they go outside for a cup of cider, and I thought, *Oh, well, that's it.*" Maggie chuckled. "But wouldn't you know. Within minutes Dee-dee showed up, *minus* Sylvia. She slapped her credit card on my counter and told me to wrap that sucker up. No discussion, no hesitation. She got her annoying roadblock out of the way and came back to do what she wanted to do. And that was that."

"Good for her," Lia said, chuckling. "And good for you! A nice sale."

Maggie's phone pinged, a signal to get back to her booth. "And maybe another one," she said, then chortled. "Maybe Sylvia wants one of her own." The quilter packed up the remains of her lunch and hurried off.

Lia watched her go with a smile, then polished off her salad, a hearty one with chunks of Hayley's leftover chicken mixed in. She'd closed the empty container and uncapped a bottle of iced tea, when she was startled to suddenly see Pete standing outside the barn, one hand shading his eyes as he peered over the picnic area. His search stopped when he spotted her, and he began making his way over.

"Pete!" was all Lia could say when he arrived, stunned to see him.

"A red-haired lady back there told me where I could find you. When I saw your empty booth, I was afraid I'd missed you."

"No, just on a lunch break." Lia worked to pull herself together as she guessed why he must be there.

Pete slid onto the picnic bench across from Lia. "I barely recognize the place now," he said, glancing around.

"I guess you've never been to one of our normal craft fairs."

"No. But I had the afternoon free and figured I'd stop by. You got my call last night?"

"I did," Lia said and began searching for the right words.

"I realized I never said what the play was," Pete said. "*Arsenic and Old Lace.* An old chestnut, but if you like that type of humor, it can be fun."

Lia smiled. "I do like it. I just have one problem."

Pete waited as Lia shifted uncomfortably.

"You know I'm a widow," Lia began. "I'm not sure if you knew for how long. Not quite a year and a half."

She stopped, her voice catching slightly, and Pete reached over to cover her hand. "I did know, but I wasn't thinking. I'm sorry. I shouldn't have bothered you."

"It's not a bother, Pete. Please. It's lovely. I've enjoyed your company very much. It's just—and this is so awkward—I know I'm not ready yet for anything more than friendship. So I don't want to waste your time—"

Pete raised a hand to stop her there. "Don't even think of that, Lia. I'd simply like it if you'd join me on Tuesday. Nothing more. Watching a play together that we'd both enjoy would be the best way I can think of to spend an evening." He smiled. "And you'd be giving my social life a much-needed lift. Since my divorce of some time ago, it's consisted mainly of nights out with the guys." He leaned back with a mild snort. "You can guess what that added up to: sports, card games, and beer. If you can see your way to help perk it up, you'll have my eternal gratitude. And with no pressure whatsoever." He paused, then added, "But I might insist on holding doors for you. And possibly even helping you with your coat, at least once in a while."

Lia smiled. "Holding doors? And coats? Those are some stiff requirements."

"Yeah, and the guys hate when I do it."

"Then I'll swallow my feminist pride and allow it. For your mental health, of course."

Pete grinned. "Then we're good? You'll come?"

"We're good. And thank you very much."

Lia was astonished at how easily her dilemma was resolved and how nice it felt. She looked forward to the evening out, especially as their conversation turned to other subjects and flowed comfortably.

Gradually, though, her worries for Jack snuck back in.

"Remember Ronna Dickens, the woman who Len overheard arguing heatedly with Arden?" she asked Pete. "Our craft fair photographer, Mark Simmons, took photos of the area before the reenactment and had them displayed at his booth. I spotted Ronna in one, near the tent where Jack's rifle was stored. She had no reason that I know of to be there instead of in the living history section, where she'd been demonstrating how to spin flax. Mark couldn't tell me exactly when he took that shot, but he was going to check and get back to me."

"He's already given us all those photos," Pete said. "I'm pretty sure our techs have already retrieved the time each was taken."

"Good! Then you can tell if Jack's rifle was in the tent at the time Ronna was hanging around. Maybe there's another photo with her there but after Herb left the rifles unguarded."

"If there is, we'll know. Those photos are getting close scrutiny."

"One other thing," Lia said. She shared how Ronna had claimed she'd managed to prevent Arden from destroying the area of endangered plants. "When someone lies to cover up a motive, even if it's only to someone unofficial like me, I find that suspicious."

"It's definitely worth noting," Pete agreed.

Lia nodded, pleased, but suddenly realized that a lot of time must have gone by. "I'd better relieve Olivia from watching over my booth."

She grabbed her thermal lunch bag, and Pete walked her back to the craft fair barn. When they came to the side door, he made a show of holding it for her and waving her in, then said he'd be on his way. "I'll pick you up at a quarter past seven on Tuesday," he said. "If that works for you?"

"That works very well." Lia said good-bye and continued on to her booth in an upbeat mood, almost annoyed to see a customer approach, which required her to switch into business mode. But that, too, could be most agreeable. Depending, of course, on several possible variables. As did, of course, just about everything.

Chapter 22

Lia had just sat down to knit during a quiet period when her phone rang. It was Beth Daniels, the neighbor of Candace Carr.

"Hello, Beth," Lia said. "Questions about the sweater?"

"I haven't stopped thinking about it," Beth said, laughing. "No final decision yet, but I wondered about picking out the yarn. How do we go about it?"

"Well, first you'll have to decide on the pattern. That will come with recommendations for the kind of yarn. If alpaca yarn works, there's a wonderful place, the Weber Alpaca Farm, that processes its own yarns, and we could go together to pick out the color you like. For other types of yarns, there is a lovely shop in Crandalsburg that carries those."

"You'd be willing to come with me for that?"

"Certainly! It's my second-most favorite thing to do," Lia assured her. "After knitting."

"That's great to know."

Hearing lingering hesitation in Beth's voice, Lia said, "I know it's an investment. But the cardigan patterns you were interested in will be in style for a long time. You'd wear yours and love it for years."

"I'm sure you're right," Beth said. "I think Candace has had hers for some time. Not that it's a splurge for her, I'm sure," she added. "Her wardrobe in general looks to be pretty high-end. Well, I'd better go. I'll think about this a little more and get back to you, okay?"

"Sure. I'm glad you called." They disconnected, and Lia pocketed her phone. She resumed her knitting until a few browsers showed up. That ended with a single sale, coincidentally of a headband, similar to what she'd just been working on.

She had just completed that sale when Lia had her second surprise of the day. Heidi Sprouse had come to the craft fair and was making slow progress through it. She apparently had something to say to nearly every vendor along the way, reminding Lia of her first appearance among them on that fateful day of the reenactment. This time, Lia was sure Heidi heard multiple expressions of sympathy, which she appeared to accept graciously before she turned to the craft items at hand.

When she made it to Olivia's both, Heidi oohed and aahed over Olivia's scented soaps and bought a pack of three. Then she turned with a smile to Lia, who had set aside her knitting to step up to her counter.

"Hello again!" Lia said.

"I was hoping you'd be here," Heidi said as she came closer. "I wanted to let you know I spoke to the police about having noticed Jack around the reenactment tents looking extremely pale. I told them I was sure he was coming down with a migraine."

"Thank you for that."

"I don't know that it helped any, but at least it's on the record as a bit of backup for Jack. You mentioned you were trying to help him out. Any progress?"

"Some." Lia hesitated. "Do you mind me talking about it?"

Heidi waved a hand dismissively. "Please, don't concern yourself. I've heard the worst already from the police. What I care about is having this murder solved. The sooner it is, with the *actual* person convicted, not Jack, the sooner my life can take on some semblance of normalcy."

She then swallowed as her voice quavered. "Someone took my Arden from me. He was the joy and center of my life. I know it will never be the same without him, but I can't even hope to have peace until someone, the *right* someone, pays for what they did. So please, don't keep any progress toward that end from me. I want to hear it."

Lia nodded, satisfied. "Well, it's very little at this point, but it might lead to more." She explained what she had learned about Ronna Dickens, how strongly the environmentalist felt about the changes Arden intended to make on the Hubbard Hotel grounds. "I recently found evidence that she was lingering near the tents where Jack's rifle was stored."

"Ronna Dickens," Heidi said. "I didn't know about her. But Arden didn't talk that much about business. Would she feel strongly enough about digging up plants to commit murder?"

"She's passionate about things like that. She's taken part in protests that led to violence, and she was seen arguing vehemently with Arden before the reenactment."

"Really? Well, that says something," Heidi said, though she sounded doubtful. "I should ask Lucas what he knows about her."

"That could be helpful. And coincidentally, I just learned

about someone else who worked for Arden and might know about Ronna. Candace Carr."

"Candace?" Heidi shook her head firmly. "No, she's only a clerk. Very low-level. What? Has she claimed to be more?"

"Not at all," Lia hurried to say. "I apparently got the wrong impression. Candace's neighbor was here, interested in ordering a sweater like hers, and implied that Candace might be in upper management. That's all."

"I see. No, Lucas is the one I'll need to go to," Heidi said. "Though that doesn't thrill me," she added with a tight pinch of her lips. "He's taking over, you know."

Lia nodded, having learned that from Hayley.

"He hasn't wasted much time, either," Heidi said. "Yesterday, boxes of Arden's personal items from his office were delivered. Cleared out so that Lucas can move in." She sighed. "No invitation for me to come in and help— you know, to make sure nothing that I might want to keep got tossed. Just boxes dropped on my doorstep."

"I'm sorry," Lia said.

Heidi shook her head. "I guess I should have expected it. Arden saw only Lucas's business smarts. I suppose setting it up for his son-in-law to step in was Arden's way of looking after me, financially. And of course it's a benefit for Julie." She grimaced. "But money isn't everything, is it? A happy home, and someone who . . . Well, never mind. Perhaps Lucas's satisfaction with his new position will brighten things up."

Lia had no idea what to say to that. Herb had also suggested that the marriage between Lucas and Arden's daughter was a less-than-happy one. But it was none of her business. Instead, Lia asked if Lucas intended to stay with the reenactors group.

"I don't know," Heidi said. "I had the impression he joined mainly to please Arden. But then he seemed to get interested. He invested a lot of money into a uniform and that rifle."

Perhaps so, but Lia remembered how he'd scoffed at Jack for being what he called nitpicky about historically accurate details. Sharon had heard him claim that the purpose of the battle reenactment was simply to give the crowd an exciting show. Obviously not a person who cared about history.

As if reading her mind, Heidi said, "I think Lucas might find he's too busy to keep up with the group. Its usefulness for him is over."

Heidi began looking through the items spread over Lia's counter, exclaiming over the knitted tree ornaments Tracy had made. She bought a set that included a miniature snowman, gingerbread man, and Santa Claus, then said she wanted to check out Maggie's booth across the way.

"We'll have to go for coffee again," she said. "Soon!"

"Absolutely," Lia said. Her attention was then taken by more shoppers. By the time she finished with them, Heidi had moved down the line of vendors beyond Maggie, chatting and adding more parcels to her tote.

Later, after Heidi had exited the barn, Maggie came over to Lia's booth. "So, what did she buy from you?" she asked.

Lia had just answered a woman's string of questions about caring for a particular sweater, so her response to Maggie was, "Nothing. She decided handwashing was too much trouble."

"Not that one," Maggie said. "Sprouse."

"Oh! Uh, Heidi bought a set of Christmas ornaments."

"Yeah. She's been picking up stuff from just about every

vendor. Mine was a quilted pocket-pack tissue holder. What's with that?"

"Planning ahead for stocking stuffers? Or just being nice?"

"Maybe." Maggie gazed at the open exit door. "But she's a Sprouse."

"A Sprouse widow," Lia reminded her.

"Yes, but . . . Oh, I don't know. I just wonder . . ." Maggie shook her head, then grinned as she asked, "So, did that good-looking man find you at the picnic table?"

Lia smiled. "Didn't you recognize our Crandalsburg police chief?"

"Is that who it was? No, I didn't. He wasn't in uniform. What did he want? You're not in trouble, are you?"

"Trouble that required our chief of police to personally come by and deal with?" Lia asked, laughing. "No, Pete's a friend. He, uh, just stopped by to say hello."

"Is that right?" Maggie gave her a look but didn't press, though Lia expected she hadn't heard the last of it.

She hadn't intended to hide the fact that she'd be seeing Pete. Maybe because *seeing* implied more than it was? *Going out as friends*, on the other hand, was awkward and seemed like unnecessary explaining. She expected she'd eventually feel more comfortable with the whole thing, assuming, of course, that Pete invited her to more than one evening out, and that she accepted. Until then . . . well, she'd just wait and see.

Chapter 23

Lia was sifting through her mail the next morning—mostly junk—when one advertising circular stopped her: Macy's at the Cranberry Hill Mall was having a big sale. Pictured prominently on the front page were towels.

She had noticed the towels she'd brought with her in her move were getting raggedy. And none had gone well with the colors in her bathroom. Maybe this was a good time for replacements?

It took her only minutes to decide, most of it spent checking out what else was on sale—just in case. Soon she had grabbed her purse and jacket and was on the road to the shopping mall.

It turned out Lia wasn't the only one drawn by the sales, and as her search for a parking spot took her farther and farther away from the stores, she began to have second thoughts about bothering to stay. But visions of her newly updated bathroom kept her going until she finally spotted a car backing out close enough for her to grab its spot.

She made her way to the bed and bath department and joined the rummaging masses. Before long she'd found two nice sets of towels—one navy blue to go with her light blue bathroom, and one white, to alternate or mix as she liked. She added a pair of kitchen towels, then stood in line to pay for it all, thankful that the clerks were ringing things up efficiently.

Her shopping bag in hand, Lia hesitated a moment, then veered toward the women's department. The circular had announced nice sales going on there, too, which made Lia think about her own wardrobe. It had been quite a while since she'd added to it. She probably could make do with what was on hand to wear to the play on Tuesday. But something fresh and new—and on sale—appealed. She'd just go take a look.

The "look" ended up with Lia carrying a second shopping bag, having found a simple but stylish skirt-and-top outfit that she could dress up or down as needed. She exited the store with a smile on her face, then paused, realizing she was famished from all her efforts and wondering if she should grab something to eat at the mall or just head on home.

"Hey, Mrs. Geiger!" a familiar voice called from the surrounding crowd.

Lia turned to see a red-haired young man dressed unfamiliarly in a mall security uniform. "Brady!"

"Looks like you had some luck with the sales," Brady said.

"I have," Lia said, holding up her bags with delight. "And now I'm starving. It's good to see you, Brady! It's been a while."

"Good to see you, too," Brady said. "I'm actually due for a break. Want to grab something with me at the food court?"

"That'd be great!" Lia said. "We can catch up."

Brady took Lia's bags from her and led the way through the throngs, explaining that a table was always reserved for security employees. "It saves us time on our breaks. And having security people visible there helps keep things orderly at the court."

"Makes sense."

Within minutes they had their lunches—a burger and fries for Brady and a chicken wrap for Lia. Lia had feared that the noise level common in food courts would be too high for a good conversation but was pleased to find that Brady's table was set far enough to the side to allow them to hear each other.

They exchanged small talk as they enjoyed their food until Lia, thinking of Hayley's recent laments, eventually said, "You've been putting in some long hours, I hear."

Brady nodded, wiping his mouth on a napkin and leaning back in his chair. "I have."

"I hope you're getting enough rest."

He grinned at her mom-like comment. "I am. Mostly I miss my workouts. But I figure the walking I do around here makes up for the runs I liked to take. Especially the ones with Hayley."

"I imagine it might," Lia said. She took a sip of her iced tea. "Not as much fun but still exercise."

"And I get paid for it," Brady added.

"Good point," Lia said with a smile. She munched a bit on her chicken wrap, then said, "Hayley has missed your jogs together, too, but she's started running with the girl across the street."

"Yeah," Brady said, nodding. "She told me."

Brady's sad look as he responded to that prompted Lia to ask kindly, "Is it worth it? I mean all the free time this second job is taking away from you?"

Brady shifted in his plastic chair. "I think it is. And it won't be forever. Just until I've saved enough."

"Well, Hayley's dad would probably approve, since he was the highly practical one in the family. But I'm looking at a young man who I think could use more fun and relaxation than he's currently allowing himself."

"I suppose I could cut down on the hours a little," he conceded. He stirred the straw in his chocolate milkshake, then sucked up the last of it. "On the other hand, if I kept at it as is, for now, I could stop for good sooner."

"That'll be your decision, of course," Lia said with a smile. Feeling she'd said enough on that subject, she moved on to one that was never far from her mind. She told Brady about looking into the Sprouse murder and asked if he could possibly help her on one point.

"Sure, if I can," Brady said. "What is it?"

"I'd like to know if Ronna Dickens, who owns the Eco Alley shop, has a record of arrests." She explained about the dispute between Ronna and Arden Sprouse. "And if you have the time, maybe see what you can find on Lucas Hall?" At Brady's questioning look, she explained why she was interested in the Sprouse son-in-law. "With Ronna, I'm interested in signs of past violence, but with Lucas, I'm curious about any possible iffy business dealings. Maybe lawsuits."

"I'll see what I can do," Brady said.

Lia noticed he hadn't suggested, as he had a few times before, that she leave any investigating entirely up to the police. Had Brady become more assured of her abilities and common sense? Or was he simply glad to get away from the topic of his extra job?

A voice suddenly crackled from Brady's two-way radio, calling him to an area of the mall. He responded as he quickly stood.

"Sorry, Mrs. G. Gotta go."

He glanced doubtfully at the remains of his lunch, but Lia waved him on. "I'll take care of it."

He made his thanks and hurried off as Lia watched, impressed as always with the man, who'd already shown his good sense and bravery. But as highly as she thought of his professional side, Lia couldn't help worrying about his personal side.

Was Brady making a mistake to count on Hayley's patience and understanding as he pursued some unexplained goal? Lia hoped not but feared otherwise. She sighed and finished the last of her lunch. Then she cleared the table tidily, which, unfortunately, was the only kind of help she could give for the time being.

Lia hauled her bags to her car and loaded them in the trunk. After getting behind the wheel, she checked her phone and found she'd missed a call from Herb. He'd invited her to stop by for the mustard greens he'd promised her from his garden. "They're ready now. Come on by anytime," he'd said.

Lia pondered that for a moment. What about right then? Herb's place was convenient to the mall, and she had no other plans for the day. She returned the call and checked if that worked for him, getting an enthusiastic response from Herb.

"Just come around back to the garden," Herb said. "That's where I'll be."

Lia mentally ran over the route she'd need to take as she put her car in gear, then told herself she'd need to find recipes and directions for fixing mustard greens. That wouldn't be a big problem. Enjoying them might be another thing, unsure as she was of how they tasted. But a small serving or two would be worth a try. And she'd get to visit again with that lovely man.

When Lia arrived at Herb's house, she pulled up behind another car, a white SUV. A second visitor? Perhaps the grandson who helped Herb work his garden? But when Lia followed the voices to the back of Herb's house, she saw a woman standing with the older man, holding a large bag of greens. A woman who looked vaguely familiar to Lia.

"Well now!" Herb cried, catching sight of Lia. "There she is. Come on over. Lia, do you know Julie?"

Lia smiled and headed over to the two. "I don't believe I do," she said. "Lia Geiger," she said, holding out her hand to the thirty-something woman, whose face kept reminding her of someone.

"Hi! Julie Hall," the younger woman said, taking Lia's hand.

"Hall?" Lia repeated. "Are you Heidi's daughter?" The resemblance suddenly became clear. Though slimmer than Heidi, and with brown hair that reached her shoulders instead of Heidi's shorter, gray-streaked style, Julie had her mother's green eyes and dimpled smile.

"I am. And I just recognized your name, Ms. Geiger," Julie said. "My mom mentioned you."

"Please call me Lia," Lia said, quickly offering her condolences for her loss. "Your mom has mentioned you, too.

She came by the craft fair yesterday. And left with a load of items."

Julie laughed softly. "She told me about that. I can't wait to see them."

Julie resembled her mother physically in some ways, Lia noticed, but her manner was more subdued. Perhaps it had to do with her father's recent death. But Lia remembered both Heidi's and Herb's comments about Julie's husband. It didn't seem a stretch that being married to Lucas would be dispiriting.

"Julie's come for some of my mustard greens, too," Herb said. "And I've cut and packed up some for you." He reached down for what looked to Lia like a huge bag and held it out to her.

"That's far too much for me," she protested. "And to tell the truth, I've never fixed them before."

"Oh, they're easy," Julie said.

"My wife just threw them in the skillet with some bacon and stuff," Herb said.

"And stuff?" Lia asked.

Julie smiled. "I have lots of recipes for mustard greens. I could email them to you if you like."

"That would be lovely, thank you," Lia said. "I need specifics when I cook. Otherwise I end up with disasters."

"You can't go too wrong with these," Julie said, shaking her bag. "But they are an acquired taste, I guess. My husband won't touch them."

"He doesn't know what he's missing!" Herb said. He looked a little more upset than the idea of someone not appreciating Julie's cooking warranted. Lia could guess what might be going through Herb's mind.

"It's okay," Julie said, though a shadow crossed her face, making Lia wonder if Julie's thoughts had matched Herb's.

But Julie pulled up a smile. "These won't go to waste," she assured Herb. "I'll share with my mom."

She asked Lia for her contact information and typed it into her phone. "Very nice meeting you," she said, then thanked Herb before walking off toward her car.

As Lia and Herb stood quietly watching Julie leave, Lia heard Herb sigh.

"Nice woman," he said. "Deserves better." Then he shrugged and coughed. "But what do I know? A crusty old guy like me?"

A horn suddenly beeped, and Herb perked up and clapped his hands together briskly. "Must be the Andersons. Having a run on mustard greens today! Gotta get 'em when they're fresh."

Lia bid him good-bye with thanks and headed back to her car as the next of Herb's multitude of friends arrived for his generous bounty. *Crusty* didn't describe Herb at all, she thought. *Caring* fit a whole lot better.

Chapter 24

That evening Lia had a call from Beth.

"I found a cardigan that I love," she said, excitement coming from her voice. "I'm hoping you could make it from alpaca yarn. Can I send a photo I took of the pattern and materials list for you to check out?"

"Sure, go ahead," Lia said. "I'll look it over and get back to you."

When Lia got the photo, she saw that Beth had moved past wanting a cardigan to match Candace Carr's. Lia had seen that happen often as a shopper discovered the vast number of possibilities. Her new choice was a lovely one. Lia called Beth back within minutes.

"I love that sweater, and yes, it can definitely be made with alpaca yarn. Would you like to buy that at the Weber farm? I'd be happy to help you with it."

"Oh, that'd be so great! Would tomorrow work for you?"

"Perfect." Lia gave directions to the farm after Beth decided it would be more convenient for her to drive on her own, rather than ride with Lia. They picked one o'clock as the meet-up time, Beth ending the call with, "I'm so excited!"

Lia was, too. She'd have a wonderful new sweater commission and get to wallow in the luscious yarns at the alpaca farm again. There was one more possibility: With luck she'd get to meet and talk with Gil Hubbard.

Lia shot off a text to Hayley to let her know her plans, then sank into her knitting chair to knit yet another headband. If all went well, she'd have an amazing new project to work on soon—and possibly more information about Gil Hubbard to think about as she knitted.

As Lia drove to the Weber farm the next day, her thoughts wandered to Julie Hall, who had sent links for several mustard green recipes. It turned out the leafy vegetable cooked down quite a bit, much like spinach, so the large bagful Herb had given her made more sense. Lia was also glad to know that after the initial cooking of the mustard greens, she could then freeze the result to use in recipes later on. She looked forward to her first experience with the vegetable.

As for Julie, Lia had detected an undercurrent of sadness in the young woman. Not the expected sadness from the recent loss of her father, but possibly something deeper, more ingrained. Did that impression come from the striking contrast between Julie's personality and that of her much livelier mother? Possibly. But the negative opinions of Julie's husband that Lia had heard from three people—Herb, Heidi's cousin Marlaine, and Heidi herself—certainly were an influence.

What would happen in the Hall marriage now that Lucas had taken Arden's place in their business? Perhaps more importantly, what might Lucas have done in order to reach that position? Lia knew nothing concrete at this point. Was there anything beyond motivation? If so, how could she find it?

Lia put her questions on hold as she turned in to the Weber farm. Tensions quickly melted away as she anticipated the afternoon ahead. She climbed out of her car and glanced around. The few cars parked nearby were unoccupied. If one was Beth's, she'd already gone over to the barn, where they'd arranged to meet, with this being Beth's first visit to the farm.

"You have to see the alpacas first," Lia had said. "It's part of the experience. Later on, you'll think of them every time you wear your sweater."

As she arrived at the barn, Lia saw that Beth hadn't hesitated. She stood surrounded by three alpacas, each eager to be petted by her.

"Hi, Mom," Hayley called, keeping watch from a slight distance.

Beth turned, laughing as the alpacas maneuvered among each other for first place. "They're so friendly!" she cried. "I had no idea. And so fluffy."

"Their coats are filling in nicely from their spring shearing," Hayley said. "You should have seen them back then. They looked more like groomed poodles." She went over to her favorite, Rosie, and gave her a squeeze. "But you were still adorable, right, Rosie?"

Lia let Beth have her fill of alpaca nuzzles, then suggested they head to the gift shop to look at yarns. Beth gently disengaged from her new fleecy friends, and Lia thanked Hayley for coming over. She held back a moment as Beth left the barn.

"Is that Gil Hubbard?" she asked Hayley, nodding toward an older man working in the outer corral that she could see through the open back of the barn.

"Uh-huh. Want me to introduce you?" Hayley asked.

"Maybe later. Will he be around a while?"

"He generally works until four."

"Good. We'll be done well before then."

Lia caught up with Beth to chat about sweaters and yarns. When they walked into the yarn shop, Beth's eyes popped.

"Wow! Every color in the rainbow and then some!"

Lia agreed and also recognized the signs of someone quickly overwhelmed.

"Don't worry," she said. "We already know the colors you're considering. We'll just start there." She led the way to the shelves of tans, beiges, and lighter cream colors and pulled out a few skeins to let Beth feel the softness. Lia then suggested she hold various skeins against her skin. "See which shade you'd enjoy wearing."

"I love the feel of it," Beth said, then went from dark to light, holding the skeins as Lia suggested. "I like this the best," she said at last, holding out her choice to Lia.

"Now let's pick out the contrast trim. Brown? Or another color?"

"Would green go with it? Or maybe blue?"

"Let's see."

They pulled out a few skeins. Beth dithered a bit, saying she liked them all. But in the end she chose a dark brown. "If I could afford five sweaters, I'd have one in each color. But I think the brown will be classic."

"I think so, too," Lia said. "Settled?"

"Settled," Beth said, her eyes shining.

"Great." Lia counted out the number of skeins the pattern called for and added them to the red shopping basket Beth held. Beth took them to be rung up, then handed the bag over to Lia.

"Thank you so much for doing this with me. You made it so much easier. I can't wait to see it all stitched up!"

"And I'm eager to work on it. I think you picked what will be a beautiful sweater."

Beth beamed. She thanked Lia again as she said good-bye and headed to the parking area. Lia considered dropping off the bag in her own car, but the yarns were light. Instead, she walked over to the barn, hoping to find Gil Hubbard. After glancing around and not seeing him, she was about to check the corral when she heard "Mom!"

Lia turned to see Hayley walking toward her. "Gil's taking a break in the café," she told Lia. "I could go there with you and get things started with him if you want. Then maybe take off?" she asked.

"I think that'd be good," Lia agreed. "Sometimes one-on-one conversations are more productive."

She followed Hayley to the small café, set up for visitors but open to employees. As they walked in, she saw the few tables taken, but sparsely, most with only one or two chairs filled. Gil sat alone at his, and Hayley went directly to it.

"Hi, Gil! Mind if we share?"

The older man had been gazing down into his mug. Strands of his thinning gray hair drooped over his brow as he appeared deep in thought. He started at Hayley's words but managed a smile as he looked up.

"Hello, Hayley." He gestured toward the vacant chairs. "Please do."

Hayley introduced Lia as they sat, and Gil nodded politely. A waitress hurried up, and Lia and Hayley each ordered an iced tea.

They made small talk with Gil, and after getting her drink, Hayley asked about one of the alpacas who'd been seen recently by a vet. Gil was assuring her all was well when Hayley's phone signaled a text.

"Oh shoot! Mom, I've got to go." Hayley stood and picked up her iced tea glass to take with her. "Stay and finish yours. This might take a while. I'll call you later, okay?"

Lia did her part and gave Gil a smiling shrug after Hayley took off. "At least I had her for a few minutes," she said.

"Hayley's a nice girl," Gil said. "Always polite." Gil nodded toward the bag that sat at Lia's feet. "Yarn shopping?"

"Yes, for a client." She explained about the Ninth Street Knitters and the booth she ran for them all at the craft fair. "A special commission."

Gil nodded. He took a drink from his mug, then stared down at it.

"Hayley and I are fairly new to the area," Lia said. "Have you worked here long?"

Gil gave a short laugh, somewhere between mirthful and bitter. "This is what you might call my retirement job. Do you know the Hubbard Hotel?"

"I've heard of it."

"Used to be mine. Sold it."

"I see. Well, this is quite a change, I'm sure. Hayley loves it here, partly for the animals."

Gil smiled. "They're good to be around. Different. I grew up on a farm, a regular one with pigs and chickens, a few cows. Not quite the same as here. We didn't give names to our livestock. It wasn't good to get too attached to them, especially when you're a kid. Not where they were headed."

"No, I imagine not," Lia said.

Gil leaned back, his hands clasped in his lap. "Actually, I never got past that. It's why I didn't want to be a farmer. I left as soon as I could and worked my way up in the hotel business."

"And eventually owned one," Lia said. "Quite an accomplishment."

Gil smiled at that. "I had help. My wife, Ava. She was actually the better businessperson. I liked dealing with people more. But then she got sick. And I lost her. I couldn't do it all."

"I'm sorry."

Gil drew a deep breath. "It was hard." His expression turned bitter. "It would have been better if . . . well . . ." He grabbed his mug and drained it. "Neither here nor there," he said, clearly straining to sound upbeat. "Guess I'd better get back to work."

"I enjoyed talking to you," Lia said as Gil stood.

He paused, then smiled. "Thank you," he said, sounding almost surprised. "I did, too. If . . . if you're here again, for yarn, or, you know, to see Hayley, look me up."

"I will," Lia promised.

Gil nodded at that, then left. Lia watched, unsure what she'd learned, if anything. Under normal circumstances she would have felt only sympathy for how this man's life had taken a major downturn. But, though he hadn't mentioned Arden Sprouse by name, Lia had caught the lingering anger. Enough to lead to murder? She suspected the thought had crossed Gil's mind. But to follow through? That was a hard one.

Chapter 25

When Lia came home from the Weber farm, she saw Jack out in his yard raking leaves, at least the few that he'd missed the several other times she'd spotted him there. He truly was at loose ends, as Sharon had said, which hurt Lia to see.

He lifted one hand in a weak wave as she got out of her car. Lia pulled out the bag of yarn and walked over to him.

"How are you, Jack?" she asked.

"Bored," he answered with a grimace. Then he grinned lopsidedly. "Need anything done at your place? Sharon refuses to let me touch anything more indoors."

"I'm afraid not. But I can certainly ask around with others."

Jack waved that away. "Don't bother. That Carr woman has turned my name to poison in the remodeling business."

"How can one person have so much influence?" Lia asked, sad and indignant.

"Oh, it's easy nowadays," Jack assured her. "Just post bad reviews online wherever my business might be listed.

None of those are ever verified. Make it sound the least bit credible and the business is toast."

Lia shook her head in disgust. "Then my next question is, Why? Why is she acting like this? According to her neighbor, Candace was thrilled with your work. I know she's withholding payment. Is it because she can't afford it? Did you get any clue that might be the case?"

Jack shook his head. "None at all. She agreed to the partial payment without a flick of an eyelid, and that check cleared with no problem. She has good furniture, a nice car. I think she just sees an opportunity to get my work for free. She's probably hoping I'll be so tangled up with this Sprouse murder that I won't be able to fight her on it when she takes me to court for a refund."

"Has she filed anything yet?"

"As a matter of fact, yes. Small-claims court. The notice came yesterday. Sharon is fit to be tied."

And Jack, too, Lia was sure, though he was doing his best to cover it. "I'm so sorry," she said. "You haven't done any remodeling for me, but if you need a character witness I can certainly do that."

"Jack?" Sharon suddenly called from their front door. "Your phone's been ringing a lot."

"Probably nothing," he called back, but he tossed his rake onto the small pile of leaves. "I'd better check." He took a step, then turned back to say, "Thanks, Lia."

Lia watched Jack hustle inside, her heart aching for him, and returned Sharon's wave. When they both disappeared into their house, she moved on.

Pete had said he'd pick her up at seven fifteen. Lia was ready at seven. She'd fussed a little over her new outfit, exchanging a necklace for a scarf, then changing that for a second necklace until she was satisfied. But that wasn't unusual for her, especially with something new. Or so she reminded herself.

Daphne had run over when Lia sat down on the sofa, which caused Lia to instantly pop up.

"Not tonight, Daph, sorry," she'd said. "You're a little too furry for me right now. I don't want to be picking cat hair off all evening." Lia remained upright after that, wandering about as Daphne watched, looking bewildered.

When the doorbell rang, Lia was in her kitchen, and she hurried out.

"Hi!" Pete said when Lia opened the door. He looked very nice in a dark sport coat, an open-collar shirt, and gray pants. "Ready to go?"

"I am, unless you'd like to stop in for a bit?"

Lia took a step back, but Pete checked his watch. "We probably should be on our way. It's—oops!" Daphne had suddenly appeared at the open doorway.

Pete acted fast to scoop her up. "I'm guessing you don't want him to get out?"

"Her," Lia said. "Definitely not. Please bring her in. This is Daphne," she explained as Pete carried the cat, who'd gone limp, past her. "And I'm so sorry, but she might have just shed on your jacket."

"No bother." Pete set Daphne on the sofa and brushed at his sleeves. "That's a big cat!"

"She's a ragdoll," Lia said. "They tend to be large. They're called that because—as you noticed—they wilt when they're picked up. They're also very affectionate."

Lia gave Daphne a quick pat, then reached for the light coat she'd draped over her stair rail. Pete quickly took it from her. "Remember?" he said. "I get to help you with your coat."

Lia laughed. "I believe we agreed on once in a while."

"True," Pete agreed, holding the coat. "So this is once."

"Thank you," Lia said, turning to slip her arms into the sleeves. "And I think you had been about to say that we'd better be going?"

"Yes, we should. Will Daphne stay where she is?"

"I think she'll be fine, now that her curiosity is satisfied," Lia said.

They slipped out without incident, and Lia took a long breath of the crisp air filled with the scent of autumn leaves. "I love this time of year, don't you?"

"It's great," Pete said, adding, "While it lasts."

"Maybe that's what makes it so special," Lia said. "Knowing that these perfect days are fleeting." She thought of their excursion to Parkridge and how glad she was that she'd gone on it.

Lia slipped into the Equinox as Pete held the door, then said as he got in behind the wheel, "I forgot to ask. Where is the play?"

Pete started the car and put it into gear. "The Tucker Playhouse. It's just outside Gettysburg. About a thirty-minute drive."

Lia nodded and smiled. It was a beautiful night for a drive.

Once on the road, conversation between them flowed easily, and thirty minutes sped by before Pete pulled into the playhouse parking lot. Lia felt a little thrill seeing the bright lights and the posted playbills. It seemed ages since she'd been to a live performance, and no, this wasn't Broadway or Philadelphia, but it would still be very special.

They had good seats—center front and four rows from the stage. The rest of the theater filled steadily, and before long the lights dimmed, and a rich, disembodied voice welcomed them to the Tucker Playhouse. Then the curtain rose.

Lia let herself sink into the world of the Brewster family, both lovable and bizarre, enjoying it as the familiar story-line played out. It wasn't Cary Grant or Raymond Massey on the stage, but the actors who took those roles, along with the others, did a creditable job, and she laughed often along with the rest of the audience and shared amused glances with Pete.

During intermission, Pete brought two paper cups of ginger ale. "No champagne, I'm afraid," he said, handing one to her, and Lia told him it was just as well. Champagne usually gave her a headache. The lobby doors were open, and they followed others outside for a short stroll until the flickering lights called them back in.

The second half of the performance was just as much fun, and by the final curtain the audience showed their appreciation with enthusiastic applause.

"That was so good!" Lia said as they joined the throng heading back to the parking lot.

"Not bad at all!" Pete agreed. "I admit I was a little worried, never having been to this playhouse before." He used his key fob to flash his car lights and locate it.

It was on the tip of Lia's tongue to express gratitude to the friend Pete said had passed on the tickets. But Hayley's having laughingly referred to it as a familiar "ploy" stopped her. Did it matter? However it came about, they'd had a great time.

As Pete drove them back, discussion of that evening's play, followed by other performances they'd each enjoyed, filled much of the time. When they fell into a comfortable silence, Lia's thoughts wandered to her conversation with Gil Hubbard earlier that day.

Should she bring it up with Pete? They'd already gone over Gil's lingering presence near the rifle tent. Lia hadn't gained anything more from her talk with Gil other than that she now struggled to consider him a possible murderer. Had Pete ever arrested a person who appeared incapable of a particular crime but that evidence proved they had in fact committed? She wanted to ask but at the same time didn't want to find out how rare that might be.

She also didn't want to spoil the pleasant mood of the drive. Pete wasn't on duty, and he likely would appreciate being allowed to simply enjoy his time off. As she had. Finding facts that would clear Jack was hugely important, and she would continue to work at it. But taking a little time away from that couldn't hurt and might actually help. She glanced over at Pete, who was tapping his fingers lightly to the beat of the music coming softly from the car's radio. Yes, let him enjoy his time off, she decided.

Pete parked in front of Lia's house, then came around to open her door. As Lia climbed out, she caught movement out of the corner of her eye. Someone was walking in their direction. It wasn't until he reached the brighter area of the streetlight that Lia realized who it was.

Jack stopped short, obviously recognizing her at the same time but seeming confused. Because of who she was with? Should she have given Jack and Sharon a heads-up about Pete ahead of time?

"Good evening, Jack," Lia said. "Out for a stroll?"

"Uh, yes. Hi, Lia." Jack paused, then nodded to Pete. "Chief Sullivan."

"Nice night for a walk," Pete said.

Normally, Lia would have gone on to say something about the play she'd just been to see, perhaps recommending it. But not then. Not with the expression she saw on Jack's face.

"Night," he said brusquely before turning into his yard.

As Lia stood watching Jack head up to his house, arms tight against his sides and hands jammed in his pockets, Pete gently took her arm.

He then walked her quietly up to her own house.

Chapter 26

The next morning, Lia got a call from Brady.

"I had a chance to look up those people you asked about," he said. "Came up with a couple of things."

Lia, who had started up her stairs, turned back to her living room to jot down notes. "What did you find?"

"Ronna Dickens had an arrest in Harrisburg during a protest."

"I knew about that. But I couldn't find what it led to," Lia said.

"Nothing," Brady said. "No charges. But there was another incident."

"From another protest?"

"No, this was with a neighbor."

"A neighbor?" Lia scribbled that down. "What happened?"

Brady chuckled. "It was a dispute over lawn mower usage."

"What?"

"It happens," Brady said. "More than you'd think. But it doesn't usually lead to somebody getting hurt."

Lia's brows shot up. "And this did?"

"Yup. It seems Ms. Dickens thought her neighbor ran his lawn mower far too often and too early in the day. She called us several times to complain. We had to explain that he wasn't breaking any laws. The noise ordinance laws mostly cover things like loud music and crowds past reasonable times. Yard maintenance is vague, but the neighbor wasn't running his mower at the crack of dawn. One of our guys tried to explain that to her, but he said it didn't go over well."

"I can imagine," Lia said. "I'm guessing she didn't let it go?"

"Not at all. But then, the neighbor didn't help much. Two of a kind butting heads, probably. Not only did he not want any compromise, he went out and got himself a motorcycle, maybe to annoy her even more."

Lia shook her head but couldn't hold back a small grin, picturing it. "And then?" she asked.

"Well," Brady said, "you've seen Ms. Dickens?"

"I have."

"So you know she's a tall woman."

"She is," Lia agreed. "Probably in good shape, too."

"Possibly more so than her neighbor," Brady said. "Who should have considered that before he decided to escalate things."

"Oh-oh."

"Right. One day, Ms. Dickens apparently had reached her limit. Mr. Kessler—that's the neighbor—was running his mower back and forth, close to their property line and near one of her bedroom windows. He was wearing headphones at the time. Ms. Dickens surprised him by running over and tackled him, grabbed his mower, and pushed it into a ravine. Mr. Kessler suffered a cracked rib."

"Yikes!" Lia cried. "Did she get jail time?"

"There was a plea agreement," Brady said. "Community service, anger management classes, and expenses paid. Oh, and the neighbor has since moved, I understand."

"Wise decision," Lia said, jotting that down. "Wow. That's it?"

"That's it on her," Brady said. "Now to Lucas Hall."

Lia flipped the page on her notepad and waited.

"I didn't come up with any business-related problems—no lawsuits, tax issues, things of that nature."

"But . . ." Lia prompted.

"There was a domestic assault claim eight years ago made by a girlfriend."

"Uh-oh." Lia wrote that down. "Arrested?"

"No evidence. He might have been rough with her, as she said, but there was no blood, obvious injury, or witness. No prior report or restraining order. He stated it was strictly a verbal argument and she was overreacting. The responding officers advised her to leave the premises and stay with a friend. No charges."

"Hmm. A familiar story," Lia said. "Does it sound like he got away with something?"

"Hard to say," Brady said. "It might be true that the girlfriend overreacted. But it could also be emotional abuse. That's not something we can handle other than to advise the victim and give resource information."

Lia pictured Julie Sprouse's downtrodden demeanor. "So, nothing current on Lucas? To do with his present relationship?"

"No."

Lia laid down her pen. "Okay. Thank you, Brady." She

heard voices in the background and let him get back to his job, then sat for a while mulling over what she'd learned. Daphne nudged her knee until Lia picked her up. "Any idea what to do with this?" she asked, but she got no help from her furry friend.

A few minutes later, Lia saw Sharon pass by her house at a brisk pace and thought she might be out for another stress-releasing walk. Lia fixed herself a coffee and carried it out to her front porch to wait. By the time she'd drained most of her mug, she spotted Sharon returning from the opposite direction, probably having made a circle of the immediate neighborhood. Lia wandered down to the sidewalk to meet her.

"Good morning," she said, once again startling Sharon out of her thoughts. Lia gestured to her porch. "Want to sit?"

Sharon smiled, saying, "Sure," and followed Lia to the chairs on her porch.

"I won't ask how things are," Lia said. "Jack already told me about Candace's small-claims suit. For what it's worth, I don't think she has a case. She's probably hoping Jack will just settle to get it over with."

"That's what I've told him," Sharon said. She uncapped her water bottle and took a swig from it. "But she doesn't know Jack. He'd rather fight to the bitter end when he knows he's right. Unfortunately . . ."

"Yes?"

"Well," Sharon sighed. "I see what it's doing to him. He didn't need this on top of everything else. And if people hear about this claim against him, it's just one more blow against his already ailing business, a business he built from the ground up and was so proud of."

"And rightfully so," Lia said.

"So," Sharon continued, "sometimes I think it'd be better for him to just settle to avoid more publicity. But then I know how devastating that would be, personally. He couldn't do it. I just don't know what the answer is."

"I wish I did," Lia said, shaking her head.

Sharon reached over to squeeze Lia's hand. "Just letting us unload once in a while helps so much. And we know you've been doing a lot on his behalf."

"One thing I wanted to explain," Lia said. "In case Jack thought I'd given up on him or"—she laughed lightly—"gone over to the enemy. Not that Chief Sullivan is the enemy."

Sharon waited, curious.

"Pete, Chief Sullivan," Lia said, "invited me out last night—purely social, and nothing to do with Jack or the Sprouse murder. When Pete brought me home, Jack seemed startled to see us together and maybe a bit upset. I just want Jack to know that Pete is aware of the digging around I'm doing and has only asked that I inform him of anything they need to know."

"You went out with Chief Sullivan?"

"As friends," Lia said. "Jack didn't tell you?"

"No. So this was around eleven?"

Lia nodded.

"Jack's been going out for walks around then. Sometimes even later. I guess he doesn't want to run into anyone. I can imagine the last person he expected to see was Sullivan. If he looked upset, he was probably just trying to make sense of it."

"You can tell him Pete isn't jumping to any conclusions on the murder. Although I don't know everything the police are doing, I believe they're investigating all the possibilities."

"Can you tell him to hurry up?" Sharon asked with a lopsided grin. She then switched focus. "You and Pete Sullivan?"

"Don't jump to any conclusions yourself, please," Lia said, smiling.

"I won't." Sharon seemed to mull that over a while before looking back at Lia. "But you'll keep me updated, right?"

Lia smiled again. If Lia's relationship with Pete gave Sharon something else to think about beside Jack's troubles, that was fine with her.

"Of course," she said.

Chapter 27

Lia was studying the pattern for Beth's cardigan around lunchtime when she got a call from Hayley. She set the directions aside to answer.

"So, what did you think of my super-clever move to leave you alone with Gil?" Hayley asked.

Picturing her daughter's laughing face, Lia smiled. "A sudden text? I'm sure he never suspected. Not that he had any reason to think it was prearranged. At least I hope so." Lia remembered Gil's distracted air and decided any thought of that kind had surely been far from his mind.

"How did it go after I left?" Hayley asked.

"Well," Lia said, thinking back, "we chatted. He was very polite. He talked a little about his former life with pride but also understandable sadness. And I detected bitterness toward Arden Sprouse, though he didn't mention him by name."

"You didn't ask why he was at the reenactment and hanging around the rifle tent?"

"No, I didn't see anything to gain by that. I know he was there. I doubt he would tell me if he'd snuck into the rifle tent. And questioning him would only put him on his guard if he had something to hide. I mainly wanted to form an impression of him."

"And?" Hayley asked.

"And . . . I probably feel the same as you right now. I don't want him to be a murderer."

"And as you once said to me . . ."

Lia sighed. "Wishing won't make things true."

"Something like that," Hayley said. "Doesn't stop us from doing it, though, does it? Well, I'm glad we feel the same about Gil and hope we're not wrong. On a different subject, I had another chat with Marlaine."

"Did you?"

Hayley laughed. "She must love raking leaves. She sure is out there doing it a lot. But I got a little tip on where to easily find Lucas Hall in case you'd like to track him down."

"I would," Lia said, reaching down to pat Daphne, who'd wandered over to her chair. "The only time I've seen him was on television, when he made those baseless accusations."

"He might be in a softer mood when he's dining out. Marlaine, who doesn't like him, you know, complained this time about his rigidity. 'Everything has to be his way, how he wants it and when he wants it,' she claims. One of those things happens to be visiting a particular restaurant regularly on Wednesday nights. That would be tonight."

"Indeed it would," Lia said, leaning forward with interest. "Would that restaurant be in Crandalsburg?"

"It would. Hoffman's. And I'm free tonight." Hayley then laughed, since, as Lia knew, she'd been free most every night lately. "Would you like to have some German food?"

"I believe I would," Lia said. "Did Marlaine happen to mention the time Lucas rigidly sticks to?"

"Eight."

"Hmm. Not too late for you?" Lia asked.

Hayley laughed. "I wouldn't miss it. Pick you up around seven forty-five?"

"Perfect. I'll make a reservation."

They ended the call, and Lia retrieved her sweater pattern, though her thoughts stayed on the evening's plans as well as Marlaine's description of Lucas. Such demands, if true, were often a sign of a controlling person. One who needed to be headman, rather than second-in-command at his father-in-law's business? she wondered. And one who couldn't stand to wait?

Hayley walked into Lia's house a few minutes before their arranged time.

"You're early," Lia called down from her bedroom as she worked at attaching an earring.

"I was ready and thought I might as well be here as at my place," Hayley called back. "Gives me a little time with Daphne."

"Enjoy. I'll be down in a minute." Lia had put on her recently purchased skirt and top but dressed it down a bit with a casual cardigan and flat shoes.

Hayley looked over as Lia trotted down the stairs. "That looks nice. Is it new?"

"Yes. I picked it up on sale the other day."

Hayley grinned. "Just in time for your big night out with the chief, huh?"

"I just happened to see it," Lia insisted.

"How was it? The play, I mean," Hayley asked.

"Fun! We saw *Arsenic and Old Lace*. It was good to get away from real murder and just laugh over absurd ones."

"And now I've dragged you right back into the real one." Hayley set Daphne down gently on the sofa.

"Not dragged," Lia said. "It's a perfect opportunity, and I'm delighted you came up with it. Plus, we'll get a good dinner out of it."

"I'm already thinking about those fried pickles I had the first time we went there," Hayley said.

Lia smiled, remembering that evening. They'd gone to the restaurant after Hayley had run into Brady for the first time since high school. A lot had happened since then. Quite a lot.

Hoffman's was about three-quarters filled, not bad for a Wednesday evening. As the young hostess got ready to lead them to a table, Lia glanced around the room but didn't see Julie and Lucas Hall. Of course, she and Hayley had arrived a few minutes early. From Marlaine's description of the man, he might walk in with his wife as the clocks chimed eight.

Hayley stopped the hostess before she left her station to ask, "Will the Halls be here tonight? Julie said they might be."

"Probably," the woman said. She glanced down at her list to check. "Yes, they have a table reserved. Did you want to be seated with them?"

"Nearby would be fine," Hayley said. "I just wanted to say hello, not to intrude."

"Certainly. Follow me, please." The hostess led them to a table for two that had just been freed up, tucked into a nook near a fireplace with a single crackling log. "The Halls always request that table," she said, pointing to a larger one closer to the fireplace. A third table stood between them with two occupants who would partially screen Lia and Hayley.

Perfect, Lia thought. "Thank you so much," she said, taking her seat and accepting a menu.

"So far, so good," Hayley said once they were alone. "Now we just hope they show up." She glanced over her menu. "Oh, good. They still have the fried pickles."

Though food had been the last thing on her mind, the tempting aromas she picked up as they walked through the restaurant made Lia's stomach rumble, and she made her choice quickly, wanting to pay more attention to the Halls once they arrived. Having dined at Hoffman's before, she knew anything she was served would be good.

As expected, when the minute hand on the large clock on the wall ticked to the hour, Julie and Lucas Hall walked in and were immediately led to their table. Lia kept her menu up high, not wanting Julie to notice her just yet.

"That's them?" Hayley asked, and Lia nodded, realizing Hayley hadn't seen Lucas on TV and of course never met Julie, despite having breezily implied so to their hostess. Had the woman noticed the silence at their table as the Halls approached? Doubtful. Lia was sure she had more to keep track of than the social interactions between the tables—and more to actually care about.

Julie looked very nice, Lia thought. At Herb's place, she had worn jeans and a flannel shirt, and her hair had been simply parted and brushed to hang smooth and straight. For dinner out, she'd pinned it up and curled a few wisps next to her face.

She was also a bit overdressed. Her sequin-studded jacket over a silk skirt might have been perfect for an upscale restaurant in Philadelphia, but Hoffman's in Crandalsburg was more casual. Julie had struck Lia as more comfortable in her flannels and jeans. But perhaps Lucas, who wore a perfectly tailored suit and tie, had pushed for sequins?

Their waiter handed a wine list to Lucas, who engaged him in a long discussion. Lia and Hayley's own waiter arrived, and their full dinner orders had been placed while Lucas continued to toss out questions on wines. Julie, Lia noticed, gazed down at the table as she fiddled with her utensils and water glass.

Eventually everyone's food was served, though Lucas had also turned choosing that into a major event. Surely he'd memorized Hoffman's menu by then. Julie, once again, had refrained from any input, seemingly willing to eat anything Lucas decided she should have.

But Lia thought of the multiple recipes for mustard greens that Julie had taken the time to send her. They indicated an interest in food and cooking that wasn't on display that evening. She also engaged with their waiter when he served her meal. Showing up weekly must have made for enough familiarity to ask about the man's new baby, which lit up his face, though it became Lucas's turn to gaze at his tableware with disinterest.

Between bites of her own meal, Lia noticed there was little conversation between Lucas and Julie. What took place were mostly brief comments, possibly on the food or wine. Lucas occasionally launched into longer speeches, which seemed more like lectures than conversation. Julie would listen and nod but give little response.

"They're not having much fun over there," Hayley said at one point, keeping her voice low.

"I'd have to agree," Lia replied. The only genuine smile she'd noticed so far had come during Julie's chat with the waiter.

Lia and Hayley dragged out their meal to coincide with the Halls' slow pace, but when Lucas signaled for the bill, Lia did the same, managing to get theirs settled quickly. "Time to make contact," she said to Hayley as she grabbed her purse.

"Why, hello, Julie!" Lia said, hoping she looked surprised as she veered toward her. "How nice to see you again."

Lucas's immediate reaction was to scowl, while Julie smiled with genuine pleasure. "Hello, Lia," she said. Introductions were quickly made, which Lucas responded to more politely.

"Thank you so much for the recipes," Lia said. "I can't wait to try them."

"Oh, they came through okay? I'm so glad. We keep getting new computers, and I'm not always sure about what I'm doing."

Lucas snorted. "That's an understatement."

Hayley jumped in on Julie's behalf. "You're not alone. You should have seen me trying to handle my new phone the first few days. Disaster!"

A vast exaggeration, Lia knew, but Julie looked at Hayley gratefully. Lia caught the quick sneer on Lucas's face.

"Lucas," Lia said, "I understand from Heidi that you'll be taking over Arden's position in the business."

"Yes, that's right." Lucas ran a hand over his hair as he sat up a little straighter.

"Big shoes to fill, I'm sure," Lia said with a kindly glance toward Julie. "But it shows how much confidence Arden had in you." As Lucas acknowledged that with a slight dip of his chin, Lia asked, "I wondered, with so much more to handle, if you'll have time for the reenactment group."

"Oh, I'll manage somehow," Lucas said. "Can't let them fall apart over what happened, you know. Besides," he said, "I sank a good chunk of cash into that rifle I bought."

"Oh?" Lia attempted to appear impressed. "A genuine collectible?"

"One hundred percent. Course I'll recoup it in time. The value only goes up." He then scoffed. "About ten times better than that piece of crap Jack Kuhn has. Had. It's in the police evidence locker now, where it'll stay."

Julie had a pained look on her face, and Lia didn't care to hear more of the same from Lucas. "Well, we'll be on our way. Thank you again, Julie, for the recipes."

Julie pulled up a smile, and Lucas gave a quick nod before reaching for his wineglass to drain its final drops.

"What a jerk," Hayley said as soon as they were out of earshot. "Marlaine is right about him." She held her tongue as they passed close to others, then added, "He sure benefited from his father-in-law's murder. Any way we can prove he did it?"

"I'll be looking," Lia said, still dealing with her own reaction to the man's crass rudeness. "Believe me, if there's anything to be found," she said, "I'll be doing everything I can to dig it out."

Chapter 28

Settled in Jen Beasley's living room, Lia described the interaction with the Halls to the knitting group. "What a jerk," Maureen cried, unwittingly echoing Hayley's own stated opinion of Lucas.

"I'm sorry for his wife," Tracy said, pausing her circular needles. The lavender baby sweater she was working on had grown significantly in the past week.

"*I'm* not," Maureen said. When the others turned to her in surprise, she said, "I mean, yes, I'm sorry if she's unhappy. But why doesn't she do something about it? This isn't the Victorian age, for gosh sakes. She can leave."

"True," Lia said. "And I don't know why she doesn't."

"She must have loved the man enough to marry him," Diana said. "Maybe she's hanging on to that with some hope."

"He probably didn't show his true colors right away," Jen said, managing to continue working on a cable-knit hat as she followed the discussion. "That's usually the case, you know, I mean with controlling personalities, and Lucas sounds like he has one."

"Definitely," Maureen said, her eyebrows twitching.

"And some women gravitate toward the kind of man they're used to," Jen said. "Unconsciously, that is. I read somewhere that women whose fathers were alcoholics were twice as likely to marry an alcoholic."

"Really?" Tracy asked. "How sad."

"But Heidi, Julie's mother, indicated her marriage was happy," Lia said. "I don't think Julie grew up with a bad example."

"Then she had bad luck," Maureen said. "But she can still get out."

"That might happen," Lia agreed. "But right now it might be, for whatever reason, too much for her."

"Perhaps she's too beaten down," Jen said. "Emotionally, that is."

"Gaslighted," Diana offered.

Jen nodded. "Exactly."

"One of the reenactors," Lia said, thinking of Herb, "thought Lucas might have married Julie to gain access to her father's business. And now he's running it."

A collective "Ohhh," sounded from the group.

"And what do we know about his movements around the time his father-in-law was murdered?" Jen asked.

"Nothing out of the ordinary," Lia said. "He was one of the reenactors, so he was in and around the battle area, where he was expected to be."

"Good cover," Maureen said. "If, of course, cover was needed," she acknowledged.

Lia told them about Mark Simmons's photos and how they'd been turned over to the police. "I can only assume there were none showing Lucas sneaking in or out of the rifle tent, or he would be in jail by now."

"I'm wondering about something," Tracy spoke up, and all heads turned her way. "Did Lucas automatically replace his father-in-law in the corporation after the murder?"

"Arden set it up for Lucas to replace him," Lia said.

"So why the rush?" Tracy asked. "I mean, if he was sure to get what he wanted anyway. Why resort to killing the man?"

"Good question," Diana said. "Arden wasn't that old, though. Early sixties, maybe? And seemingly healthy." She glanced at Lia for confirmation.

Lia shrugged.

"So maybe Lucas saw too long of a wait ahead of him and decided to shorten it," Diana said.

"That's a pretty big risk to take for impatience," Jen said.

"On the other hand, he might have married someone he doesn't care about. That can make two or three years feel like twenty or thirty," Diana argued.

"Could be," Lia said. She hadn't knitted a stitch on Beth's cardigan since arriving, her thoughts focused on Lucas. "Or," she added, "maybe there was a business-related reason for the hurry."

"Possible, of course," Jen said. "Then again," she added, her expression serious, "maybe Lucas saw a danger that Arden would change the head-honcho replacement plan."

"Aha!" Maureen cried. "Maybe Arden lost confidence in him, and Lucas had to act before he did anything about it."

Tracy nodded. "That would explain it for me. But I would imagine the police have looked into that, wouldn't they?"

"But there's only so much that would be findable," Maureen said. "If, for instance, Lucas and Arden had an argument—just between them—about Arden's future plans or maybe something Lucas did—the police wouldn't necessarily know about that."

"And even if they did," Lia said, wondering at the same time if she could ask Pete about it, "it would still be just a motive. They need proof for the actual murder."

Sighs ran through the room as the knitters were reminded of that annoying but critical need for proof.

"There's one more thing." Lia told them about the assault claim made against Lucas eight years ago. "But there wasn't enough evidence to warrant an arrest," she said. "He claimed the argument with the girlfriend was only verbal."

"A bad sign, though," Jen said, knitting a bit more furiously. "When added to the type of person he's shown himself to be." The others nodded.

"On the other hand," Lia said. She paused to take a drink from her mug of cooling coffee. "Ronna Dickens has things in her background that reflect badly on her as well." She related Brady's account of the escalating problems between Ronna and her neighbor. Serious as it was, it had the knitters chuckling by the end.

"Oh my stars!" Maureen said, wiping her eyes. "She really shoved his lawn mower into a ravine?"

"I've had the urge, sometimes," Diana said. "With certain noisy neighbors. But I never acted on it."

"But it certainly shows what she's capable of," Tracy said, reaching for a pretzel from one of the snack bowls.

"Indeed it does," Jen agreed. "That on top of what she did during the protest in Harrisburg."

"And she was in photos that show her hanging around the rifle tent," Lia said. "With much less reason to be there than Lucas."

"Not to forget," Jen said, "the argument she had around

that time with Arden Sprouse that Len told us about. A 'sparks flying' argument, as he described it."

"That's right," Maureen said, setting down the half-finished sweater she'd been working on. "So does that make her our prime suspect? Replacing Lucas?"

Lia shook her head. "I can't say who is prime at this point. I wish I could, and that we were closing in on that person. But right now, I'm pretty much hopping from one to the other as more information comes up. Oh, and I met our third suspect, Gil Hubbard, in person the other day." She described their conversation and what she got out of it.

"An angry person," Diana commented.

"But a sad one, too," Tracy said.

"And maybe," Jen pointed out, "someone who has nothing to lose by getting his revenge."

They fell into a silence, mulling over all they'd heard that evening, five sets of knitting needles slowly resuming the creation of beautiful things, while thoughts of murder flowed through five separate minds.

On her drive home, Lia stopped for gas outside Crandalsburg, then ran into the convenience store on-site for milk. She went directly to the dairy section in the back, grabbing a quart of one percent. As she debated if she needed anything else, she heard a raised voice coming from the front checkout area. A familiar voice. Stepping around the cookies and crackers aisle, Lia peered toward the front and spotted Ronna haranguing the scrawny man at the cash register.

"How can you carry things like these?" she asked, holding up a child's toy packaged in a plastic blister pack. "Don't you know what these are doing to the planet?"

The man, who looked tired, shrugged. "Do you want it?"

"Want it?" Ronna raised her voice. "I'm telling you things like this are destroying the very earth we live on, and you ask if I want to buy it? And this isn't the only poisonous thing in here. Just look around—"

"Lady, you're holding things up," a burly, bristly-faced man growled. "Wave your flags some other place. I gotta get going."

"Oh, I'll wave my flag whenever I please," Ronna said, turning on the man, who probably outweighed her by more than a hundred pounds.

"Oh yeah?" the John Deere–hatted customer slammed his six-pack of Coke on the counter; Lia saw the clerk jump back, his eyes wide.

"Ronna," Lia suddenly called, hurrying toward the two. "How nice to see you."

Ronna and her burly challenger turned, confusion on both faces at Lia's cheery tone.

"Uh . . ." Ronna said.

"Lia Geiger," Lia supplied. "I was in your shop the other day."

The burly man picked up his Coke and pushed past Ronna to slap his cash on the counter. The scrawny clerk scrambled to make change.

"Well, I just stopped in for this milk," Lia said, thankful that it was in a carton and not a plastic jug. She slid it toward the cash register. "I was on my way home from my knitting group. Did I tell you about my knitting?" Lia babbled on, not letting Ronna get a word in and wondering how she could drag the woman out of the place with her.

But Ronna seemed to have run out of steam. When more customers got in line, apparently holding environmentally acceptable items, she moved out of their way and left when Lia did.

Lia wished her a cheery good night and hustled to her car, taking a deep breath as she did so, relieved to have successfully de-escalated what might have turned into another "Ronna situation."

What was going on in that woman's head to get herself into a face-off that could only have ended badly? Ronna wasn't a stupid person. In fact, Lia thought she was probably quite bright. But had she gone off the rails? If so, when had that begun, and where might it have led?

When Lia finally got home, she pulled up in front of Sharon's blue Impala, parked where it usually was. Her thoughts still on Ronna, it wasn't until she got to her porch that Lia happened to turn back and see the empty space behind the Impala. Jack's pickup was gone. She didn't think much of it and greeted Daphne with an affectionate head rub, put away her milk, and got herself ready for bed.

Sleep came soon but not deeply. Sometime in the middle of the night, Lia gradually woke as her brain churned with myriad thoughts. When those thoughts began running in circles, she gave up and decided to warm up some of that milk she'd brought home.

From long habit, established during the odd working hours of her nursing days, when she did her best to avoid disturbing Tom, Lia navigated through her house by the brightness of the streetlights and moonlight coming through her windows rather than switching on lamps. She'd made it downstairs and was about to turn toward the kitchen when she heard the sound of a car door closing. Her digital clock had already told her it was two fifty-five. Curious, she peeked out her front window.

That space behind Sharon's car, she saw, was filled. Jack was home and had parked in his usual spot. What she saw next was much less usual. Jack had apparently *just* returned home—the car door slam must have been his. She saw his familiar figure heading up his walk, head down and hands jammed into his jacket pockets.

Lia winced. The sadness and stress coming from him were almost palpable.

Chapter 29

L ia woke late the following morning, a little bleary-eyed after her disturbed night. But the sight of the bright October sun shining through golden leaves stirred her. After feeding Daphne and herself, Lia put on her walking shoes and stepped outside. She enjoyed a deep breath of the crisp air and set off, feeling her energy level inch up with every step.

She knew this was good for her. If she was going to help Jack—and her heart still ached over the sight of him looking so down—she needed to be at her best. Lia had covered several blocks, enjoying the sight of carved pumpkins and Halloween decorations on porches along the way, when she came to a familiar sight. A white house on the corner with a tall privacy fence surrounding the backyard. It belonged to Muriel Burgess, the elderly woman who had played a big part in returning Daphne to her that stressful day some weeks ago.

Lia paused, thinking about that time, and was about to turn and retrace her steps, when Muriel's front door opened.

"Why, hello!" Muriel called as she stepped outside. "How nice to see you again! Won't you come in for a cup of tea?"

Lia smiled and came partway up the front walk. "Hello, Miss Burgess. It's very nice to see you, too. Thank you for the invitation, but I really can't."

Muriel's white hair was as perfect as it had been in the early hours of that previous day. Lia was impressed that the woman remembered her and now wished she'd stopped by much sooner.

"How is that little kitty of yours?" Muriel asked, coming off her porch to meet Lia.

Lia smiled, thinking that might be the first time Daphne had been described as little, at least for some years. "She's very good, thank you," Lia said.

"And your daughter?"

"Hayley's fine." Lia had second thoughts about just dashing off. She could certainly spare a few minutes with this sweet woman, who obviously hadn't forgotten her. "Now that I think about it," Lia said, "I probably have time for a quick cup of tea. That is, if you're sure?"

"Lovely!" Muriel clapped her hands. "Come right in. I actually have a batch of cookies I baked just yesterday." She lowered her voice conspiratorially as she held open the door. "The little boy next door loves the peanut butter ones."

Lia smiled. "Then I'll try not to have too many."

"Oh, don't worry." Muriel led the way to her kitchen and bustled about filling her teakettle and setting it on a burner, then spooned loose leaves into a tea ball.

How long had it had been since Lia had fixed tea that way? She remembered the richer flavor but had given it up in favor of quick and easy. Muriel filled the extra time with pleasant chatter as she pulled delicate, flowered-painted cups that Lia was sure never saw the inside of a microwave out of a convenient cabinet and poured the tea.

"Well, there you are," Muriel said, setting down a plate of cookies and joining Lia at the table. She tested her tea before setting it down to cool a bit more. "So, what luck brought you all this way?" she asked. "You live some distance from here, I believe, don't you?"

"I do, but the perfect weather pulled me out of the house for a bit of exercise. I spend a lot of time exercising my fingers—I'm a knitter—but not enough on the rest of me."

"Oh, you knit!" Muriel's eyes lit up. "How lovely. What kind of things?"

Lia explained about her knitting group and how it had led to stocking and running a booth at the Crandalsburg Craft Fair.

"My goodness! That's quite impressive." Muriel tried her tea again and took a sip. She set her cup down carefully, looking thoughtful. "Wasn't that where the Battle of Crandalsburg reenactment took place?"

"It was," Lia said. She sipped her own tea and found it delicious, as expected. "The reenactment was on the Schumacher property where the craft fair barn is located."

"And where Arden Sprouse was murdered."

Lia hadn't been about to bring that up, but since Muriel did, she nodded.

"Interesting situation, wasn't it?" Muriel said.

Lia looked at Muriel, a bit startled at her choice of words. She would have expected *tragic*, or perhaps the milder *unfortunate*. But interesting?

"Certainly a complicated one," Lia said.

"Yes, especially since he had a finger in so many pies," Muriel said. "Arden, I mean."

"You knew him?" Lia asked, surprised.

"Oh, not personally, dear. Only as a stockholder."

"A stockholder?"

"Why, yes. I realized long ago that I'd need to supplement my pension—I taught math for years, but at a parochial school, which doesn't pay particularly well—and started looking into the stock market for added income. It became quite absorbing." She chuckled, adding, "And addictive. It's a lot like gambling, you know."

Lia had heard Tom make a similar comment, but it was startling coming from Miss Burgess.

"So you hold stock in the Sprouse corporation? I know about his buying the Hubbard Hotel, but what else did he invest in?"

"It was all hotels, dear. Buying, improving, then selling. But for some reason, Arden wanted to hold on to the Hubbard. Maybe because he'd moved here? He might have seen it as a way to display his wealth and importance to the locals."

"Could be," Lia mused. "He was also in the process of taking over the reenactment group." *If he'd lived, would he have moved on to running the town?*

"The only problem with his plans for the Hubbard," Muriel said, "was the cost to the corporation for the improvements he had in mind. Big ones and quite costly. Some might call them grandiose."

"Could the corporation afford it?" Lia asked.

"In my opinion, it would have been overextending. Major. As a stockholder, I was concerned."

And Muriel might not have been the only one. Lucas might have seen a serious danger that he was helpless to prevent, other than by—

"But what do I know?" Muriel tittered lightly. "I'm just an old lady who dabbles in things that are probably over my head."

Lia had begun to doubt that. She had seen the change on her hostess's face as her talk shifted from tea and cookies to finance, a sharpness that told Lia her hostess knew exactly what she was talking about. But that look faded just as quickly as it had appeared.

"More tea?" Muriel asked, smiling sweetly as she lifted her teapot, illustrating Lia's thought very well.

Lia was heading back home, filled to the brim with tea, peanut butter cookies, and things to think about, when her phone rang. It was Tracy.

"I might have a little something of interest for you," Tracy said.

"What is it?" Lia asked. She returned a wave from a neighbor raking leaves as she continued walking.

"It's about Heidi and Arden Sprouse," Tracy said, surprising Lia. "And it might be just gossip and unreliable, but I'm passing it on because of what Jen said last night. We were wondering why Julie married her husband when he seems like such a bad choice, and Jen offered how some women gravitated toward the type of man they were used to, meaning the father they grew up with. But you had the impression that the Sprouse marriage was a happy one. Well, maybe not."

"What did you hear?" Lia asked.

"Again, it might be a big nothing, and if so just forget I ever said anything."

Lia understood that this was a struggle for Tracy, who normally was not one to spread gossip. "Whatever it is," Lia said, "I promise it won't go any farther, unless it has to."

"Great." Lia heard Tracy take a deep breath. "So, my twins, you know, are on their middle school soccer team.

They had practice last night, and Jon stayed to watch after driving them to it. A few other parents hung around, too, and they mingled and chatted like they always do. Jon heard two moms talking about the Sprouse murder, and one of them said her friend had catered several dinner parties for the Sprouses. Tessa's Table or something like that. It's located in Crandalsburg. This friend commented that while Heidi Sprouse was a great client, paying promptly and always considerate, the caterer dreaded seeing Arden, that he was interfering and critical. He once brought one of her staff to tears, and the girl might have quit altogether except that Heidi smoothed things over after Arden left the room."

"That sounds like something Arden might have done," Lia said.

"Well—again according to this caterer—Heidi seemed to be always walking on eggshells around Arden. The woman's opinion was that Heidi always put on a cheery front, but that she showed plenty of signs of being anxious."

"Not just from the usual stress of hosting dinner parties?"

"Not according to what Jon was overhearing. Supposedly there were longtime signs, like nails bitten to the quick and jumpiness. But," Tracy emphasized, "I don't know these women or their caterer friend, so I can't say how much weight to give to this."

"I understand," Lia said. "I didn't see any of that in the woman I met, though I admit I didn't notice her nails."

"Well, it might be way off base," Tracy said, "or mean nothing. I just thought I should pass it on for what it's worth. I hope I didn't get you at a bad time? I forgot to ask."

"No, this was good," Lia assured her. "I'm just coming to the end of a lovely walk."

"Oh, that sounds nice. I should get out, too."

They finished their call, and Lia slid her phone into a

pocket as she turned into her yard. She picked up her mail and carried it inside, thinking of Tracy's tale and wondering about its accuracy. Heidi had always struck her as an in-charge person, so it was hard to picture her the way her caterer had described. So Lia tucked the story away as her thoughts turned back to what she'd learned from Muriel: Arden's business plans and how they might have affected Lucas.

As she sorted through her mail, Daphne sauntered down the steps, looking drowsy.

"Just got up from a nap?" Lia asked, used to asking the cat questions that never got answers—not verbal ones, anyway. She picked Daphne up for a hug, then carried her to the sofa, where she clicked the remote to get the local news.

"Of course. Just in time for the weather report," Lia said with a laugh. "No need. I've just been out in it." She turned to Daphne. "I ran into an old friend of yours." As the cat looked up, looking interested, Lia talked about her visit with Muriel, running her hands over her pet's thick fur as she chatted until something on the television suddenly stopped her cold.

The weather report had moved on to breaking news, preceded with a bit of fanfare to catch viewers' attention.

WOMAN DIES IN FREAK ACCIDENT, text on the screen announced, followed by the newswoman's explanation. "Crandalsburg resident Candace Carr died this morning when a section of her newly installed deck suddenly broke away, causing her to tumble to her death."

Daphne protested with a squeak as Lia's hand clenched on her.

"Candace Carr," Lia repeated. "Dead." She sat back, astounded, her thoughts quickly adding *from the deck that Jack built.*

Chapter 30

Lia searched online for any details of Candace's deck collapse but found nothing. It was apparently too soon to find more than the bare-bones report she'd already heard from the television. Then she thought of her sweater customer, Beth Daniels. She pulled the woman's number up from her phone contacts and called, remembering that Beth worked from home. Beth answered on the second ring.

"Hello, Lia," Beth said. "You saw the report on the news?"

"I did. But there wasn't much information. Did you see what happened?" Lia asked.

"No." There was a long pause. "But I heard the scream."

Lia winced. "I'm so sorry. Would you rather not talk about it?"

"I'm okay. It was awful, but at least I didn't witness it. Other neighbors got to her right away, and they called 911 for help. But it was too late."

"The TV report said a section of her new deck had given way. Was that correct?"

"Yes. An entire section between the posts broke away." Beth sighed. "Candace would take her morning coffee out to her deck on warm days. She had a great view from there. Her house is a split-level, and her backyard slopes down pretty steeply, so her deck was up high. Sitting there, she could see a little pond with ducks in the distance.

"But because of the steep slope, the previous owners had put a rock garden close to the house. It was to prevent erosion." Beth paused, and Lia waited. After several moments Beth continued. "She must have leaned against the railing. When it broke, she fell headfirst into the rock garden."

Lia gasped. "How awful."

"I know," Beth said. "Terrible. If it was mulch or grass below, she might have broken something but still survived. And I feel horrible to think this, but I was on that deck when she had that open house, along with others. It could have happened to any of us."

"I don't think so," Lia said. "That rail section must have been tested and leaned against many times."

"So why did it break today?"

A good question, for which Lia didn't have an answer. But after ending the call, Lia was flooded with a series of terrible thoughts that she couldn't dismiss. Jack was a skilled and careful carpenter. No way would he have built a deck railing in a shoddy manner, especially one up high above rocks.

And the railing had held for Candace and others who used it before the accident. Worse thoughts came to Lia, as she remembered Jack's return home in the early hours of the morning, but those she pushed away, not willing to confront them. At least not yet.

* * *

L ia spent the afternoon working on Beth's cardigan, glad
for the escape that the knitting offered, with the need to
focus carefully on the pattern, along with the satisfaction it
provided as the piece grew.

But knitting for hours without a break wasn't possible.
When her hands begged for rest, she set the needles down
and flexed them as she checked the television for any news.
Hearing only repetitions of what had already been reported,
she turned to searches online, but with the same results.

Lia was sure thorough investigation of the accident was
going on while she knitted, but she, of course, wouldn't be
first to hear conclusions. So she picked up her needles and
got back to work, until she heard the knock on the door that
she'd both feared and expected.

"Can I come in?" Sharon asked, standing forlornly on
Lia's doorstep.

"Of course." Lia stepped back, then closed the door behind her neighbor and friend. "Coffee?"

"Please." Sharon followed her into the kitchen but stood
wordlessly, arms crossed tightly to her chest, as Lia worked
her coffee maker.

Back in the living room, Sharon leaned forward on the
sofa, holding her mug at her knees. "They've taken Jack in
for questioning," she said.

Lia nodded. "Concerning Candace?" she asked. Sharon
nodded, and Lia added, "So it wasn't an accident?"

"I don't know. They didn't say. But they must have found
something that points to that. Otherwise, why . . ." Sharon
didn't finish.

"They must be talking to everyone who had a connection to her, Sharon. It's routine."

Sharon nodded. "But not everyone had a problem with her like Jack." She took a first sip of her coffee, swallowing with a distracted look that told Lia she'd barely tasted it. "Lia, Jack couldn't say her name without grimacing. Putting him through that ridiculous lawsuit . . . Of course, now people will think it wasn't ridiculous. That she had every reason to complain." Sharon shook her head impatiently, leaning back. "But that's the least of it now, isn't it?"

"I'm afraid so," Lia conceded. "Any railing Jack made would have been sturdy and perfectly safe."

"It would. Plus, it passed inspection!" Sharon said. "That deck and railing were built well." Sharon looked steadily at Lia. "So, we both know what that means."

"That somehow the railing was deliberately damaged."

"But in a way that wasn't noticeable," Sharon said.

"Apparently, or Candace wouldn't have been caught off guard," Lia agreed.

"So whoever did it had the skills and the tools to do it," Sharon said, looking miserable. "And that leads right to my Jack."

Lia could have argued that Jack surely wasn't the only person capable of such work, but without a specific person to name, it seemed of little comfort. Did Sharon know about Jack's predawn excursion? Lia had to ask. When she did, the tears that sprang to Sharon's eyes were her answer.

"He's been unable to sleep, Lia! He was going out later and later for walks, to deal with the stress but also to avoid running into people. He claimed he saw such fake smiles on faces that he couldn't stand it. I told him people were sympathetic but just didn't know what to say. He didn't believe it."

Going for walks, Sharon had said. But Lia had seen him return in his truck—the truck that typically held carpentry tools. She couldn't bear to say that to her already distressed friend. But if Jack didn't admit it to the police, Lia would have to. The thought was painful. She couldn't believe Jack would do anything so terrible—normally. But had he been pushed beyond that?

"I'd better go," Sharon said, setting down her half-finished coffee and rising. "Jack might be home soon."

Lia pulled Sharon close for a hug, then walked her to the door. "Call me if there's anything I can do."

Sharon gave Lia a bitter smile. "Can you turn the clock back? To before Arden Sprouse ever set foot in Crandalsburg?"

If only. Lia watched her friend head back home before sadly closing her door.

Chapter 31

When Lia arrived at the craft fair barn Saturday morning, there was plenty of chatter among the vendors concerning the Candace Carr death, which had been officially called a homicide. Jack hadn't been publicly named a person of interest, and Candace's lawsuit against him wasn't common knowledge, but Lia expected it wouldn't be long before that situation changed. Lia avoided the chatter, busying herself with her booth, until Belinda came over. Bill had just called out the five-minute warning, but Belinda's concern wasn't about the craft fair.

"Shocking news, huh?" she asked.

"Definitely," Lia said, knowing what her friend meant. She gave a quick shake to the cable-knit sweater she'd just hung up at the back before coming to the front counter.

Belinda lowered her voice. "How's Jack doing?"

"I think he might be in a heap of trouble," Lia said, matching Belinda's voice level. She told her about Jack's problems with Candace and his late-night excursion. "He was questioned yesterday," she said. "I don't know how it went other than there was no arrest."

"Yet," Belinda said.

Lia nodded grimly.

"You had Ronna in your sights for Arden's murder," Belinda said. "Does she have any connection to Candace?"

Lia shook her head. "Not that I know of. But I know very little about Candace."

"Well, you know Candace was fighting Jack over payment for shoddy work," Belinda said. "If she had no grounds—"

"She didn't."

"Then she must have been a piece of work herself. She surely had other enemies," Belinda said. She glanced at the large clock hanging over the barn's front doors. Bill would be opening those doors soon. "Let me see what I can dig up about the woman," she said. "Online first, then with Chad. He surprises me sometimes."

"And me," Lia said, remembering what Chad was able to tell her about Ronna. She didn't have high hopes concerning Candace, though. Her world was pretty remote from Chad's college situation. Then again, so was Ronna's, and look how they had overlapped.

"Here we go!" Bill called, announcing the doors' opening. Lia thanked Belinda, then got busy finishing her prep.

As she waited for shoppers to make their way to her more distant booth, Lia thought about Ronna and her strong feelings, for not just the environment but apparently everything. Had Candace crossed her in some way? But the stealthy trap that brought about Candace's death didn't seem like Ronna's style. She was a confrontational person, as evidenced by her neighbor's lawn-mowing problem.

Then again, the penalty for murder was significantly higher than that for a cracked rib and called for stealthy planning.

Lia's thoughts moved on to Gil. Could he have had—?

"How much is this?" the woman standing at her booth asked, holding up a lacy red scarf.

Lia blinked and returned to the present. "Let me see." She took the scarf Jen had made and searched for the price tag, finding it hidden among the stitches. "Nineteen ninety-nine," she announced.

"Hmm." The woman asked about the yarn and its care. She draped it around her neck for length then pulled it off and stared at it silently.

"Are you thinking of it for yourself or for a gift?" Lia asked.

"Myself," the woman said.

"It looked lovely against your dark hair," Lia said.

The woman smiled. "I just wondered about the color and what I have in my closet that it would go with."

"Red goes with more than you'd think," Lia said. "Black, white, green. It can be gorgeous with purple. And think about Christmas outfits!"

The woman's smile widened. "Right! And it's not that far away." She handed it to Lia. "I'll take it."

"Excellent." Lia was happy for both Jen, who'd made the scarf, and her customer, who would get much pleasure from wearing it. As she wrapped it up, more shoppers gathered— one person's purchasing always seemed to draw more—and Lia's morning zipped by with several more items disappearing from her stock.

She kept an eye on Olivia's booth when her craft fair neighbor was ready for a break, then took her own break after Olivia came back. The weather was mild enough to enjoy lunch outside. Lia glanced around for possible lunch companions but saw all her nearby vendors occupied. So she headed alone to a spot at one of the outdoor tables, just as happy to enjoy a bit of quiet time after her busy morning.

Lia had finished her sandwich and poured out a second cup of coffee from her thermos, when she saw Heidi walking her way, toting a large package.

"How lucky for me," Heidi said as she came up. "I thought I'd rest my feet a little before heading home, and here you are, with an empty spot at your table. Mind if I join you?"

"Please do!" Lia invited as she brushed away a few crumbs. "Looks like you bought something interesting," she said as Heidi settled across from her.

"Oh, I wish I could show you. But he wrapped it so carefully. It's an absolutely delightful metal sculpture for my garden. A garden fairy, dancing on a flower stalk."

"I've seen that," Lia said. "It's beautiful. Lou makes amazing things."

"I noticed it last week," Heidi said, "then later wished I'd bought it. So I came back for it today." She laughed. "Indecision makes for extra effort. But now I get to chat a bit with you. If you still have time, that is."

"Another vendor's watching my booth. She'll text me if I have a customer waiting."

"Great." Heidi chatted a while about several items she'd been impressed by. Then she brought up Candace Carr. "I'm sure you heard what happened," she said.

"I did." Lia set down her coffee. "And it has me very worried for Jack."

"Jack!" Heidi's eyes widened. "Why Jack?"

Lia explained about the problem between Jack and Candace as well as her neighbor's late-night excursions.

"I had no idea," Heidi said, reaching down to pluck a

blown leaf from her package. "But then, I don't know either of them well at all." Her eyes met Lia's. "I'm so sorry for Jack, especially on top of what he's already going through." She looked truly caring, which touched Lia. "Is there anything I can do?" she asked.

"Perhaps, since Candace worked at your husband's company, you might be able to learn more about her for me? Maybe she had serious problems with others besides Jack? Someone with a stronger motive?"

Heidi nodded. "I will certainly try. Even though Lucas has taken over, I still have connections with many people there."

"Thank you." Lia paused. "By the way, I've met your daughter recently."

"Julie?" Heidi's eyes brightened. "How?"

Lia told her about Herb's garden and the mustard greens. "Julie was kind enough to send me several recipes for using them."

"Julie's a wonderful cook." Heidi's dimples had appeared along with her smile, reminding Lia of Julie's resemblance to her. "When she was younger, she thought about becoming a chef and having her own restaurant. But then she met Lucas . . ." Heidi's dimples disappeared.

Lia thought about mentioning her encounter with the couple at Hoffman's, but she hesitated, partly because it hadn't appeared to be a particularly enjoyable evening for Julie. Then her phone signaled a text. "I have to go," she said after reading it. "Customer waiting."

"Absolutely," Heidi said. "Go ahead. I promise to get back to you if I have anything useful for Jack."

Lia thanked her and hurried off, grateful to have another helping hand on Jack's behalf.

* * *

At the end of her successful craft fair day, Lia was closing up her booth when Belinda showed up.

"Nothing to report about Candace, I'm afraid," she said. "But I haven't talked with Chad yet."

"Are you seeing him tonight?" Lia asked, knowing the two often had plans for Saturday nights.

Belinda smiled. "We'll be watching football. His Ohio Buckeyes played this afternoon, and I recorded it. Chad's bringing pizza. Want to join us?"

"No, thanks. I'm always happy to put my feet up and turn in early after a craft fair day." Lia emptied her cash and receipts box into a large envelope to take with her.

Belinda watched silently for several moments, then said, "You know, there's a really nice guy Chad knows at the college. Single. In case you're ready to meet someone, I mean."

Lia smiled. "I don't know about being ready, but I did go out with someone the other day."

"You did? And you didn't tell me?" Belinda looked aghast. "Who, what, and where?"

"I didn't bring it up because we don't consider it dating. We talked that over and agreed to see each other as friends. Pete had tickets to a play and kindly invited me."

"Pete? Pete who?" Belinda demanded.

"Pete Sullivan." At Belinda's puzzled look, Lia added, "Police Chief Sullivan."

"Oh! Really?" Belinda digested that for a bit. "Well, at least I won't have to worry about you."

"Worry about me?" Lia laughed.

"Well, you know what I mean. That he's trustworthy and

all that." She paused. "Does he know about your, um, investigating the murder situation?"

"He does, and he's only asked that I keep him informed about anything important."

"That sounds reasonable. Okay, I approve," Belinda said with a grin. "As friends, as you said," she added.

Lia laughed but was also happy to hear that. Navigating the waters of widowhood was still new to her. She'd had to face so many decisions, large and small, that she hadn't been prepared for. Lia hadn't consulted her friend before accepting Pete's invitation, feeling that would only inflate the situation. But now that she actually had Belinda's backing, it felt good.

"So, how was the play?" Belinda asked as they headed out of the barn.

Lia chuckled inwardly as the old chestnut *Other than that, Mrs. Lincoln, how was the play?* ridiculously popped into her head. But she then thought about how relaxed she had felt with Pete the entire evening, how easy conversation had been with him, and how comfortable the occasional silences felt. She remembered that they had laughed at the same things happening on the stage.

She smiled as she answered Belinda. "It was good."

Chapter 32

That evening, Lia was doing what she'd told Belinda she would—relaxing with her feet up after her dinner—when Hayley called.

"Guess what. I'll be going out on an actual date with Brady tomorrow night."

"How nice!" Lia said.

"Getting dressed up and everything." Hayley laughed. "It's been so long, I'll have to dust something off. But it'll be fun to eat somewhere with him besides the food court and to see Brady in something besides his mall security uniform."

"I'm sure it will. Any special reason for this?"

"Just that Brady finally has the time. I think he might have felt bad about, well, neglecting me."

"Did you feel neglected?" Lia lifted the coffee mug from the table at her side and took a sip.

"No," Hayley said. She cleared her throat. "Well, maybe

yes. A little. I mean, we had agreed to be exclusive, but that comes with some expectations, wouldn't you think? Like," she said, laughing, "actually doing things together?"

Lia smiled. "But you did know it was temporary, too."

"I did," Hayley said. "And that made it easier. Maybe we've come to the end of it. Fingers crossed." Lia heard a crunching sound as Hayley apparently bit into something. Then she asked, "So, what's new with you?"

Lia had to think about where to start. So much had happened since she and Hayley were at Hoffman's.

"I had an interesting talk with Muriel Burgess yesterday."

"Who?" Lia reminded Hayley about the woman who'd returned Daphne to them. "Oh yeah!" Hayley said. "Nice lady."

"She also surprised me with what she knew about the Sprouse business." Lia relayed their conversation and the information about Arden wanting to take his company on a financially risky track.

"Muriel invests in the stock market?" Hayley asked, surprised.

"She seemed to know her way around it pretty well. That surprised me, too. But her information gives Lucas a motive for quickly removing his father-in-law from control, at least to my mind."

"To my mind, too," Hayley said. "From what we saw the other night, I think he's much too full of himself. I can totally see him deciding he's the best person around to run that company and wanting to speed things along to take over before things went south. I got a hint of something more about him from my landlady, too."

"Marlaine? You mean more motivation for Lucas?" Lia rose from her chair and began walking about. "What did she say?" Lia faced her front window, but all she saw were images of Hayley, Marlaine, and Lucas.

"It was just a hint," Hayley cautioned, "but it had to do with that woman who died from the deck collapse."

"Candace Carr?" Lia felt her pulse rate pick up. "What about her?"

"This was when it still looked like an accident. Marlaine said something like 'Lucas wouldn't be too broken up about it.' I asked her what she meant, but she clammed up after that."

"What could Lucas have to do with Candace?" Lia asked. "Candace worked at the Sprouse company but not at the upper level, according to Heidi." She ran her fingers through her hair, thinking. "But Marlaine is Heidi's cousin, right?"

"Right."

"So I'd think Heidi would be aware of what Marlaine was talking about."

"Maybe, maybe not," Hayley argued. "Maybe it was something that would only upset Heidi. Marlaine might have wanted to avoid that."

"But she said it to you," Lia pointed out.

"It could have just slipped out, like she was thinking aloud. Then she caught herself and clammed up."

Lia retook her seat. "Yes, that's possible. But," she said, reaching for her mug, "I think it's worth asking Heidi about it. This could be important for Jack."

Lia told Hayley about having seen Jack return home in his truck in the early hours before Candace's fatal fall.

"Ooh, that's not good," Hayley said.

"It certainly doesn't look that way," Lia agreed. "But it might also have been a simple case of not being able to sleep. The trouble is, Jack was questioned by the police. I don't know if he told them about that or not. He surely must have realized how bad it would sound."

"And he could figure no one would have known," Hayley said.

"Except I did." Lia gnawed at the inside of her cheek. Then she drew a deep breath. "I might have to decide what to do about that."

"Tough spot," Hayley said. "You'd be putting him in hot water if he claimed to be home all night. Let's hope he told the truth about being out."

And hope he was just driving around aimlessly in his truck full of tools, tools that could handily slice through Candace's deck rail.

W hen Lia peered out her front door on Sunday morning, all was quiet next door at Jack and Sharon's house. Quiet and closed up. Shades had been pulled and draperies covered their living room window.

Sleeping late or hiding? Lia didn't know. But her hopes of catching one or the other to learn what Jack said or didn't say to the police evaporated. Though both of the Kuhns' vehicles were parked in front, it seemed clear a knock on their door wouldn't be answered. Lia sighed, then drew back into her house to get herself ready for the day. In the middle of that, her phone signaled a text. It was from Pete.

I'd like to bring lunch for us to craft fair. OK?

Lunch? With Pete? Did he have something to gently break to her? Or was it simply a friendly suggestion for a nice day? Conflicting thoughts bumped up against one another. In the end, Lia decided it might at least be an opportunity for her to learn what Jack had admitted to. If he'd admitted nothing, she knew she'd have to tell Pete what she saw. Exactly when was another question.

She texted back, thanking Pete and suggesting the time. He responded with a thumbs-up and a happy emoji face, making Lia smile. Perhaps this would be a social lunch after all. But, of course, Pete was a police chief. Was he ever completely off duty?

Lia's drive that morning wove through several glorious sights of red and gold leaves drifting down from trees. The narrow road to the craft fair barn was just as beautiful as the bright sun caught the metal rooster atop the barn's cupola, making it glow. The rooster had been crafted by Lou Kraus, which brought thoughts of Heidi and the garden sculpture she'd bought from him. Would Lia hear back from Heidi with information about Candace? If so, should Lia bring up Marlaine's comment on Candace's death?

All questions to be dealt with later. Lia pulled into the fair's parking lot, then joined the funnel of vendors heading into the barn. She greeted Olivia and busied herself with readying her booth. As she rose from a stoop down for a selection of knit hats beneath her counter, she came face-to-face with Belinda.

"There you are!" Belinda said. "Thought you hadn't come in yet."

"Good morning," Lia said. "How was the game?"

"Game? Oh right. Chad's alma mater. They won, I think. I wasn't paying too much attention. But Chad cheered, so that must have been it."

Lia smiled. She'd sat with Tom when he watched football, though always with a knitting project to occupy herself. But Hayley became interested enough during high school to learn the plays.

"Chad didn't know anything about Candace," Belinda said. "Sorry."

"It was a long shot," Lia said as she arranged the hats on her front counter. "But thanks for checking."

"He did bring up Ronna, though," Belinda said. She picked up a cable-knit hat. "This is cute."

"Ronna? What about her?"

"Well, remember Travis? The guy whose office is next to Chad's at the college?"

"Yes. Chad said Ronna would come by to chat with him about environmental concerns."

"Right. Well, Travis complained that Ronna's been calling a lot, pretty much making a pest of herself. He teaches environmental science, you know, which is how they first connected. Mutual interests, and he was happy to answer questions she had. But he says lately, what started as rational discussions have turned into rants on her part."

Lia winced. "I ran into her a few days ago at a convenience store. She was badgering the poor clerk over some of the merchandise and annoying the customers. It was on the verge of becoming a big problem."

"Yeah, that sounds pretty much like what Travis has been dealing with. He thinks she's gone off the deep end. He isn't sure how to handle it. Travis says he made the mistake of giving her his cell number and now might have to block her. That she called him, like, two or three in the morning the last time."

"The last time?" Lia asked. "Did he say which day?"

"Hmm, let me think." Belinda handed Lia the hat she'd picked up. "Must have been Thursday night, well, that would be Friday morning, because he complained about losing sleep when he had to teach an eight-o'clock class Friday."

"And I'm guessing it wasn't anything that couldn't wait?"

Belinda scoffed. "Total blather, he said. Furious about something. He would have assumed she was drunk except he's sure she doesn't touch the stuff. Weird, though, huh?"

Lia nodded. Weird coincidence, too, that it was around the same time Jack was out in his truck and when Candace's deck might have been sabotaged. Except Ronna didn't have any problem with Candace, at least as far as Lia knew. But in case the woman had in fact gone off the deep end, it was worth making a note of.

Chapter 33

When Pete arrived, Lia was in the middle of a discussion with a shopper. He signaled that he'd grab a table and wait for her outside. The cooler Pete carried looked far too big for a mere lunch for two, causing Lia some difficulty with focusing on her customer instead of what awaited her outdoors.

When she finally made her way out to join Pete, Lia was amused to see a red checkered tablecloth spread over the picnic table and held down by real plates and silverware. Two wineglasses graced the settings.

"Wow!" she said. "This isn't anything like the waxed-paper-and-thermos lunch I'm used to."

"All credit is due to Josie and Joe's, the place that puts together picnic and tailgating food," Pete said. "I have to return the dishes and cooler by five."

"I think we can be done by then," Lia said with a smile.

She slid onto the bench across from Pete, then tapped the empty wineglass closest to her. "But I'm not sure about—"

"No, that's fine." Pete reached into the cooler at his feet and brought out a bottle of sparkling cider. "I figured this might be a better choice for someone on the job."

Lia laughed. "Thank you for that! It happens that wine makes me drowsy. Not a good thing for long days working with the public."

"Absolutely." Pete twisted the cap and poured the nonalcoholic bubbly into both glasses. He then pulled containers of food from the cooler and spread them over the table. "These croissants are stuffed with ham and cheese," he said, tapping a plastic lid. "And this is chicken salad." He peered at a round container. "This looks like a fruit salad," he said, setting it down. "And this one, I think, is potato salad. There's pickles and olives, and there's some kind of dessert still in the cooler for later." He grinned at Lia. "Dig in!"

"No toast?" Lia asked, lifting up her glass. "How about: to the very thoughtful and creative Pete Sullivan?"

Pete dipped his head in acknowledgment. "But since I can't toast myself, here's to my charming lunch companion." He clinked his glass against hers, and each took a sip.

Lia helped open lids, and they passed containers back and forth, quickly filling their plates.

"This is such a treat," Lia said after a bite of potato salad. "What made you think of it?"

"The great weather," Pete said. He'd already polished off one ham-and-cheese-filled croissant and was reaching for another. "And I've always had a thing for picnics. I thought of you being here at the craft fair today and all these available picnic tables and thought, Why not?"

"Lucky me that it all came together." Lia added a scoop of fruit salad to her plate.

"So, how did it go with your customer?" Pete asked.

"Left up in the air for now. She might order a sweater like one I have hanging at the booth, but with a few changes. She needs to think it over. A made-to-order sweater can cost more than some people are used to paying."

Pete nodded. They continued with small talk until they got to the dessert of cookies and chocolate truffles, a perfect ending, in Lia's mind. Pete clearly thought so, too, helping himself to more than one. Lia decided to bring up Candace's death.

"One of my customers lives next door to Candace Carr," she said, naming Beth. "She didn't see Candace fall, but she told me the deck rail was broken. I understand her death has now been ruled a homicide."

"It has." Pete offered more sparkling cider with a lift of the bottle. After Lia shook her head, he half filled his own glass.

"I know Jack was called in for questioning," Lia said, then paused, unsure how to proceed. Pete helped her out.

"He hasn't been charged with anything, if that's what you're wondering."

"It was. I'm glad to hear that."

"We knew about her dispute with Jack," Pete said, "and had to check him out. But we can't place him at the scene close to the time. A witness verified that the railing was in perfect shape the day before, which narrows the window for tampering considerably. Jack was home with his wife during that time frame."

Lia looked down at her plate. The chocolate truffle sitting there was suddenly unappetizing. She propped her chin on her hands, elbows on the table, as a long silence fell between the two of them. Finally Pete asked, "Lia?"

Lia looked up, then sat back with a sigh. "I promised to tell you if I came up with anything significant." She proceeded to describe what she had seen from her window at three a.m., hours before Candace's death.

Pete's eyebrows went up. "That's unfortunate."

"What will you do?" Lia asked.

"Talk to him again, for one thing." Pete placed his arms on the table. "He should have told us, you know."

"I know."

"But unless another witness can place him on the scene or we find other evidence, this doesn't give us enough to charge Jack."

Lia felt a weight lift, though not completely. "Will you have to tell Jack that this came from me?"

Pete shook his head. "Not necessary at this time. If it came to presenting evidence in court, well, then . . ."

Lia winced. "Please find evidence on someone else. I really can't believe Jack would do anything like this." Lia thought about Ronna's disturbing late-night phone call to Chad's fellow professor and shared that with Pete. "I know it's not evidence. But Ronna has been showing signs of losing control lately." Lia described the scene at the convenience store. "I don't know what Ronna could possibly have against Candace, but maybe there's something? Maybe her behavior on top of her screaming argument with Arden Sprouse warrants looking into?"

Pete nodded, but Lia couldn't tell if he was simply being polite. On the other hand, there was nothing to stop her from doing the same with Ronna, was there?

She owed it to Jack.

* * *

That evening, Lia got a call from Heidi.

"I hope I'm not disturbing you," Heidi said.

"Not at all. I'm glad to hear from you." Lia was more than glad, remembering Heidi's promise to see what she could discover about Candace. Hoping that was the reason for the call, Lia set down her after-dinner coffee and lined up a notepad and pen.

"Well, that's always nice to hear," Heidi said, a smile in her voice. "And I wish I could just chat, but I have visitors coming soon. I wanted to let you know what I've learned about Candace Carr."

"Okay." Lia picked up her pen.

"I spoke with a woman who worked with Candace in the clerical section of the company. I know Darla, quite well. Her husband did a lot of plumbing work for us. When he was badly injured in a car accident and couldn't work, I helped her get the position. Anyway, Darla said that Candace wasn't well liked in the department."

"Why was that?" Lia asked.

Heidi chuckled lightly. "I had to really work to pry that out. Darla is a sweet person who hates to speak badly of anyone. But according to her, Candace acted like she was doing everyone a favor just to show up in the morning. She also tended to look down her nose at her coworkers and would make derogatory comments, particularly toward one older woman who struggled with new technology, although Candace wasn't exactly a whiz at navigating new software herself."

Lia wrote *unpopular* on her notepad, though it wasn't particularly helpful.

"There was one incident," Heidi said, raising Lia's

hopes. "It concerned one of the cleaning staff. Apparently Candace left a bracelet of some value on her desk, which was gone the next day. She accused the janitor on duty the night before of taking it. Darla thought that was very unfair. She said the man had once turned in a wallet that he found in one of the meeting rooms. Besides, Candace was careless. Coworkers were always coming across things she left behind in the restroom or break room."

"What happened to the janitor?" Lia asked.

"He left. Darla said he was close to retirement, and he took it."

"So he wasn't fired?"

"No. No theft was proven, but that longtime employee left under a cloud with a damaged reputation. He might have wanted revenge."

Heidi gave his name and contact information, which Lia wrote down, though she didn't hold out much hope for the lead. She'd check for a criminal record in public records and perhaps through Brady.

After a long pause, Heidi said, "I've had an idea of my own."

"Yes?"

"It concerns Lucas."

"Do you mean in connection with Candace?" Lia asked.

"I do. It's just a feeling, and I could be reading too much into things."

Lia waited. There was another long pause. Then Heidi apparently decided to come out with it.

"I've picked up on an animosity between Lucas and Candace at a few company parties, and he's even bristled at the mention of her name. I never thought much of it until now. But, well, now I wonder if Candace had something on him."

"On Lucas? Why would you think that?" Lia asked, scribbling on her notepad.

"There were hints of a problem when Lucas and Julie were first engaged. Arden actually ran a background check on him. He came up with something to do with a former girlfriend, a request from her for a restraining order. Arden said he discussed it thoroughly with Lucas and was satisfied that it was all a big nothing. He pointed out that the woman never actually got the restraining order. But Arden liked Lucas, especially his business smarts, so I'm not so sure that he didn't talk himself into accepting Lucas's version of the story."

Arden put more importance on his business than his daughter? Lia couldn't imagine Tom thinking that way, though Heidi seemed to have accepted it from Arden.

But Lia had to ask. "Was Arden right? Was Julie's marriage free of that kind of problem?" Lia didn't ask if it was happy, which it clearly wasn't.

"Julie would tell me if any kind of abuse occurred, so yes, Arden was right, on that point, at least. But I don't believe Lucas has been a good husband. I realize that might color my thoughts, but I think Candace may have had something on Lucas that he didn't want to come out."

Blackmail. Lia wrote that down, adding two question marks. "How would Candace have known this information?"

"That's a good question," Heidi acknowledged. "But I do know that she worked at the same company that Lucas did, some years ago. She might also have known the former girlfriend. They'd be close in age, I'd guess."

"What is, or was, Candace's age?" Lia asked.

"Around forty," Heidi said.

"Okay." A lot of conjecture, Lia thought, but she made

note of it. She brought up the broken railing on Candace's deck. "Is that something Lucas would know how to do?"

"Lucas knows everything about everything," Heidi said in a voice tinged with scorn. "And frankly, I wouldn't put anything that protects Lucas as being past him. If he didn't know his way around deck construction, he'd learn it. And maybe," she added, "he'd figure that no one would suspect it of him."

Maybe, Lia agreed silently, though she was still unsure. But she wrote it down.

Chapter 34

Late the next afternoon, Lia got a text from Hayley suggesting she come by after work.

I can pick up dinner for us.

No need, Lia replied. *Have plenty. Love to see you.*

Though she'd claimed to have plenty, what Lia meant was that she *would* have plenty after a quick trip to the supermarket. She wanted to fix one of Hayley's favorites, which took a little more time and effort than Hayley had after most workdays.

As Lia left the house, she looked over to the Kuhns' house for any signs of life, but all was quiet. Sharon's car was gone from its usual parking spot, and Lia wondered if the two might have gone together to speak with the police. She winced at the thought. What would come of that was a huge unknown.

As she drove the short distance to the store, she thought about her online search for information on the janitor Candace had accused of stealing. Lia had found no signs of the man in the public records and very little anywhere else. His name popped up in the caption of a photo, one that identified members of a group that had volunteered for a charity food collection, but that was all. This only strengthened the idea that Candace's accusation was false. It also made the man a less likely murderer, at least in Lia's eyes. But she had more to do.

Lia lucked out at the supermarket, having hit a slow shopping time. She was able to gather her items quickly and got in the checkout line behind only one shopper. As she waited to load her groceries onto the conveyor belt, she caught Jack's name from the discussion going on up ahead. The checker and shopper had lowered their voices, but the knowing looks and nods going back and forth between them told Lia that Jack wasn't coming out ahead. No wonder he'd taken to only going out for walks late at night.

Except that didn't explain why three days ago he took his truck instead.

The shopper ahead moved on, and Lia got her items rung up and bagged. Only the basic courtesies were exchanged during the process, including an ironic, "Have a great day!" from the cashier. Lia returned it automatically, though she wasn't feeling particularly great after what she'd overheard. She shook it off as she headed home, turning her thoughts instead to her upcoming dinner with Hayley.

Sometime later, as she filled the last green pepper cup with her ground beef mixture, Lia began to wonder about Hayley's last-minute request to stop over. It wasn't all that unusual, but something felt a little different about this visit. But Lia quickly caught herself. Hayley had texted barely ten words, and yet Lia was reading something into them? She set her oven to preheat. Whatever was up—or not— would come out eventually.

I'm here!" Hayley called from the doorway, then sniffed at the air. "What's in the oven?"

"Stuffed green peppers," Lia said as she came down the stairs. "You still like them, I hope."

"Of course!" Hayley swept up Daphne for a quick cuddle. "They're the best!" She set the cat down, gave Lia a hug, and shed her jacket. "Anything I can do?"

"All is done, thanks, and almost ready. Your timing is perfect." Lia headed to the kitchen to check on the peppers, waving at the empty water glasses on the table. "You could fill those for me."

Hayley grabbed the glasses to fill at the sink as Lia pulled their dinner out of the oven. In a short time they were seated and tucking into their meal.

Lia let Hayley lead the conversation, which began with chatter about her day at the alpaca farm, then led to questions about the murder investigation. Lia told her about Heidi's call.

"Candace worked at the Sprouse corporation and might have wrongly accused one of the cleaning staff of theft." Lia described the situation and the resulting retirement of the man under a cloud.

"I tried to find more about him online. So far, there's nothing that hints at a person who would turn to murder for revenge."

"At least it's one more possibility besides Jack," Hayley said.

"It is, but I'd love something stronger. I told Pete about Jack's late-night excursion."

"You did?" Hayley glanced up from her pepper.

"I hoped Jack would have admitted it to the police himself. It turned out he didn't."

"Yikes! Not good."

"That's pretty much what Pete said. But he also assured me that they would need more to justify a charge against Jack." Lia reached for her water glass to take a sip. "Unfortunately, it sounds like the Crandalsburg townspeople have already tried and convicted him." She described the conversation at the supermarket.

Hayley scoffed. "Gossipers. They'll say anything to sound in the know when they know nothing." She reached down to soothe Daphne after accidentally nudging her under the table.

"And without considering how that affects the person— or people—in question," Lia said. "Both Jack and Sharon are stressed to the limit. I'm getting desperate to find answers for them." She crossed her knife and fork on her empty plate. "I doubt the janitor will turn out to be a good lead. Heidi sounded suspicious of Lucas regarding Candace's death, but with no real basis for it other than her dislike of him." Lia ran her fingers through her hair. "Maybe Brady can help me with finding more about the cleaner."

"Maybe." Hayley reached for Lia's empty plate and set it atop her own. "Before you ask him, there's something I wanted to talk to you about."

"Concerning Brady?"

"Uh-huh. But let's clean up first and fix some coffee, okay?"

Lia nodded, while thinking, *Uh-oh*. But she picked up utensils and glasses to carry into the kitchen.

They loaded the dishwasher, set Lia's baking dish to soak, and brewed two mugs of coffee to carry into the living room. Lia took her usual place in her knitting chair, and Hayley settled on the sofa, where Daphne quickly joined her.

Hayley took one sip, then set the mug on the table beside her. "Okay," she said. "Here's what happened."

Lia waited, hands crossed in her lap, and tried to look composed.

"We went out last night, like I told you we would," Hayley began. "It started out great! We got dressed up. Brady made reservations at Maison Marcel. A really nice place, by the way. He ordered wine, the food was terrific, and it was so nice to be out on a real date again."

Lia waited for the *but* that was surely coming.

"Neither of us ordered dessert, so we were sitting there, just finishing our wine, when—"

Hayley's phone rang. She grabbed it from the side table and with an apologetic glance toward Lia checked the screen. Hayley shook her head. "It can wait."

Thank you, Lia cried silently.

"So, anyway," Hayley said, "we were having this really nice time, when Brady drops this bomb on me."

Hayley chose this moment to take a longer sip of her coffee.

"Okay," Lia said after what she considered a more-than-generous wait. "What bomb?"

Hayley put down her mug. "You know all this moonlighting work Brady's been doing? The extra money he never really explained why he needed? Turns out it was for the down payment on a house."

"Oh!"

"Yes, a house. But not just any house," Hayley said. "A house for the two of us."

From the look on Hayley's face, which was exasperated, even angry, a quiet *hmm* was all Lia felt safe to offer.

"How could he do that?" Hayley demanded. "We were taking things slowly, remember? We agreed on that. No hurry. And he springs a house on me?" She paused for a deep breath. "He did at least say it was my decision. He wants to get married, but if I wasn't ready for that, moving in together would be fine, too. Like that wouldn't be a huge step, too?"

Lia again waited a bit, then asked. "What did you say?"

"I told him no, of course. No to both! No way is that taking things slowly, right? How could he think that?" A glint of tears appeared in Hayley's eyes, which she quickly banished with a shake of her head. "But I feel so guilty."

Lia's impulse was to rush over and hug her daughter. But she sensed that Hayley wanted to talk out her feelings more than be comforted for them at the moment. So she asked, "Why guilty?"

"Because he had such a hurt look on his face."

That tore at Lia's heart, too, but her first concern was for Hayley. "It sounds like you weren't rejecting Brady altogether, only his sidestepping of the agreement you had. Did you explain that to him?"

Hayley puffed out her cheeks then popped her lips. "I tried to. But I think I made a mess of it. Mom, he thought he was doing such a great thing, putting in all those hours at that second job and all. For the two of us. And I quashed it all."

"I'm sure that must have hurt," Lia said. "But, Hayley, you needed to make your own decision."

"I know." Hayley lifted her chin. "I shouldn't have been

pushed in such a way, even if Brady thought it would be a wonderful surprise."

"He made a misjudgment," Lia agreed. "It was a loving one, but still a mistake." Lia paused, then asked, "Can you forgive him for it?"

"That's the thing," Hayley said. "I don't know. Well, forgive, yes. But to stay on as a couple? I don't know. If we're on such different wavelengths, maybe we shouldn't?"

"That's for you to decide," Lia said. "But think about it carefully. Be sure of your reasons, whichever way they go."

"I will." Hayley pushed herself up and turned to pick up her coffee mug, but instead she knocked it over. "Oh shit!" she cried. Her hands flew to her face, and she began to cry.

That was Lia's signal. "Never mind," she said, rushing over and pulling her daughter close for a hug. "Never mind," she repeated, patting Hayley's back. "It'll be fine," she added, referring mostly to the coffee spill. The relationship was another thing.

Chapter 35

After Hayley left, Lia's night threatened to be a restless one, until she convinced herself that whatever happened between her daughter and Brady was out of her hands. They were two sensible adults who would work their problems out between themselves and make their own decisions. All she could do was wait to hear and offer comfort as needed.

That let her get a few hours of sleep and to wake the next morning with an idea of what she could do that might actually be productive. After a good breakfast, she called Beth.

"Would you mind if I came over?" Lia asked. "I know you work at home, and I don't want to interrupt that. Perhaps I could bring something for the two of us when you take your lunch break?"

"Oh my gosh, don't do that," Beth said. "I can take breaks whenever. Just come on over. Is this something to do with my cardigan?"

"No, though I can bring it to show you how it's coming along. Would ten be a good time, then? I won't be long."

"Sure, ten is fine. Coffee or tea?"

"Neither, thanks. I'll be quick." Lia got directions to the house and ended the call, hoping she wouldn't be wasting either one's time. She searched for photos online and downloaded a few to her phone. Then she worked on Beth's cardigan, gathering her thoughts as she knitted until it was time to leave.

At ten on the dot, Lia pulled up in front of Beth's house. She glanced at it only long enough to check the address, before turning her gaze to the house next to it, Candace's house, easily identified by the scrap of crime scene tape left and flapping in the breeze. From where she stood, Lia could glimpse only a corner of the deck. A better view, she hoped, would come from Beth's backyard.

Beth had her front door open by the time Lia reached it. "Hi! Come on in."

"Thanks so much." Lia stepped through the doorway and held up her knitting bag. "I have enough of your cardigan done that you can see how the colors go together." Once in the living room, she spread the sweater out as flat as the circular needles would allow on one of the sofa cushions.

"Oooh," Beth said. "I love it!" She ran her fingers lightly over the stitching. "So soft," she cooed. "I wish I had it to wear right now with this perfect weather."

Lia smiled. "And I wish I could knit faster. But you'll have it by spring, I promise."

Beth stepped back. "Are you sure you want nothing to drink? I can make it in a minute."

"No, thanks, Beth," Lia said, rolling up the knitting to repack. "What I'd really like is to have a look at Candace's deck. Would you mind?"

"Not at all. Come on back through the kitchen. You'll get a good view from my patio." Beth led the way through a bright kitchen and out the back door. "There it is," she said, pointing upward from her patio.

Looking over the low fence that separated the two properties, Lia could see the stained-wood deck and the balustered rail edging it. A wide gap in the railing had been roped off.

"They took away the section that broke," Beth said. "You can see the rock garden through here." She brought Lia over to the fence and an opening in her shrubs.

Lia peered at the bowling ball–sized rocks, some dislodged either from Candace's fall or from the first responders and police. An image of Candace landing headfirst came to Lia, making her wince.

"You see how steeply her yard drops away," Beth said. "It's not an ideal yard for a family with kids, who'd want a play area for things like swing sets. But for a single person like her it was fine, and she liked the view it gave her. Mine slopes much less, as you see, which I like better for a little gardening."

Lia studied Candace's yard a bit more, including the side area between the two houses. Paving stones led from Candace's front yard to the deck stairs, but shrubs in both front yards had hidden most of that from Lia's view when she'd first arrived.

She pulled out her phone to show Beth one of the photos she'd downloaded. "I think you said that this man had been at Candace's open house. Is that right?" Lia displayed the photo of Arden Sprouse posing with Heidi at a charity function.

Beth looked it. "Yes, that's the guy who was murdered at the reenactment. I was so shocked when I heard the news and realized I had met him. I don't know who the woman is, though."

"That's his wife, Heidi Sprouse."

"Oh!" Beth checked the photo again. "I guess she wasn't at the open house. Or"—Beth shrugged—"maybe I just missed her. It was a large crowd."

Lia then showed a photo of Lucas. "How about this man? Do you recognize him?"

Beth studied it. "Hmm. I don't think he was at the open house, but something about him rings a bell." She puzzled over it a few moments, frowning, until her face suddenly lit up. "Oh, wait! He was at Candace's another time."

"He was? When?"

"Gosh, when was that?" Beth chewed at her lip. "Wait! It was last Tuesday, the day we met at the alpaca farm for my yarn. I remember that when I came home there was a package on my front step, though I wasn't expecting anything. When I checked, I saw it was addressed to Candace, not me. I had just trotted down my steps, intending to take it over to her, when this guy came out her front door."

"This one?" Lia asked, pointing to Lucas's photo. "You're sure?"

"Yes, absolutely. He might not have stuck in my head except he seemed really angry, mad enough that I stopped where I was. I didn't want to get in the middle of anything."

"What told you he was angry?" Lia asked.

"His voice was raised, for one thing. I couldn't hear everything, but he was definitely mad. And the one thing I did catch was him saying to Candace, 'You'll be sorry!' His car was parked at the curb beyond mine, so he had to walk past my house to get to it. He glanced toward me as he went by, so I got a good look at his scowling face."

Well, that was interesting. "I don't suppose you discussed that with Candace, did you?" Lia asked.

"Uh-uh!" Beth said, shaking her head, eyes wide. "In fact, I brought the package into my house and took it over much later. We only exchanged a few words as I handed it to her."

Heidi's suggestion that Candace might have been black-mailing Lucas suddenly seemed more plausible. But Brady hadn't found any charges pressed against Lucas after the ex-girlfriend claimed abuse. Had Candace come up with something that could prove it? Something else? How could Lia find out?

Beth's phone signaled a text, and she checked it. "Sorry, it's work-related. I'll need to deal with it."

"Yes, of course. Could you take a look at just two more photos and tell me if you've seen these people in the neighborhood?" Lia quickly pulled up a photo of Ronna that she'd downloaded from the Eco Alley website. Beth shook her head at that and also at the one of Gil. "Nope. Never saw either of them."

"Okay, thanks. I'll let myself out this way," Lia said, moving to an opening in the fence that led to the side yard. "If anything more comes to mind, would you give me a call?"

"I will," Beth promised. "And keep on knitting."

Lia smiled and did a thumbs-up. Beth hurried into her house, but Lia paused on the grassy strip between the two houses. She looked up at the gaping hole in Candace's deck railing and cringed inwardly, once again, as she pictured the woman tumbling through it.

Who had tampered with the railing to cause Candace's death? Lia couldn't believe Jack would have done such a thing, angry though he was. He had never shown any indication of such vengefulness. But, sadly, his actions of late made it seem more possible. If Lia was going to help him, she needed to get inside his head. It was past time to do that.

Chapter 36

As Lia walked to her car from Beth's yard, her phone rang with a call from Olivia. Surprised to hear from her craft fair friend, she quickly answered.

"Hi, Lia," Olivia said. "Got a minute?"

"Sure. What's up?" Lia asked as she continued to walk.

"Remember those place mats my sister-in-law, Jeanie, bought from you a couple of months ago? They were dark blue with a white daisy in the corner?"

"Yes, I do. Jeanie bought six, if I remember correctly."

"Right! Well, she wants four more. Do you have them?"

Lia got to her car and slid in behind the wheel. "I might, but I'll have to check and get back to you. I guess Jeanie's having bigger dinners, huh?"

"She loves to cook," Olivia said. "She's been working for a caterer on weekends, when Rob can stay with the kids. She loves it."

"A caterer?" *What was the name of the caterer Tracy*

had mentioned? Then it came to her. "That wouldn't happen to be Tessa's Table, would it?" *How many caterers could there be in a small town like Crandalsburg?*

Apparently not that many, as Olivia said, "Yes, that's the one. Jeanie started with a smaller caterer, but Tessa's offered more work. Plus Jeanie really likes Tessa's menus."

"I'd love to talk to Jeanie about that. Maybe I could call her directly about the place mats. Would that be okay?"

"I guess so. Are you looking for a caterer?"

"No," Lia said with a laugh. "My little house couldn't hold enough people for a caterer. It's about something else. I'll explain more at the craft fair, okay?"

"Sure. I'll send you Jeanie's number."

"Thanks, Olivia." Lia started her car. "And maybe give Jeanie a heads-up that I'll be calling. See you Saturday!"

On her way home, Lia stopped to pick up a few things at the supermarket. She wished she'd thought of them the last time she was there and hoped she wouldn't run into another Jack-bashing conversation. But her stop there this time was uneventful, and she was in and out in minutes.

Back at her house, Lia checked through her craft fair stock and found the place mats Olivia's sister-in-law wanted. Olivia had texted Jeanie's phone number and said her sister-in-law would be available to talk, so Lia gave her a call. Jeanie answered quickly.

"Good news," Lia said. "I have your place mats."

"Wonderful!"

They agreed that Lia would pass them to Olivia at the craft fair. Then Lia said, "Olivia says you're working for Tessa's Table."

"I am! We cater all sizes of events. I guarantee the food is wonderful."

"I'm sure it is," Lia said. "I believe you've catered for the Sprouses?"

Jeanie's voice turned somber. "Yes, several times, before, you know, what happened."

"Yes, that was certainly shocking. Did you see much of Arden when you were at his house?"

"Quite a bit, actually," Jeanie said, then asked tentatively, "Were you a friend of his?"

"No, I never met him. And I should explain why I'm asking. A good friend has been living under a heavy cloud of suspicion—unfairly—since Arden's murder. I'm trying to help him by learning all I can about Arden and who might have wanted to kill him."

To her surprise, Lia heard a soft laugh. "You could add me to your list," Jeanie said, "if I were the murdering kind, that is. He was an awful person."

"I've been getting that impression. Why do you say so?"

"He was a rude, obnoxious, condescending bully, for one thing. I wouldn't blame anyone for having murderous thoughts about him. But Olivia told me how you saved the craft fair from going under after that other time," she said, referring to the murder of Belinda's ex-husband. "So I'm more than happy to help you clear your friend, if I can."

"Thank you. I was told that Arden had one of your staff on the verge of quitting. Is that right?" Lia asked.

"Oh, poor Chloe. She's an excellent worker. But she gets anxious when it's crunch time. I really felt like Arden zeroed in on that and chose her to pick on. He barked at her over the antipasto platters, that they weren't perfectly arranged or something, and got her so flustered that she ended up dropping one. Then he hit the ceiling, called her an effing idiot, and claimed he wouldn't pay for any of her platters."

Lia shook her head. "Why was he in the kitchen at all?"

"Micromanaging. But he just got in everyone's way and caused problems like that one. His wife was a saint, always stepping in to smooth things over. But she couldn't keep him out altogether. I really think he enjoyed stirring things up."

"Poor Heidi, having to pick up the pieces."

"I know, right? But she kept arranging those parties that were mostly business-related and probably not much fun for her. Her daughter tried to help sometimes," Jeanie said.

"Julie?"

"Yeah. She'd be there sometimes as a guest with her husband, but she'd come early to pitch in. She liked working with food, I could tell. But when things got too tense because of her father, she'd beat it out of there. Or if her husband barked at her for not mingling with the guests. Like I said, these were business, not social events. The whole family was working."

"How did Julie's husband, Lucas, get along with Arden?" Lia asked.

"Okay, I guess," Jeanie said uncertainly. "I mean, Arden didn't get after his son-in-law like he did Chloe. But when I was out circulating with the hors d'oeuvres, I did overhear a few remarks from some of the guests, speculations about how long Lucas would be around. But I wasn't sure how serious they were."

Interesting. "How did these same guests interact with Lucas?"

"I'm afraid I couldn't say. Too busy, you know."

"Of course," Lia said. "Anything else you can tell me?"

"Can't think of anything. Not very helpful, I'm sure, for your friend."

"It might be," Lia assured her. "Bits and pieces sometimes add up. Thanks, Jeanie. Sounds like the Tessa's Table staff had their work cut out for them catering for the Sprouses."

"We did it mostly for Heidi," Jeanie said. "Yes, she paid us well, but we also knew how truly grateful she was. We catered the reception after his funeral, you know." Jeanie paused. "I shouldn't say it was the pleasantest job we did for her, since it was, you know, for a funeral. But it was definitely the calmest."

"Yes," Lia said. "I imagine it was."

L ater that afternoon, Lia pulled out the grocery items she'd picked up and got to work. She followed a recipe for chili that Sharon had given her when Lia couldn't locate her own after her move from York. Sharon had mentioned it was a favorite of theirs, which made it a good choice for Lia's needs.

She hadn't seen either of her neighbors' vehicles move from their spots since she'd been home, and most of their windows remained covered. Lia expected a phone call would either go unanswered or be cut short with a lame excuse. She therefore intended to knock at their door, chili pot in hand, until her friends got tired of the noise and let her in.

Within an hour, she did exactly that. Lia didn't have to knock long. A curtain at the Kuhns' front window twitched, and soon the front door eased open and Sharon peered out, looking puzzled. "Lia?" she asked.

"This is kinda hot and heavy," Lia said, holding up the steaming dish by her oven mitts. "Can I bring it in?"

"Of course," Sharon said, stepping aside. "Why—?"

Lia ignored her friend and headed straight for the kitchen. She set the pot on the stove and turned to Sharon, who'd followed behind. "Chili. Your recipe, to reheat whenever you're hungry." She slid a bag from her arm and set it on the counter. "Dinner rolls. Now, we need to talk. Where's Jack?"

"Thank you for the chili," Sharon said. "We were getting down to bologna sandwiches. But I don't know if Jack—"

"It's fine, Sharon." Jack appeared at the kitchen doorway, looking as though he hadn't shaved in a couple of days and possibly not slept for that long, either. "It's good to see you, Lia. And thanks." He nodded toward Lia's pot. "Come, sit down." Sharon quickly offered coffee, but Lia waved that away. She wanted to get down to business.

Once they'd settled—Sharon and Jack side by side on their sofa with Lia facing both from a chair—Lia said, "Jack, I don't believe you had anything to do with Candace's death, but I need to hear that from you."

"Lia—" Sharon began, but Jack stopped her with a squeeze of her arm.

"I had absolutely nothing to do with sabotaging that railing," Jack said, looking steadily at Lia. "As I told the police right away. Yes, there were times I thought I could strangle her," he said, then patted Sharon a second time as she let out a squeak. "But not actually. And when I heard what had happened to her, I was horrified. Much as I disliked the woman, she didn't deserve that."

Lia nodded, then drew in a breath. "Did you explain to the police where you'd gone at three in the morning that day?"

A muscle at Jack's jaw pulsed. "Chief Sullivan told you about that?"

"No," Lia said. "I told him. I had to, since I saw you return, though I dearly hoped you had a good explanation."

Jack shook his head. "An innocent but not very good one. I simply went out driving. It helps me deal with all the crap that's been going on. But I didn't stop under any security cameras, as far as I know, nor did I run into anyone I knew."

"Of course not," Sharon said. "Who else is going to be out at that time? Which is exactly why Jack chose it."

"I understand," Lia said. "And his being out at that time doesn't prove anything. But—"

"But it's one more thing to have piled on," Jack finished for her.

"Unfortunately, yes," Lia said. She leaned forward, hands clasped at her knees. "On the other hand, you might not be the only one to have a major grudge against Candace." Sharon and Jack listened intently as Lia related what she'd learned from Heidi about the office cleaner Candace had falsely accused of theft, then about Lucas, who might have been blackmailed by Candace and who was seen storming out of her house by a neighbor. "He warned Candace she'd be sorry."

Jack's brows shot up.

"I never liked that man," Sharon declared. She grabbed Jack's hand. "And I wouldn't be at all surprised if there was something about him to be blackmailed for. The way he treated Jack and some of the reenactors was atrocious and showed exactly the kind of person he is. It's a pity too many were blinded by the money he and Arden brought to the group." She scoffed. "As if their expensive gear made them something special."

"I understand his rifle, the one stored in the tent with yours during the battle, is a collectible," Lia said. When Jack nodded, she said, "I watched the bayonet demonstration, but I didn't notice a difference between the rifles. Of course, I wasn't examining them up close. Were they easily distinguishable?"

"There were differences," Jack said. "My reproduction is a good one, but you wouldn't have to be an expert to tell them apart. Lucas would never have picked up mine by mistake, if that's what you're thinking, Lia. Besides the rifles themselves, the wraps are different, too."

"Wraps?" Lia asked.

"They're for protecting the rifle during transport and when they're not in use. Mine is the basic padded camo wrap. Lucas's is leather and pretty close to authentic. Maybe not exactly Civil War but near enough to it, I think. Since wraps aren't any part of the reenactment, the affordable one works for me."

"What really bugs me," Sharon said, "is that Lucas bought all those expensive props, but they were all for show. It's the same as flashing a Rolex watch to him. He doesn't care at all about the history his pricey collectibles originated from."

"He did comment that his rifle was a good investment because of how the value would increase," Lia said.

"See!" Sharon's face radiated indignation.

"It might have given him some satisfaction," Lia said. "But I don't think showing up others in that way and treating the people around him as he did brought him any respect. Or happiness." She pictured Julie's sad demeanor at the restaurant.

Lia thought about Lucas's angry departure from Candace's house, then of Muriel's suggestion for why Lucas might have wanted to quickly take the reins of the Sprouse corporation out of Arden's hands.

Did it all add up to Lucas being a murderer? She looked at her friends. They wouldn't have an answer to that for her. But there might be someone who did.

Chapter 37

After Lia returned to her house, she fixed a hazelnut coffee and carried it to her knitting chair, where she picked up Beth's cardigan to work on. Those two things, along with Daphne circled affectionately at her feet, soothed and helped clear her head. Just like the pattern of the sweater she stitched, there were many strands of thought that needed to be knitted together. A picture in her mind had started to take shape, but several threads were still missing.

As her needles clicked, ideas began to form, until after many rows she nodded. Lia tucked her knitting away. A bite to eat first, then she'd be on her way. She needed to weave those final threads into place—if she could.

Sure, Mom," Hayley said when Lia called, asking to come over. She then asked cautiously, "This isn't about Brady, is it? I mean, nothing's changed since last night."

"No, it's not about Brady," Lia assured her. She explained what she had in mind.

"Okay," Hayley said, her interest piqued. "We'll need something to keep her around a while and to maybe soften her up. Got any dessert-type things to offer? I don't."

"Good thought. I'll pick something up."

"Great! See you soon."

Lia made a quick call, then gave Daphne a pat and grabbed her jacket and keys. Heading down the walk to her car, she saw both Sharon's and Jack's vehicles parked where they'd been for some time, now, as their owners huddled inside their house. Lia badly wanted to see her friends get back their old lives. She felt that was getting closer, but the truth was often a slippery thing to grab hold of. Sometimes, though, it was simply a case of asking the right questions. She slid into her car and buckled up, crossing her fingers that those would come to her.

Hayley met her at the base of the stairs leading to her upstairs apartment. "I called Marlaine when I saw you pull up," she said. "She'll be over as soon as *Jeopardy!* ends."

"Good." Lia followed her daughter upstairs, holding the chocolate-frosted devil's food cake she'd bought on the way from the one person guaranteed to have something luscious at hand.

"I told Marlaine about the dripping showerhead, which has actually been going on for some time, now. It was just something I didn't think about too much—until now. She said she could fix it herself, which I figured. She takes care of a lot of things around the house."

"Good work." Lia set the cake box on Hayley's kitchen counter and started opening it. "Got a plate for this?" she asked.

"Oh, yum. Chocolate!" Hayley said, spying the cake. She

bent down to search through a lower cabinet, coming up with an aluminum tray. "I carried something home from the Food, Fun, and Alpacas event last summer. It's all I have."

"This'll work," Lia said, setting the cake carefully on the tray. "I have more than I need at my place. You can take your pick anytime you want." She licked frosting from her finger. "I had a choice between this and a coconut cream. I figured everyone likes chocolate. I hope Marlaine isn't the rare exception."

"She has her own strong dislikes about a lot of things," Hayley said with a smile. "But I'd be surprised if chocolate was one of them. I mean, really. Chocolate?"

"We'll find out soon enough. I think I hear her coming now."

Hayley went to her door to welcome in her landlady, who held a toolbox in one hand. "Thanks so much, Marlaine. That drip has been driving me crazy."

"Should have called me sooner," the landlady said brusquely. "Drips like that only get worse. And they waste water." She pulled up short, apparently surprised to see Lia.

"Hello, Marlaine," Lia said pleasantly. "Good to see you again."

"Evening. Didn't know you were here."

"I came just a minute ago to bring Hayley this cake. I hope when you're done, you'll have a piece with us?"

Marlaine's expression remained stony, but Lia caught a spark of interest in her eyes. "I just might," Marlaine said. "Thanks." After she turned toward Hayley's bathroom, Hayley did a thumbs-up, then got busy pulling out plates and forks as the clank of tools sounded down the short hall.

Lia and Hayley chatted as they waited, mostly about Hayley's work and the craft fair as Lia carefully avoided any mention of Brady. She hoped Marlaine's job wouldn't drag on and that parts wouldn't be needed. Luckily, within half an hour, Marlaine reappeared with her toolbox.

"All fixed," she announced.

"Wonderful," Hayley said, popping up from her chair. "Let's celebrate with this fantastic cake. Please have a seat, Marlaine. Coffee, anyone?"

Marlaine and Lia both accepted, Lia letting Hayley handle the coffee pods as she began slicing the cake. Soon the three were digging their forks in. Marlaine wasted no time. She was scraping up the last of her crumbs before Lia had barely finished half of her own piece.

"That's the best chocolate cake I've had in a long time!" Marlaine declared, setting down her fork. "Did you make it?" she asked Lia.

"Goodness no," Lia said. "This is a Carolyn Hanson cake. Carolyn is one of our vendors at the Crandalsburg Craft Fair, where she sells all sorts of baked things."

"Is that a fact? Well, I just might have to head over there sometime."

"Oh, you'll love it," Hayley said, reaching for her coffee mug. "Lots of really amazing crafts." She turned to Lia. "Didn't you say Marlaine's cousin Mrs. Sprouse shops there?"

"She's come more than once," Lia said, grateful for the opening. "And left with stuffed shopping bags. We chatted a couple of times over coffee," she said to Marlaine. "I admire her resiliency, considering what's happened."

Marlaine nodded. "Heidi is someone who could always roll with the punches. Me? I'd rather punch back." She cackled. "But we had plenty of other things in common. I picked up on that early on."

"There are a few years between you, right?" Lia asked. "But you still became close friends?"

"Yeah, we really connected, once we were older," Marlaine said. "I was glad when she moved to Crandalsburg."

"I was glad when Hayley moved here, too," Lia said. She took a sip of her coffee. "There's only so much you can understand about someone's life from phone calls and texts, isn't there?"

"That's the truth!" Marlaine nodded firmly.

"More cake?" Lia asked.

"Well." Marlaine hesitated, then handed over her plate with a wicked grin. "Maybe just a small piece."

Lia popped up to quickly slice one, asking as she served it, "I imagine you hadn't really gotten to know Julie and her husband very well until they moved here as well."

Marlaine shook her head, already working on a forkful of cake. She followed it with a swig of coffee. "Never met Lucas before the wedding," she finally said. "And you know how those things are."

"Oh, I do!" Lia cried, flapping a hand. "Crowds of people. Noise. You hardly get to say two words to the bride and groom."

"That was it. Always hated those things, but I went for Heidi's sake." Marlaine forked up more cake. "But I got to know him once they were here." She scowled. "Sorry I did."

"You don't like him?" Lia asked, already knowing the answer through Hayley but hoping for more details.

"I think Julie got hoodwinked," Marlaine said, leaning back in her chair. "Good looks, and charm when he felt like it, but inside nothing but a con man, in my opinion."

"How unfortunate." Lia paused. "But I guess he ultimately got what he wanted. I mean, taking over the family business. Heidi told me Arden had written Lucas in as next in line."

Marlaine harrumphed. "He conned Arden, too. Something I never thought could happen."

"That's surprising, isn't it?" Lia said. "Arden must have been pretty smart to garner as much business success as he did over the years. Why didn't he see through Lucas as you did? Was he slipping?"

Marlaine shrugged. "Heidi mentioned there'd been arguments between them lately, Arden and Lucas, I mean. I suppose Arden was still sharp enough to catch on to his son-in-law, even if it took a while."

Interesting point. That would have put pressure on Lucas if it was the case. Lia was considering what to ask next when Marlaine popped up from her chair.

"Well, nice chatting with you," she said, carrying her plate and mug over to Hayley's sink. "But I've got things to do. Can't sit around forever. Thanks for the cake." She grabbed her toolbox, and Hayley walked her to the door.

"And thank you for fixing my shower drip," Hayley said.

"No problem. Just don't let something like that go again."

As her landlady thumped down the stairs, Hayley turned to Lia. "What do you think? Get anything good?"

"Food for thought," Lia said. She began scraping the cake plates before loading them into Hayley's dishwasher.

"Yes, she—" Hayley's cell phone dinged. She checked it and let out a deep sigh, which made Lia glance over. "It's Brady. He wants to talk."

Lia read Hayley's expression and covered the leftover cake with foil. "I've got a few things to do, too," she said. "One of which is mulling over tonight's conversation with Marlaine. I'll talk to you later."

She grabbed her jacket and gave her daughter an encouraging hug. They both had things to work out, and the outcome of each was decidedly iffy. At the moment, Lia couldn't say for sure which mattered to her the most.

Chapter 38

The next day, Lia thought about giving Herb a call but decided to run over to see him instead. Her questions were best asked face-to-face but also might require a bit of memory jogging. Lia knew her own recall of minor details was never one hundred percent, and who knew what Herb was capable of with his extra decades? She might come away with nothing after all.

She found the older man in his front yard, picking up windblown papers. He brightened when he saw her pull up.

"Well, look who's here!" he called as Lia climbed out of her car. "Come for more mustard greens? There's plenty more."

"No, thanks, Herb. I'm good. I really came to talk about a few things. Do you have time?"

Herb laughed good-naturedly over that. "You're looking at someone who has nothing but. Come on in." He waved her to the house. "I'll make us some coffee."

Lia followed him in and offered to help with the coffee but was immediately ordered into the living room. She spent her wait time looking over Herb's collection of Civil War buttons and medals arranged in their glass case.

"Here we are." Herb returned carrying two steaming mugs and placed one on the coffee table for her before heading to his own overstuffed chair. "Now, what's on your mind, young lady?"

Lia smiled at the *young lady*, which, coming from an eighty-year-old, seemed more genuine than patronizing. "I need to get a better picture of what happened around the time Jack handed you his and Lucas's rifles."

Herb's brows twitched at that, but he said, "Okay." He took a sip from his mug before carefully setting it down. "Shoot."

"So," Lia began, "after the bayonet demonstration, Jack carried both rifles to your tent. Did he hand them directly to you?"

"He did. And I think I asked how the demo went, but that was about it."

"He transferred them to you outside the tent?"

"Uh-huh."

"And didn't go into the tent himself?" Lia asked.

"Nope, just handed them over and left. I carried them in myself."

"And then put each in its rifle wrap?"

"Just set them on top. There was no use packing them up since there was going to be another demo after the battle."

"There was?" Lia asked, then remembered Sharon had mentioned that.

"Oh yes," Herb said. "There're always two, before and after. It keeps more people around for the living history. Of course, this time . . ." Herb grimaced and reached for his coffee mug.

"Of course," Lia said kindly. "So, after the police arrived, you were the one who found the blood on Jack's rifle bayonet?"

"I did." Herb's voice turned gravelly. "I couldn't believe it at first. But I know those bayonets were clean when I got them. That spot wasn't there before."

"Just a spot?" Lia asked, and Herb nodded.

"Only about so big." Herb held his thumb and index finger about half an inch apart. "It was like someone had wiped away most of the blood but missed that."

"But the rifle was right where you'd left it?"

"Exact same place," Herb said. "No sign at all that it'd been moved, except for the blood on it."

"If Jack had used his bayonet on Arden Sprouse, as some believe he did, is it likely he would have left that spot of blood on it?" Lia asked.

Herb shook his head firmly. "Absolutely not. If he'd only so much as dropped it, he wouldn't have left a speck of dirt on it. That bayonet was used on Arden by someone who didn't know how to care for it."

"Or wanted to implicate Jack?"

"That could be," Herb said. "Though I can't imagine who that scumbag could be."

Lia had guesses. Too many, and she needed to pare them down.

"One more thing," she said. "Can you tell me who you saw nearby when you left the tent to get a johnnycake?" She was sorry to bring up that painful reminder of Herb's mistake but needed to ask.

Herb winced but nodded understandingly. "Sure," he said. "The battle was just about to start. Most of our guys were already lined up for it. But there are always the stragglers. Let me think."

"Anything you can remember might help Jack," Lia nudged.

"Let's see. One of the drummers came running back. Left his drumsticks behind or something. A few of our guys in uniform were taking their time getting to the field. I would have said something to hurry them up, but then I spotted Lucas among them and kept my mouth shut."

"Did he see you?" Lia asked.

"Must have, but I can't say for sure." He cleared his throat and shifted in his chair. "A little farther on, Mrs. Sprouse— Heidi—was standing with her daughter, Julie. Heidi said if I was looking for a johnnycake they were going fast and I should hurry. I remember those two split up as I passed by.

"I got my johnnycake. I forget the woman's name, but she does the camp cooking demo, and she'd set aside a bunch that she'd made for us reenactors. Heidi was right. They were going fast."

"While you were in the living history area, did you see Ronna Dickens at her spinning station?"

Herb shook his head. "No, I didn't."

"You didn't happen to see her, or she wasn't there?"

"She wasn't there. I remember because a young kid was playing with the wheel. I went over and stopped him. Told him it wasn't a toy, and he went running off. I glanced around for Miss Dickens but didn't see her. But no other kids were around, either, so I left."

"Okay," Lia said, making a mental note of that. "On your way back, then, who did you see?"

"A couple more uniformed fellows. No Lucas this time, so I hustled them over to the battlefield."

"You told me when we first talked that you didn't see Gil Hubbard near the tent. Now that you're thinking about it again, does that change?"

Herb concentrated, then shook his head. "No, I don't think so. That doesn't mean he wasn't there, of course."

"Right," Lia agreed. "When you got back, did you go right into the tent?"

"No, I stayed out front from then on. It was a nice day. The tent could get stuffy."

"So you didn't check on the rifles at that time?"

Herb's face fell as he shook his head. "I just didn't think of it. It seemed like I was barely gone a minute, and I didn't think of it."

Lia thought he'd likely been gone longer than that—long enough for someone to slip in and out of the tent—but didn't say so. It was clear to her that Herb greatly regretted his mistake.

"Thank you, Herb. I appreciate your going through this with me."

"Anything I can do, especially if it might help Jack," Herb said, though he looked doubtful. He offered Lia more coffee and another visit to his garden, both of which she declined politely as she got up to leave.

Herb walked her back to her car with an invitation to come back anytime. Lia nodded automatically, her thoughts on what she had just learned. What she did with it all was her next challenge.

L ia had just walked into her house when her phone rang. She dug it out of her purse and saw it was Pete.

"Hi," she said, slipping off her jacket. "What's up?"

"I just had a couple of free minutes and thought I'd say hello. Were you on your way out? I heard a door close."

"No, on my way in, actually. I just came from a visit

with Herb Weaver." Lia hung her jacket over her stair rail and reached down to scratch Daphne's head.

"Ah, Weaver," Pete said. "The man who discovered the bloody bayonet. And who grows an impressive vegetable garden. Let me guess. You weren't there to discuss rutabagas."

Lia smiled. "Not exactly. I asked him to walk me through his actions from the time Jack turned the rifles over to him."

"Anything interesting come up?"

"Probably nothing you didn't already know." Lia sank into her knitting chair. "I just wanted to get a complete picture." She ran over the major points of Herb's account.

"Right, we got all that from him. Couldn't help feeling sorry for the guy. He obviously felt terrible about having left the rifles unattended."

"He does," Lia said, patting her lap to invite Daphne up. "But they've done those bayonet demonstrations for years, and I'm sure tucking the rifles out of sight of wandering crowds was all he felt was necessary to keep them safe. After all those years of being an active participant, being left behind with a boring job must have been tough. All because of his bad hip."

"And his cataracts," Pete added. "But yes, what he did was understandable. The crowd had gone to watch the battle. Why not run over for a johnnycake while they were still available?"

Lia nodded. "On another note, I learned a few things about Candace Carr that could have a connection to her murder." She told Pete about the office cleaner who might have had a vendetta against Candace because of her theft accusation. "I couldn't find much online about the guy. I wonder if you want to check into him?" Pete asked for the name and promised to have someone look into it.

"Then there's Lucas Hall," Lia said. "Did you know he visited Candace three days before her death and threatened her as he was leaving?"

"No, I didn't. Where did you hear this?"

Lia explained about Candace's neighbor, Beth. She was ready to lead into her conversation with Hayley's landlady when Pete interrupted her in mid-sentence.

"Sorry, I have to go, Lia. Something's come up over here."

"Of course."

Pete promised to get back to her when he could and ended the call. Lia lifted Daphne off her lap in order to pick up Beth's cardigan to work on, her thoughts eventually flying as fast as her needles.

By the time her fingers begged for a rest, she'd made up her mind. She packed away the sweater, then placed a call, and after some negotiation got the response she'd wanted. With a bit of time to kill, she fixed a bite to eat and worked on a plan, aware that it depended on many variables and could totally fall apart at any stage. But she could only try.

When it was time to leave, Lia grabbed her jacket and purse and ruffled Daphne's ears.

"Have to take off again," she said as the cat looked up. "But," she promised, "I'll be back."

Chapter 39

Lia gradually left the bright but congested part of Crandalsburg to enter the more remote area her GPS guided her to, surprised at how far that side of the town's border stretched. After missing a turn onto a narrow road and needing to circle back, she reached the address she'd been given, the numbers glowing on one of two stone pillars supporting an open gate.

A long driveway led to an impressively large gray stone house, its outdoor lighting illuminating beautiful landscaping. The doorbell she pressed at the double front door produced an echoing gong. Though Lia had expected a housekeeper to respond, Heidi soon appeared at the door and invited her in.

"Thank you for seeing me," Lia said.

"It's lovely to see you! Thanks for coming all the way out here," Heidi said, taking Lia's jacket. "I couldn't leave because of my lawyer bringing the documents I mentioned, a bunch of things for me to go over. It turned out they didn't take as long as I expected. We finished up, and he left a few minutes ago. Let's go to the den." She led Lia through the large foyer, past a curving stairway, and into a spacious living room with tall windows and gleaming hardwood floors. A long balcony overlooked the aggressively white room with splashes of scarlet. Heidi kept walking, her steps echoing through the open area, until they came to a small room with barely enough seating for four.

"This is much cozier," she explained. "And closer to the kitchen. Now," she said, clasping her hands, "I can make us coffee in two minutes. Any flavor. What would you like?"

Lia hesitated, but before she could answer Julie appeared in the doorway.

"I'll make it, Mother. Hello, Lia."

"Julie was here to help me with all that lawyer stuff," Heidi explained.

"I was on my way out," Julie said. "But I wanted a coffee to take along with me for the road. No trouble to fix two more. Lia?"

"Oh, um, hazelnut, I suppose. Thank you, Julie."

Heidi smiled and headed toward one of the wing chairs, waving Lia to the plump-cushioned love seat.

As the coffee maker's hisses and gurgles came from the kitchen, Lia made small talk. She commented on the striking decor of the house, which Heidi dismissed with a shrug.

"None of my doing. Arden hired a fancy decorator from Philadelphia. Frankly, it's a bit cold for me. I'll probably cozy it up with things from the craft fair." Heidi chatted about items she'd bought and particularly liked until Julie reappeared.

"Here you are." Julie carried in two steaming mugs, handing one to her mother and setting the other on the low table in front of Lia. "Anything more I can get you? Cookies? Something else?"

Lia shook her head with a smile.

"I think we're good for now, dear," Heidi said. "Thank you so much. Drive carefully!"

Julie leaned down to give her mother a kiss on the cheek, then bid them both good-bye.

As Julie left the room, Heidi asked, "So, what's come up that you wanted to talk over with me? Something that might help Jack?"

Lia heard a distant door close. "Yes," she said. "I think it might very well help Jack." She picked up her coffee for a sip and held on to the mug. "I've been doing a lot of thinking. Trying to put together all the information that has come out surrounding Arden's and Candace's murders and trying to make sense of it."

"I'm sure it's not easy," Heidi said, setting her mug down carefully on the small table beside her. "Did you look into the information I gave you? Concerning Candace and Lucas?"

"I did. It was quite interesting, especially the suggestion that Candace might have been blackmailing Lucas. Unfortunately, that might be difficult to prove." Lia took a longer drink from her mug as she organized her thoughts. "I was talking to your cousin Marlaine recently. I mentioned that she's my daughter's landlady, didn't I?"

Heidi smiled. "Yes, and Marlaine told me Hayley has been an excellent tenant."

"Marlaine is a good landlady. It's very handy that she's able to make many of the repairs herself. Besides often being quicker, it saves the expense of hiring someone."

Heidi chuckled. "Marlaine probably has every home repair tool imaginable. I don't know what the cost of it all comes to, but I do know she'd sooner work on a project for days than call in anyone else to do it. It's a matter of personal pride."

Lia nodded. "I got that impression. She said you two had a lot of things in common. Was that one of them?"

"Me?" Heidi flushed. "Oh, well, I liked to tinker, some, when I was younger. But not since I was married. No time!" She flapped a hand, laughing.

"Arden wouldn't have liked it, would he?"

Heidi shifted in her chair. "Arden preferred that I stick with what he considered more feminine pursuits."

"I imagine Lucas has strong opinions, too, about what a wife should and should not do. Marlaine doesn't like Lucas. She was quite definite about that."

"Lucas doesn't like Marlaine, either," Heidi said with a wry grin.

"Perhaps because she sees through him?"

"And doesn't hang on his every word. Lucas doesn't like to be argued with."

Lia nodded. "In that regard, I suspect she felt the same about Arden. Is that right?"

Heidi's head jerked up. "I couldn't say. We never discussed Arden. He was my husband, after all. Some things need to stay private."

"But Marlaine told me the two of you were close," Lia said. "She must have hated to see how Arden treated you. Surely she urged you to leave him?"

Anger flared in Heidi's eyes, but Lia held her gaze, half expecting Heidi to jump up and order her out. But then something in the woman seemed to sag. Perhaps she had grown tired of the pretense?

"Yes, my dear cousin thought I deserved better. But," she added, making a last grab for her increasingly shaky facade, "She didn't see the finer side of Arden, as I did. He could be very generous."

"Did that make up for the overwhelming control?" Lia asked. "The humiliating put-downs?"

"Sometimes," Heidi said in a near whisper.

"But there was a limit," Lia said. "And you reached it."

"No," Heidi said. Her eyes suddenly hardened. "Lucas did. He saw what Arden was doing to the company. Money was going down the drain. He thought he had to stop it before there was nothing left for him to take over."

"Yes, I think he saw what was happening. Arden was making poor business decisions, costly ones. And then there was Candace."

"Yes, Candace was blackmailing Lucas!"

"I don't think so. Yes, I believe Lucas must have treated his ex-girlfriend badly, but she had no proof of anything other than verbal or emotional abuse. Fortunately for him, those aren't prosecutable offenses. No, the tension between Lucas and Candace came from how she was affecting the Sprouse Corporation, didn't it?"

Heidi shook her head firmly. "She was nothing but a low-level clerk with no influence whatsoever."

"But she was much more, wasn't she? A low-level clerk doesn't move several towns away for a job of that sort. She can't normally buy a nice house and immediately start expensive renovations, nor can she afford international travel and high-end wardrobes. Not unless she's being supported in other ways."

"Then I guess there was family money!"

Lia shook her head. "The money came from Arden, didn't it? And the demands for it and for more and more of his attention escalated, badly affecting both Arden's business and personal decisions. That's why the company's stock values were dropping. And it was why Arden was at Candace's open house party, but not you. There must have been many other similar occasions."

Heidi remained silent, but her reddening cheeks and set jaw were all the confirmation Lia needed.

"If there was tension between Lucas and Candace," Lia pressed, "it was from the damaging effects of Candace's recent affair with Arden."

"It wasn't recent. It went on for years!" Heidi burst out. "Years of having to see that smirking face at company parties. Years of her sucking him dry with demands for more and more luxuries. Lucas saw it all. He knew he had to put a stop to the money drain she was causing. So Lucas killed her!"

Heidi had leaned so far forward with her furious accusation, she was close to falling out of her chair. When her tirade ended, she fell back, exhausted. Lia waited, quietly lifting her coffee mug to her lips during the silence. Then she spoke.

"No, Lucas didn't kill Candace. You did."

Heidi stared at Lia. When she said nothing to contradict her, Lia went on, her tone softer.

"It must have been hard. All those years, living with a man who didn't value you."

"I tried," Heidi said, her voice barely audible. "I thought it was me, that I was never good enough, that I kept failing. It wasn't until Julie married Lucas that I began to realize that the damage hadn't only been to me. I'd taught my daughter to see herself the same way, to accept the same kind of abuse as deserved. Yes, I finally recognized it for what it was. Abuse. But it was so much worse to witness my daughter going through it."

"So Candace was an afterthought. But you first killed

Arden for turning his daughter over to an abusive man. It was the final straw after all that you had suffered."

Heidi opened her mouth as though ready to admit that. But a noise from the kitchen stopped her. She and Lia looked up as a figure appeared.

"Mother didn't kill my father," Julie said from the doorway, backlit from the overhead kitchen lights, which left her face in shadow. "I did."

Chapter 40

Julie!" Heidi cried. "Don't!"

"It's too late, Mother. She knows."

Lia tensed, caught in a situation she hadn't expected.

"Yes," Julie said to her. "It was me, though that apparently spurred my mother to take care of Candace once and for all. Right, Mother?"

"She came to Arden's funeral," Heidi said, her voice barely audible. "That horrible woman actually came to the funeral, behaving as if she belonged there. It was then that I realized I couldn't bear the thought of her existence anymore, of her sitting smugly on that deck that Arden paid for."

"But I was the one who stole the rifle," Julie said, "and used it against my father. I'd had enough, too." She laughed bitterly. "Took me a while, didn't it? All those years living under the thumb of a monster who made my life miserable, overruling every decision I tried to make for myself.

"When I thought I was finally escaping by making my

own choice, it turned out I was only doing precisely what he wanted. I ended up marrying a man exactly like my father!"

"It's my fault," Heidi whispered. "I should have—"

"Mother, stop taking the blame for everything Father did. Just stop it!"

Julie was blocking the only exit from the small room. Lia didn't see a weapon, but the kitchen surely offered many lethal possibilities. Plus, it had become two against one. Her only hope was to convince them to be sensible.

"I can only imagine all you've gone through, Julie," Lia said. "And I'm so sorry."

"That was all I wanted from my father," Julie said. "An apology. I told him how miserable I was with Lucas."

"When was this?" Lia asked.

"At the reenactment. Before the battle. He'd asked me to bring the sash he'd left behind." Julie put one hand on the doorway molding but held her other hand behind her. Was that a glint of metal Lia caught?

"We were in a quiet spot," Julie continued, "away from the field. I had so few opportunities to talk to him alone that I grabbed at the chance. I knew he wouldn't like what I had to say—that I wanted to leave Lucas. But I didn't expect the fury that lashed out at me. Once again I was a terrible daughter who thought only about herself, who hadn't the brains to do anything right. That and all the other abusive accusations that I heard for years, hateful things I thought I'd put behind me but which came rushing back.

"He forbade me—yes, forbade!—to even think about leaving Lucas." Julie's eyes blazed. "He told me if I thought I was miserable then, I'd find out just how miserable he could make my life. Nice, huh?"

"Oh, Julie," Heidi moaned.

"It was then that it clicked. I'd never be free of his control as long as he lived."

"And that's when you got the rifle?" Lia asked.

"Don't say any more," Heidi begged.

"It doesn't matter anymore, Mother. Yes, Lia, I knew where the rifles were kept, and I knew Herb wasn't a reliable guard. I thought I could rid my life of two monsters at one time. I grabbed Lucas's rifle when I could and caught my father after he stepped away from the battle and into that clump of trees. Nobody saw us or heard us, what with all the smoke and noise going on.

"It only took a minute," she said, looking oddly surprised. "I wiped off most of the blood. But not all. I planned for Lucas to be accused of it." She laughed. "Two birds with one stone."

"Except it wasn't Lucas's rifle," Lia said.

Julie shook her head in frustration. "It should have been. Both rifles looked the same to me, but his was lying on his rifle wrap. At least I thought so."

"Herb mixed them up," Lia said. "His eyesight isn't good."

Julie nodded. "That's what I realized. Eventually." She straightened and leaned away from the doorway, one hand still held behind her. "Herb was how I knew you had figured it all out," she told Lia. "When I went for more mustard greens, he told me about the questions you were asking."

She turned to Heidi. "It's over, Mother. For both of us. But at least we got our revenge on two horrible people who wrecked our lives."

Heidi stood, and Julie set something down, then stepped over to her. She wrapped both arms around her mother as Heidi wept, then looked over to Lia.

"Please go."

Frozen for a second, Lia quickly pulled herself together.

She eased past the two, picking up her pace as she reached the living room, then dashed through it as she struggled to keep her flat-heeled shoes from slipping on the hardwood floor, half expecting one of the women to reach out and grab her. But she made it unchallenged to the foyer, which gave rise to another panicky thought.

Would the front door be locked? A turn bolt was its only hold, though Lia's shaking fingers fumbled until she managed it. She threw the door open and flew out, scrambling down the steps and down the walk to her car. Once inside, she set the locks, then took a moment to breathe. But only a moment. There was no sign of either Julie or Heidi coming after her. Perhaps they had no intention of doing so. But Lia wasn't counting on it.

She turned on the ignition, put the car in gear, and headed down the long driveway, her only thought being to get as far away from that house as fast as she could. She would call someone—Pete?—as soon as she'd put some distance behind her.

In her haste, Lia neglected to turn on her GPS and after a few minutes she realized she didn't know where she was. Had she taken a wrong turn? She reached over to reset the GPS, causing the car to drift. An oncoming car blasted its horn, shaking Lia as she quickly righted her wheels.

Her GPS properly set, Lia drove on, holding off on a phone call until she felt in better control. Except something was wrong. The road ahead seemed to blur, then clear, then blur. She blinked, then flipped on her windshield wipers, followed by the washer. Neither helped. She blinked again.

Woozy, so woozy. A car passed from behind, blasting its horn. Lia's head jerked up. What was that? Why was the road so hard to see? Something was wrong. Very wrong. She should pull over before she ended up in a ditch!

Lia eased onto the shoulder, braked, and turned off the ignition. She stared out her windshield for several moments, then reached for her phone. She needed help.

Lia's hands shook as she struggled to think. How did you make a call? What did you press? Nothing was coming to her. She let out a scream in frustration only to drop the phone to the floor. In her scramble to reach it, it slipped under the seat. She righted herself and in her helplessness began to whimper. What was happening? What could she do?

Headlights flashed in her rearview mirror. Someone had pulled up behind her. Lia's hopes lifted. Someone could help!

Lia watched expectantly through her mirror, but no one stepped out of the car behind her. Why not? Did they want her to come out? Could she? She managed to unbuckle her seat belt, which caught one arm as it shot upward. With some effort she managed to free herself and open her door. Getting out was another problem. She couldn't seem to swing her legs out.

A light flashed on from the car behind. The driver had opened the door, climbed out, and was walking toward her. Lia tried to speak or at least lift her hand in greeting but could do neither. She was close to paralysis, and this stranger was her only hope.

The figure came near enough to be caught in the interior light of Lia's Camry. Instead of relief, the sight caused Lia to gasp.

"Hello, Lia," Julie said. "Having trouble?"

No! Lia tried to speak, but nothing came out. She tried to pull her door closed but couldn't grasp the handle. All she could do was return Julia's gaze, silently begging. Then she saw the knife.

Julie hadn't gone to the trouble of hiding it. Of course.

Why bother? They were in an unlit section of a sparsely traveled road.

"I see you drank enough of the coffee I fixed. Amazing the drugs you can find online nowadays, isn't it? I hoped you wouldn't feel the effects too soon. I needed you out of the house. This has to look like a random attack," Julie said. "Nothing connected to either Mother or me. I'm sorry, Lia, but it's how it has to be. I wish you hadn't butted in."

Julie lifted the knife, then quickly lowered it as headlights approached from the oncoming lane. Lia's hopes rose as she spotted the markings of a patrol car. She watched it—silently pleading for help—until it passed them by. Julie released a soft *aah*.

Lia closed her eyes and braced herself for what was to come, what she was so helpless to defend herself against. Then she heard the crunch of tires on gravel. Julie slipped the knife under her coat.

Lia heard faint squawks of a car radio coming from behind. It was from the patrol car, which must have doubled back to check out the stopped cars. Lia's hopes soared. But nothing happened for what felt like an eternity. Finally, the patrol car door opened and the sound of boots on gravel approached.

"Having a problem?" a male voice called out.

"No, Officer, we're fine," Julie responded.

The man's steps came closer.

"It's just my aunt," Julie said. "She started to get a little sleepy after our family get-together. Luckily I was right behind her and noticed. I called and told her to pull over. I'll drive her home now. Come on, Auntie," she said, nudging Lia. "Move on over."

The officer stepped closer. He flashed a light inside the car. "Ma'am?"

"She's really out of it," Julie said. "She has a few health issues. Good thing I got her to pull over."

"What is your aunt's name?" he asked.

"Marlaine," Julie said. "Marlaine Griffith. Look, I really should get her home. It's not good to—"

"And your name?" he asked.

At first, Lia hadn't recognized the voice. But as he spoke more and drew closer to her, she knew. Her heart leaped up. It was Brady!

When Julie hesitated to give her name. Brady spoke more firmly. "Please show me your identification."

"I—"

No! Lia tried to shout. *Watch out. She has a knife!*

"Ma'am?"

Julie turned slightly and reached inside her coat. But instead of an ID she pulled out a long kitchen knife. She lunged at Brady.

Lia heard an *unh*. Had she stabbed Brady? There was a scramble, including frightening bumps against her car.

"No!" Julie cried.

Gravel scraped as they both went down. Suddenly all went quiet.

Lia held her breath.

Then she heard, "Ma'am, you have the right to remain silent—"

Lia didn't hear the rest. Whatever Julie had put in her coffee finally overwhelmed her. She sagged against the car seat.

Chapter 41

"Lia," Jen said as she sat in Lia's living room, "I hope you've learned not to ever, ever meet with a murderer on your own."

Lia smiled but shook her head. "In hindsight, I realize that was foolish, but I honestly hadn't considered Heidi dangerous. I expected her to be alone or with a housekeeper. Julie's presence, as well as what she confessed to, was unexpected."

"A pair of psychos!" Hayley cried as she returned from her mother's kitchen with two mugs of tea. "Make that two pairs. The entire family. I wish they'd never set foot in Crandalsburg."

Lia couldn't disagree with that. The Sprouses and Halls, despite the money they brought to the town, had caused pain, disruption, and death. What Lucas would do next remained to be seen, but she dearly hoped to have seen the last of him. Lia reached gratefully for the tea. Her time in the hospital and all the necessary but disagreeable things they had to do because of Julie's doctored brew had turned her off coffee for the time being.

But she was grateful to be back, both to her fully functioning self and to her home, where she'd been receiving an ongoing stream of visitors, a situation that highly pleased Daphne, particularly when her former owner, Jen, appeared. They'd been cuddling practically from the moment Jen arrived.

"Hayley," Jen said as she took her mug, "I'm so impressed with that smart young man of yours, who acted so courageously. If it weren't for his quick action, I hate to think how it would have ended." She shivered and received a chin lick from Daphne in response. Hayley's cheeks flushed at mention of Brady. Lia knew her daughter was proud of what he did, and grateful as well, but she didn't know what other thoughts Hayley had concerning him. She would wait until Hayley was ready to talk about it.

Thankfully, Brady had emerged from his struggle with Julie with only minor cuts. A bandaged hand was the only visible sign of injury. Before leaving the hospital, he'd checked in on Lia in the emergency room, but he'd shrugged off her concerns about his well-being. Lia didn't press.

Sharon and Jack had also visited Lia at the hospital and again once she was home, each filled with a mix of gratitude and guilt.

"Lia," Jack began as he stood beside her hospital bed, "if I had known—"

Lia had quickly stopped him. "I'm fine. It all worked out, and you've been cleared. That's what matters."

"But you could have—"

Sharon interrupted, looking as wretched as Jack. "We

should never have allowed you to get in the middle of all this."

"And how would you have stopped me?" Lia asked with a mild laugh. "You know what a busybody I am."

"No! You're a generous and helpful friend," Sharon cried. "Who I hope from now on will stick to her knitting."

"That's my intention," Lia assured her. "And I can't wait to get back to it."

But the flow of visitors, once she was home, kept putting the knitting on hold. When Jen got up to leave, Maggie arrived with Belinda and Olivia.

"Please tell the other Ninth Street Knitters that a phone call is perfectly fine," Lia said to Jen, thinking that poor Hayley could surely use a break from the hostess duties she'd taken on. Hayley, however, greeted all arrivals warmly.

"I heard Ronna has temporarily turned Eco Alley over to a manager," Belinda said as she and the other two settled down. "While she takes a mental health break. Whatever that entails."

"I'm glad to hear it," Lia said. "Ronna was clearly stretched thin. I hope a break will help. Her heart and her intentions—protecting our environment—were in the right place. But her way of dealing with opposition could use some tweaking."

"Tweaking?" Maggie barked. "Belinda clued me in on Ronna. Sounds like the woman needs a complete overhaul!" She softened her tone. "Well, anyway, I wish her the best."

"My sister-in-law, Jeanie, is heartbroken," Olivia put in. "She truly liked Heidi."

"I can understand that," Lia said. "There was plenty in Heidi to like. And to sympathize with because of the obvious abuse she was suffering. I wish she had found help, either to stand up to Arden or to leave him, instead of letting her anger build up over the years. That only led to striking out at Candace."

"So Heidi's the one who sabotaged Candace's deck railing?" Maggie asked.

Lia nodded. "She dropped all pretense after Julie confessed to her father's murder."

Lia drew a deep breath. "Heidi must have been desperate to cover for her daughter. Since Julie failed to throw suspicion for the murder onto Lucas, Heidi did her best to do so. She might truly have wanted to clear Jack as well, after the mix-up with the rifles caught him in the middle, but her main goal was to put Lucas in prison, which would have released Julie from both a murder charge and a miserable marriage."

"Without the hassle and expense of a divorce," Maggie said, her lip curling. "Win-win."

Olivia winced, then nodded. "A horrible perversion of motherly love."

Lia turned to her craft fair friend in surprise. Normally one who reached far to find something worthy of sympathy, Olivia had zeroed in on the bald truth.

"It was," Lia agreed. "But there was likely a lot of guilt in Heidi as well. Guilt over the terrible example she'd set for her daughter by failing to take charge of her own life. Guilt over not protecting Julie from Arden's bullying. Julie had surely been reminded of her worthlessness her entire life, convinced that she needed to follow her father's every demand. Until the dam finally broke, and she struck out viciously."

A silence fell over the room until Maggie coughed. "Makes one grateful to have lucked into having two sensible parents, doesn't it?"

"Amen," Belinda said as Olivia nodded solemnly.

After the three left, Hayley plopped onto the sofa with a loud *oof!* She coaxed Daphne to come join her. "Think that's the last?" she asked Lia.

"Who knows? But this would be a good time to make your getaway. Thank you so much, but I'm sure I can manage now."

"How? By locking the door?" Hayley grinned. "I'm going to grab a snack. Want something?"

Lia asked for grapes from Jen's gift fruit basket. Hayley brought them out along with a dish of ice cream for herself.

"I think I'll look for another place to live," Hayley said as she retook her spot on the sofa. "Marlaine and I might be better off with more distance between us."

"You're welcome to stay here if you want," Lia said. "Unless . . ."

"No, I haven't changed my mind about moving in with Brady. But I have come around to forgiving him his, um, rash assumption." Hayley smiled and scooped a spoonful of cherry vanilla ice cream. "And not just because he did such an amazing, intelligent, and courageous thing by saving you, although that's no small part. But you don't marry people out of gratitude, do you?"

"Hopefully not."

"But it reminded me how lucky I am to have such an amazing guy. Someone who I'm willing to stick with to give us a chance to know and understand one another better."

Lia smiled and was about to comment when Hayley added, "You know what was the biggest thing holding me back?" She set her spoon down. "I wasn't sure I could deal with the dangers that come with Brady's job." Her voice wobbled and she coughed to clear it. "And I'm still not sure. But I'm willing to try and to trust that he knows what he's doing. And hope for the best."

"That's all anyone can do," Lia agreed as she wondered exactly when her daughter had become that mature.

Their talk was interrupted by a knock on the door. "Here we go!" Hayley said, hopping up with a grin. As she started to pass Lia's chair, Lia pulled her down for a hug that lasted just a little longer than usual.

L ia had had several conversations with Pete, initially in person at the hospital but the rest by phone, which she understood as his thoughtful way of not interfering with her visits with Hayley and her friends. He also sent flowers, much to her surprise and delight. The bouquet was just starting to wilt when Pete called to ask if she would like to go out to dinner.

"That would be lovely," Lia said, feeling fully recovered by then and eager to take a step toward normalcy.

He took her to a quiet restaurant a short distance from town, chosen, Lia suspected, as a place where they were less likely to run into acquaintances with more questions. The peaceful atmosphere felt luxurious to her, and she marveled at Pete's apparent ability to read just what she could use and when.

It didn't take long for their conversation to lead to the Sprouses, though Pete began with good news.

"Gil Hubbard will be managing the Hubbard Hotel again."

"Really?" Lia waited for the waiter to finish refilling their glasses before asking, "How did that come about?"

"Looks like Lucas put a stop to the grand plans Arden had for the place. He's packing up to leave Crandalsburg altogether and probably wants the hotel off his mind. I don't know what arrangements were made, but at least Gil will be back in the place and work he loved." Pete lifted his wineglass for a sip.

"I'm so glad for him," Lia said. "Gil was on my suspect list, you know, but I really didn't want it to be him."

Pete's eyebrow twitched at Lia's mention of her suspect list, though he kept silent. Lia had already heard his thoughts on the risks she'd taken. Instead he said, "I have an explanation for that scene Candace's neighbor reported, when Lucas warned Candace that she'd be sorry."

Lia set down her fork, ready to listen.

"According to him, she demanded that the company continue supporting her as Arden had been doing. When Lucas balked, she threatened to go public about the affair. He claimed to us that at the time he didn't want his wife and mother-in-law hurt by that. Frankly, I suspect Candace might have learned a few things from Arden about the inner workings of his business, which would have been Lucas's greater worry.

"Of course," Pete continued, "with Heidi's confession, Lucas is off the hook for Candace's murder. But we'll be taking a close look at the Sprouse business."

"Good."

They returned to their dinners for a few moments as soft music flowed from the restaurant's audio system. Then Lia brought up Brady.

"He did well that night," Pete agreed. "When the opportunity for promotion comes up, I guarantee Brady will be first in line. With no bias involved," he added. "I'd feel the same if it had been any other victim involved." Pete reached for Lia's hand. "Though in this case, I'm particularly grateful for his actions."

Lia felt a warmth she hadn't had in some time, and she left her hand in Pete's. Hayley's words when she'd spoken about Brady came back to her. *How lucky I am to have such an amazing guy. I want to give us a chance to get to know each other better.*

Pete had been showing himself to be an amazing guy, and Lia wanted the chance to know him better. Gradually, like developing a fine wine.

But how long did that take? she wondered, as she took a swallow from her glass. Months? Years? She reminded herself that she and Tom had thought they had years ahead of them until the unexpected intervened. Was it foolish to take things slowly, especially at their age, and risk missing out altogether? Or was it wiser in order to be sure?

"Dessert?" their waiter asked, breaking into her thoughts as he offered the menu. Lia smiled. That was one question she could answer confidently.

"Yes, I believe I will," she said.

Lia then turned to Pete with a smile. "But only if you'll join me."

Acknowledgments

Many thanks, once again, to the excellent team at Berkley: editor Sarah Blumenstock; her assistant, Liz Sellers; copy editor Eileen Chetti; cover artist Mary Ann Lasher; and the many behind-the-scenes people whose amazing skills turned my story into a polished book and worked to promote it.

Special thanks to my agent, James McGowan, whose able skills set it all in motion.

I've been grateful for many years to my long-running critique group, some of whom have been with me from the beginning: Shaun Taylor Bevins, Becky Hutchison, Debbi Mack, Sherriel Mattingly, Lauren Silberman, Marcia Talley, and Cathy Wiley.

My family, of course, has been my greatest support—and cheerleaders—which has made such a difference. I can't thank you enough for it all.

Ready to find
your next great read?

Let us help.

Visit prh.com/nextread

Penguin
Random
House